SACRIFICE

Linda Lane McCall

Writers Club Press

San Jose New York Lincoln Shanghai

Sacrifice

Published by Writers Club Press
an imprint of iUniverse.com, Inc.

For information address:
iUniverse.com, Inc.
620 North 48th Street
Suite 201
Lincoln, NE 68504-3467
www.iuniverse.com

ISBN: 0-595-09745-6

Printed in the United States of America

PROLOGUE

The man pulled the hardback book from the bookstore's plastic bag and laid it on his kitchen table before he went to the freezer to get something to nuke for dinner, a diet something. His nice shirts were straining at the seams, and he had promised himself he wouldn't give in and get some in the next size up.

No, it was simply a matter of exercising a little self-control. A diet dinner and maybe a piece of fruit for dessert. To show his sincerity, he took the rocky road ice cream tub from the freezer, put it in the sink and started running the hot water into it.

There. Just a little self-discipline, that's all.

While he scanned the selections stacked on the freezer shelves, he began to shake. It had been three hours since his last cigarette. Practically a lifetime record of clean living, by his measure. He left the freezer standing open while he shook a cigarette from the pack in his shirt pocket and lit up.

Well, good God, you can't give up everything at once. You simply cut down on the food for awhile. Later we'll deal with the smoking issue. Hell, if I give it up now, I'll blow up like a balloon. That's no good, no way to project a hero's image.

Can't wait to see if he used me this time. Damn that Det. Larson! Thurston draws him like some black heroic stud, when he looks like a giant couch potato. And a wrinkled one at that.

And Wojenski, Adair and Lobo. Damn! What did they ever do to get written into a novel? There's so much more skill involved in my job. But they don't see it, of course, always taking me for granted. What's it take to get a tiny piece of the spotlight?

The man plucked a dinner of chicken in pasta from the shelf and closed the freezer. He was humming when he read the instructions absently and tore open the box. *In the Shadows* was Bailey Thurston's fifteenth murder mystery. Odds were very good that a character patterned after the man would show up in this one. If not, he would find a way to show that he deserved his fifteen minutes of fame.

Yes siree, I'll bet I'm in there this time.

Part I

FORESHOCK

CHAPTER ONE

The deck doors were open to the late June breeze off the Pacific, a short distance to the west. The deck off the office faced the neighbor's garage wall to the north. It was a mass of guinea vine and yellow flowers, giving Bailey a sense of privacy even though the neighbors were only a few yards away. There was the faint whine of an MD-80 rising from nearby LAX and climbing the cloudless air over the blue water.

Bailey hated his speakerphone, so his neck was getting stiff from holding the phone to his ear with his shoulder while he scrolled alternately through his calendar and the Airline Guide on computer. Mary Zada was on the other end of the line in her Century City office.

"Gads, Mare, enough a'ready! The kids'll be in college by the time I get done with such a tour."

"Don't be such an old maid!" came back her laughing response.

"If I were an old maid, I wouldn't have any problem with it. You know my rule. Two weeks away, max."

"Aw, Bailey! You've built up a real following in Asia. The Japanese in particular have got the leisure bucks to spend on hardbacks, and the publisher's given us the bucks to cover a lot of territory, for a change. You have to strike while the iron's hot, as they say. Four weeks isn't a lifetime."

"Two weeks, max. You pick the cities. Since I've never been to any of them, I really don't have any preferences." He swiveled his chair away from the deck and toward the open hall door. Across the hallway, in the family room, the two boys were at the coffee table, cooperating on a new Lego construction that was beginning to resemble a spaceship.

Marissa was on the floor, in front of the television. From the fact that she was slumped like a sack of four and that the program was a demonstration of how to change a car's fan belt, Bailey guessed that his four-year-old had nodded off.

He was only half listening to his publicist and was wondering when Sara would return from Ralph's Market, when it sounded and felt as if a small truck had slammed into the side of the house.

In a split second, he dropped the phone on the desk and started toward the deck to see if Sara's van had somehow hit the side of the house by the carport, heard Bammer outside join the panicked chorus with the other neighborhood dogs, saw the light standard next to the Luft's house nodding furiously....

A quake!

Bailey changed directions toward the shrieks of the children. The planters, books and figurines on the family room shelves were doing a flamenco. The boys had dived headfirst under the coffee table and were screaming for their younger sister to join them.

She had been startled awake, hopped to her feet and was running in terror toward her daddy. He saw the accident in the making, but he couldn't get to her in time to prevent her tripping on the bunched-up throw rug and falling headlong into a pile of the hard plastic Lego pieces scattered on the wood floor.

"Stay there, you guys! You did the right thing! Just stay there till I tell you it's okay! You okay?" Bailey hollered breathlessly toward the table as he swooped up his daughter to sit with her in the doorway in case there was an aftershock.

"Yeah, Dad, we're cool," Scott answered.

Bailey didn't know whether to laugh or cry at the blasé response of his eleven year old. Bailey was shaking so badly he almost couldn't get his handkerchief out of his shorts pocket to press against the bleeding wounds on Marissa's forehead. The child buried her red curls in his chest, cried and clung desperately to Bailey's short pony tail with her little fingers for nearly five minutes as he tried to comfort her. Bailey had forgotten he had left Mary Zada on the phone in his office.

By the time Marissa had calmed down to a sniffling whimper, Bailey and the boys were watching the television announcer who had interrupted the program. He was preoccupied with fears for his absent wife.

There wasn't any apparent damage to the house. Not so much as a book had fallen to its side on the bookshelves, and the news announcement said no damage had been reported yet. Still, Bailey had visions of heavy glass pickle jars raining down on Sara as she shopped. He slumped with relief when he heard the kitchen door bang shut.

"In the family room, Sara!" he called, and Marissa started up howling again.

Sara arrived in the family room doorway still holding a plastic bag and blowing a stray strand of strawberry blond hair out of her face as she surveyed the room's occupants with obvious puzzlement. One hand went onto her hip, and she addressed the legs extending from under the coffee table, "You two gang up on your little sister?" She was putting down the grocery bag.

"No, Mom, no, honest!" they pleaded together.

Mike, barely eight, crawled out and looked desperately at his father still huddled in the doorway with the crying child. "Tell her, Dad! Didn't the man say it was all San Andreas' fault?"

$$* \qquad * \qquad * \qquad *$$

Mary Zada plucked one of Bailey's long, auburn hairs from his linen dress shirt and straightened his tie.

"You look good," she said. "Stop worrying. They love ya, and you always do fine."

He reached to loosen the tie; she tightened the knot, straightened the tie again, and he swatted impatiently at her manicured hand. "You know I hate this part."

"I know."

"I hate ties and shirts with buttons, and shoes. Next time see if I can't do it barefoot. Gads, I hate this!"

The director motioned urgently for Bailey to take his place on the sofa next to the talk show host's desk while the commercial was running. He felt like a jerk, tripping on one of the cables as he tried to comply.

"I'm sorry!" he whispered to the ulcer-ridden director—Bailey Thurston, the ever-polite prisoner, apologizing to the hangman for tripping on his way up the steps of the gallows and delaying the execution.

As many times as Bailey had been interviewed by the press or appeared at book-signings or on various talk shows, he was never comfortable at the outset. Though he was friendly enough, he didn't like having the spotlight on himself—especially literally and especially when the broadcast was nationwide as this morning's was.

None of Sara's or the kids' or the neighbors' pride in him helped. He wanted to be home in his office, the deck doors open to the coastal breeze, hammering away at his keyboard in shorts and a T-shirt. And bare feet. Most of all, bare feet.

But, as always, once things had begun, the knot in his stomach reduced to tolerable size. Perhaps the flattering and perceptive remarks of the host, Phil Hunter, had something to do with it.

"*In the Shadows* is much more tense than your previous fine work, much more urgent. Most of all, it's a much more intimate look at the villain than in any of your previous murder mysteries. I'd like to hear about that aspect," Hunter said.

"What would you like to know?"

"Well," the handsome, white-haired host said, opening the book at a place he had marked with a slip of paper, "in this section where Ralph is in his semi-dark workshop, we overhear his thoughts. That's the first time you've taken us inside the villain's head in any of your works. That change in style was deliberate, I assume."

"I see. Yes, I did want *Shadows* to be, as you put it, more urgent. By showing Ralph's careful planning, I think it makes the reader more aware of just how dangerous he is—and how sick, since his sick actions don't match the reasonable, almost noble way Ralph perceives himself."

"Yes, that part was quite chilling, when you describe him thinking in the mundane terms of removing an ugly stain from a priest's robe, when what he's doing is gathering up tools for the removing of a person from the face of the earth." Hunter shuddered.

Bailey smiled and nodded appreciation that the host had reacted as the writer intended, but his head went down a little as the host's praise continued, "Bailey, this book was so real to me that I have to wonder if you based it on some real life case."

Bailey looked up and responded, "*In the Shadows* is strictly fiction—as my eight-year-old says, a pigment of my imagination. If I had seen anything on a real case, believe me, I would have done some homework so I could capitalize on its being based in fact."

Bailey shifted in his seat and said with a smile, "I can see that my publicist is standing offstage ready to strangle me because she can't do that now that you all know the truth." Hunter and the audience laughed before Hunter resumed the discussion of the book.

As a parent and as a television viewer, Bailey despised commercials. As a talk show guest, he felt like falling down and kissing the ground when one came on and terminated his fifteen-minute interview.

*　　*　　*　　*

In spite of his Irish first name, Bailey Thurston was neither Irish nor Catholic. Nonetheless, he couldn't help occasionally referring to Mary Zada as Sister Mary Z. The steel-haired, vibrant woman took a nun's zealous interest in the well-being of his career, seeing that he got good press and lots of it.

Today, she insisted on lunch after the interview, during which time she tried (as she always did) to convince Bailey that he should have a bigger ego.

"Listen, kid, when someone gives you a flattering comment, don't change the subject like you're embarrassed. Keep them expanding on it," she said, stretching the air with her hands. "Ask them leading questions, like, 'Can you give me an example from the book?' Or, say, 'I always worry that this book's not as good as the last,' and then let them smother you with kind reassurances. Believe me, they will. You're good, Bails."

"Okay, okay," he agreed insincerely as the waitress set his pasta salad in front of him.

"And another thing—you've gotta learn to watch for reader perceptions that we can use, like that bit about your book being based on a real case."

"That was a *misperception*, Mare, in case you weren't listening to the interview."

"No matter. If you hadn't blabbed to several million viewers, we coulda milked the life out of it. Might still yet," she said with a wink and attacked her nearly raw steak.

"Listen, Bailey, why don't you change your mind and put in an appearance at Spago tonight. You can bring Sara. There'll be tons of press for the party. I know we can get a mention in the *Times*, maybe even a picture if you'll put your tie on just one more time."

"Thanks, but no thanks. Scott has a softball game at six."

Bailey finished lunch with Mary just after two. Since an interview always blew a day of writing by blowing his concentration, he devoted the rest of the day to a string of nuisance chores. They took him to the Marina for his bank and dry cleaners. From there he swung south, picking up an iced Mariposa mocha at the Blue Butterfly in El Segundo, which he carried with him to the body shop a few blocks away.

Bailey's restored '53 Jaguar roadster looked in factory-fresh condition compared with the other classic cars in various stages of work on the shop's crowded property. That is, until you noticed the missing front fenders. Bailey had done much of the restoration work himself, particularly the mechanical work. But his talents didn't extend to the metal work required to fashion a new fender from scratch. All his and the shop's efforts to find an existing replacement—even a battered one—had been in vain.

"Hey, Mr. Thurston, caught you on the tube this morning. Lookin' good, man!"

"Thanks, Randy, but don't tell me it's gonna run the price up?" Bailey sauntered, iced coffee in hand, from his convertible toward the skinny, surprisingly bald twenty-year-old wiping his hands with a hopelessly greasy rag.

"Nah! Might cost you a coupla beers some day when I wanna impress some fox with one of my more literate friends."

Bailey smiled and followed the loose-limbed man toward the cluttered desk that Bailey assumed was somewhere under the teetering pile of parts and paperwork.

"Angelo's not in today?" Bailey asked, looking around for the man of fifty who had volunteered to create the fender.

"Out—like a light," Randy volunteered in response and found the paperwork under about six inches of invoices.

Bailey muttered, "Gives one just loads of confidence in the workmanship."

Randy grinned. "Not to worry. Angelo's got enough confidence for the whole species. When he finished, he bought us all beers to celebrate the creation of the newest masterpiece by the self-proclaimed Michael Angelo of the auto body business."

Randy was still grinning as he led Bailey through the noisy shop to the wall where various hoods, doors, fenders and trunk lids were lined up, each separated by old bed sheets. Randy unwrapped one and turned it to read the chalk mark on the inside before unwrapping the other, a mirror image of shiny, black metal.

"Here's the original, right one, and this is the new one for the left."

"Wow, looks great!" Bailey said, picking up the new one and examining it as they carried the fenders toward his car. "Has Angelo tried it on another Jag to see if it'll fit?"

"Nah, waste of time. No two cars exactly alike. Heck, not even two sides of the same car are exact opposites."

"I guess not," Bailey agreed and watched Randy grab his tools to install the old fender.

"Just like people," Randy said.

"How's that?"

"My sister's got one blue eye and one green eye. I got a size eight left foot and a size nine right foot. Same thing." He shrugged.

For all Randy's youth and casual approach, he had a gift for car bodies, and the first fender was on in only a moment. Bailey didn't expect the second to be quite as easy, and he exclaimed, "Well, would you look at that!" when the new fender was quickly in place.

Randy shook it hard to make sure it was secure before he stood, handed Bailey the paperwork from his pocket and began wiping his hands. "If Angelo ever asks you, it took an hour and a half of my personal labor and ingenuity to get that sucker on there, okay? The drunk ole genius is hard enough to live with as it is."

It was five-fifteen when Bailey pulled up the western-most hill in Playa del Rey and into the driveway of the two-story house on Trask. He parked in the carport at the rear, threw the cover over the Jag and charged through the back door, into the kitchen. Sara was stacking up the stadium cushions and received her husband's quick kiss as he sped through the room.

"Scott's putting on his uniform," she called after him. "You were great. We got the show on tape."

"Swell!" he answered sarcastically and hurried through the house and upstairs to change into one of *his* uniforms—faded Hawaiian shorts and a Lakers tank top. He kicked off the dress shoes and, because he had stepped on one of Brad Nollan's hot cigarette butts during the last game at Rauch Field, slipped into another pair of shoes. These were brown leather moccasins that Marissa had decorated with fingerprints one day when he had left them outside on the deck to air out.

"Yo, dudes and dudette! Let's hit the van on the double!" Bailey hollered as he thundered down the stairs and strode the length of the house toward the children's rooms near the rear of the house. Wise, wise architect.

Marissa raced toward him along the hallway, the bill of the too-large Dodgers cap flapping down over her eyes then up again as she ran with arms outstretched.

"Daddy, daddy! Mommy put you on the TV today! Where you been? You missed it."

Bailey shook his head with a smile, received her bear hug and carried her the few steps to the boys' room, across the hall from hers. Mike was coming out in a rush, with Scott following at the more reserved pace of an eleven-year-old who doesn't want you to know he's dying to get somewhere fast.

Bailey caught a glimpse of the room. "Whoa, guys! Who picked up the room and shook it, Godzilla? You're gonna have to spend drag time putting things away after the game."

Scott rolled his eyes in disgust and pulled his cap on. Mike said, "It was San Andreas' fault again. You were cool on TV. I told everybody I'm famous 'cause you quoted me. Can I have two hot dogs? I'm starved. Gimme my hat, Rissa!"

Bailey found that following the ping-ponging conversation of children frequently distracted him, and so it wasn't until the second inning that he remembered what he had meant to ask Sara at the house.

"Was there a quake today?"

"None I heard of, why?"

"Oh, I thought maybe I'd missed it while I was driving, like you did the last one. Mike blamed the mess in their room on a quake."

"Bailey Thurston!" she said, her creamy face breaking into an astonished smile. "I can't believe you haven't noticed."

"Noticed what?"

"That ever since we laughed our heads off at his misunderstanding of the quake announcement three weeks ago, he's claimed that every mistake or spill or mess-up is San Andreas' fault. The poor saint has replaced his old scapegoat, Not Me."

Bailey couldn't believe he hadn't noticed either, but he said nothing, because Mike had just come bounding up the bleachers and plopped down next to him.

"I guess he's just jealous," the boy said unexpectedly.

"Who, Mike?"

"Dustin's dad, Mr. Nollan. I tried to cheer him up by telling him one day he'd be just as famous as you, but he just got gnarlier and started using big words. Just jealous, I guess. That was a ball, you dummy!"

"No name-calling," Sara said quietly, "even if it is well-deserved."

Bailey threw her a quick smile and turned back to Mike. "What kind of big words, Mike? Cuss words?"

"No. At least I don't guess so. Something like 'cosmic social complications.' I don't know." The boy shrugged and kept his attention riveted on the game.

"Oh, that again," Bailey muttered and turned to answer the question stated in Sara's look. "I assume what Brad flung at Mike was his usual argument: 'Thurston has no appreciation of the cosmic social implications for mankind inherent in the written word.'"

"Huh?"

"My sentiments exactly. We shouldn't be too hard on him, though. He seriously believes it's his destiny to write a novel that will change the universe."

"Oh," she responded.

"Meanwhile, it must be very frustrating for him to see me succeed with 'meaningless commercial thrillers,' while he, a true genius, works nights assembling aircraft parts."

Sara nodded and looked with sympathy toward the angry man in the front row who was screaming at the umpire for calling his son out. The yelling match that ensued got most of the kids and many of the parents totally wound up.

As a result of the adrenaline, Scott hit the winning run. The downside was that it only produced more adrenaline in Mike, so that, on the way back up the hill in the van, the two boys were bouncing up and down and talking full volume. Bailey's thought was that it would probably be near midnight before the boys would settle down and go to sleep. That meant it would be near midnight before he and Sara could feel safe about making love.

Oh, sure, they had a lock on the door. But twice before when Mike had not been asleep and had discovered their door was locked, the racket of his pounding on the door and his threats to summon the fire department had doused the flames of passion posthaste. Once Mike was asleep, he generally stayed asleep. They would wait.

The phone was ringing when Bailey pulled Sara's Toyota van into the carport, next to his Jaguar. Scott opened the van door almost before the vehicle had stopped rolling.

"Let voice mail get it," Bailey said. "Help your mom with the cushions. I'll carry Sleepyhead in."

Reluctantly, Scott complied and muttered under his breath when the phone stopped ringing. Inside the house, Bailey carried his sleeping daughter to her room, pulled the cap off the head that was now a sweaty mop, pulled off her shoes and laid her in her bed under the sheet. Next to the sight of his slender wife's naked body, a sleeping child was, in Bailey's opinion, one of the most beautiful sights on earth.

Other people might have thought that the Thurston kids were rather ordinary, slightly edited versions of their parents. Marissa, for instance, had her mother's delicate build and porcelain complexion that would probably never need makeup any more than Sara's did.

Their eldest, Scott, had Bailey's sturdier build, well-chiseled jaw and dark auburn hair, though Sara insisted that he could not let his grow long and wear it in a pony tail as Bailey did. Writers could get away with that. Bailey often wondered whether Scott might take after him in that regard later. Quiet, serious-minded Scott certainly loved his books as much as his bats, balls and computer games.

The 'serious' ingredient had been left out of the Michael Thurston formula altogether, however—probably through the same divine goof-up that had put a double dose of energy into the curly-headed strawberry blond.

All different kids. All the very finest heaven could make.

As Bailey pulled Marissa's door almost shut, he could hear the springs of Mike's bed squawking above Mike's replay of the ninth inning.

"Hey, sport, no jumping on the bed! And pick things up in there!" Bailey called toward the room and walked rapidly toward the kitchen to pick up the ringing phone since Sara was making a beeline for the children's bathroom.

"Hello?" he answered after snatching the blue phone off the wall beside the refrigerator.

There was a second's hesitation from the calling party then a muted sound that Bailey recognized as the sound of a smoker who had been interrupted in the midst of a drag.

"Well, well, well! You finally decided to lower yourself and pick up the phone." The man's voice was unfamiliar and the sarcasm unmistakable.

"Who've I got?" Bailey asked as he straightened the series of kids' drawings plastering the refrigerator door.

"You haven't got anybody, Thurston. I've got *you*."

"Okay, but you're gonna lose me fast if you don't give me a name and tell me what you want." Bailey wondered if this were Brad Nollan calling. Bailey only knew him by sight and through the rather bitter comments Nollan had made to the two boys or other parents.

How immature! Bailey thought. "Your name?" he politely insisted.

There was another drag from the cigarette, then, "A name? Levi. I thought you were smarter, Thurston, but you're as blind as the rest...."

By now, Bailey's warm spine had turned cold, and he stood up, alert and suddenly frightened by the tone of the caller as the faceless voice continued, "...and I will have to teach you about offering up sacrifices."

"Hey, Dad, I need the phone. I promised Darren...."

Whirling toward Scott, Bailey had the sudden, panicked feeling that the caller had actually invaded his kitchen. He slammed the receiver down.

"Thanks," Scott said and stepped toward the phone.

Bailey was too shaken and confused by the call to resist his son's nudge as he took up the phone to call his friend. Scott was chattering quietly away to Darren and Bailey was pouring himself a glass of cold herb tea when Sara walked into the kitchen a moment later.

"Who called?" she asked as she got a glass for herself.

"Some turkey."

"What was he selling, porno stuff? I heard you nearly smash the phone through the wall."

He forced a smile. "I overreacted to a bit of criticism. Mary will be pleased to learn I have an ego after all."

The two of them took their teas and headed for the deck off the office. As they peeked into the family room, Mike was lying on his stomach on the floor watching the baseball game, his legs crossed in the air behind him and pumping up and down like an oilrig.

As they frequently did on warm summer nights, Bailey and Sara left the lights off in the office, the doors open, and sat in the night air while they murmured back and forth. Heading up tonight's list of monumental topics were whether Scott was starting a mustache already, whether it was their turn to supply the cold drinks next game, and how many hours Bailey wanted to put in on the next book tomorrow before taking them all to the beach for the afternoon.

Finally, at just before eleven, Sara said, "I guess this morning's TV appearance drained you more than you anticipated."

"Why do you say that?" Bailey asked through a yawn.

"Because I can see that the flames of passion you mentioned to me earlier are, as fire reports put it, under control with full containment expected at any moment."

He smirked and shook himself out of a near doze. Sara stood and kissed his forehead.

Bailey mumbled, "I guess that means I have your permission to crash tonight."

"Tonight," she replied with emphasis and a sly look as she tugged at his hand to pull him from the deck chair.

He willingly surrendered his empty glass to her. As he headed for the living room and the stairs up to their bedroom, he heard her scolding Scott about tying up the phone and reminding him to take Mike and straighten their room. Less than two minutes later, as Bailey sat on the edge of the bed, pulling off his shirt, the phone rang.

To cut off Scott before he could wriggle out of room clean-up again, Bailey grabbed up the phone and sighed, "Hello?" into the receiver.

"How dare you hang up on me and leave it off the hook like that!" the gravely voice said.

Bailey felt a jolt of fear run through his body, now suddenly upright and alert again. "Listen, creep, I don't appreciate your calling this number and bugging me and my family!"

"You certainly *don't* appreciate me, Thurston—that's the problem. You didn't get me right in your book at all."

"What?"

"You heard me. I'm nothing like you said. You and everybody else just think the equipment does everything, that it's some engineering or scientific process. It's art! I offer it up like some holy sacrifice, and they don't even see what it is they're holding in their hands."

I must be dreaming! It almost sounds like it's Ralph calling!

"I was going to just kill you outright for your irresponsible journalism…"

"What journalism?" Bailey stuttered with a dry mouth. "The book is fiction—total, utter fiction!"

"…but since you've shown such irreverence, my office requires that I exact a sacrifice from you—"

"What kind of insane…? I'm hanging up."

"—your children. One at a time."

The dial tone sounded like a death wail.

*   *   *   *

CHAPTER TWO

Sara was just coming into the bedroom when Bailey nearly ran into her.

"Whoa!" she said and stepped aside. "Where did all that fatigue go?"

"Oh, uh," Bailey stammered, placing a shaking hand on his wife's shoulder, "I just got an idea for a change in the new book, and I need some technical information from Hume before I lose the essence of the idea."

"Bailey," Sara said with a hand on a hip, "it's nearly eleven. If he's working tonight, you'll wake up Cynthia and the kids."

"It's really important to me, Sara. Please make sure everything's locked up, then go on to bed."

He left her standing beside the bed looking peeved and muttering about playing second fiddle to his work, as he dashed barefoot and bare-chested down the stairs and into the office. With the hall door closed, he didn't have to worry about one of the kids eavesdropping. He had had the room insulated for sound so that, when the kids were home and noisy, he wouldn't hear it if he didn't want to.

Bailey was willing to wake his friend from a coma if necessary. He was glad when Hugh Larson picked up after the first ring and Bailey could hear the low murmur of television in the background.

"Human, hey, I'm sorry to call so late."

"No problem. Stevie tells me Scott was the big hero tonight. Sorry I had to miss it."

"Yeah," Bailey answered absently and wondering whether he was panicking unnecessarily. "Listen, Hume, maybe it's nothing, maybe just

19

some crackpot testing out a plot for a sequel to my book, but I had a couple of calls tonight that've got me spooked."

"Give me the details," Hugh Larson said, his voice switching noticeably from that of friend to police detective. The television noise terminated abruptly, and Bailey described the two phone calls.

"Recognize the voice, Bailey?"

"No...."

"Why the hesitation?"

Bailey pulled at his hair for a moment before he laughed nervously and answered, "Just because I was once unjustly accused of making an obscene phone call, and the memory of the accusation is still with me."

"You're not accusing anyone, all right? Just tell me if you have any idea who might make such a call."

"Well, I don't know the man well enough to know...."

"Just spit it out, Bailey."

He sighed. "Do you know Brad Nollan, Dustin's dad?"

There was a hesitation, then, "Unhappy man, I recall. Wife left him recently."

"Yes." Bailey held his breath, hoping he didn't have to say any more.

"Also jealous of you, as I recall," Larson blurted out. "Don't you know his voice, Bailey?"

"Only his screaming voice, and that's no help. Every time I've tried to approach him at the field to do anything as simple as compliment his son's good play, he's glowered at me and stomped off. What's the deal about checking phone records to see if a call came from his number to mine?"

"Phone numbers that geographically close won't show up on the bill. I haven't started your book yet, so tell me if there's any physical or behavioral similarity between Nollan and the Ralph character you mentioned."

"The only connection I see is the mention of engineering. Nollan works for some company that manufactures aircraft parts. Ralph is a psychopathic engineer that murders people who criticize his engineering creations."

"Touchy, touchy!" Larson joked.

"Yeah, well, Ralph looks upon himself as one with the priestly duty to eliminate such irreverence. This Levi that called wanted more credit for *his* work, claiming it's a 'holy sacrifice' and people don't know what they have in their hands."

"But you said the caller was mad because he wasn't *like* the character in the book. That doesn't make sense."

"It does if you understand that the caller, this Levi somebody, didn't feel he was the way the narrator and the other characters looked at Ralph. They all looked down on him, while Ralph considered himself a gifted holy man. Nollan gives a similar impression, always talking about his work having 'cosmic social implications' and nobody agreeing with him."

"Got it," Larson said with a sigh of weary understanding.

"Good, what do we do?"

*   *   *   *

It was too early for the neighborhood to be stirring on Trask, too early for the neighborhood dogs to be greeting the loud slap of the Wednesday L.A. *Times* on the sidewalk. Very little of daybreak had penetrated the hallway leading to the children's rooms, and so an exhausted Bailey Thurston was having trouble figuring out the scene before his blurred vision. There was a large, dark mass next to him, looming in front of his face.

The Santa Monica Mountains? Dirty laundry?

But the mass was emitting heat. Another second of Bailey's trying to figure out the bizarre landscape, and the mass sighed and stirred.

It's alive!

At that instant, Bailey felt a painful kick to his right kidney. Still fearing the dark mound in front of him, Bailey rolled quickly away and felt his arms swing out wildly as he scooted on his back and tried to get his bearings in the dim space. Bammer woofed once in the boys' room, and his tail whammed the floor several times.

The hall light came on, and Bailey's eyes clenched shut in defense. In a flash, he found himself with his back against the wall listening to Mike scream and Hugh Larson saying, "Shh, Mike! It's okay, it's just us. It's okay."

"What're you *doing*, Mike?" Bailey demanded, shaking with leftover fear.

"Goin' to the john. What're *you* guys doin' sleepin' in the hall?"

The large black man next to Bailey looked sheepish. Both men had thought they would awaken before anyone else and that Larson would be gone before the family even knew he had been there.

Bailey patted his son on the rear of his jockey shorts. "Research for the new book."

"You got a coupla characters that sleep in the hall? Together?"

"Maybe. I might not use it. Go on."

"I didn't know you wrote stuff that weird," Mike said with a suspicious look at his dad before he trotted off to the hall bathroom.

Bailey squinted to read his Rolex. Five thirty-two. "Now that our stakeout's blown," he said facetiously and pulled himself up, "how 'bout some coffee?"

"Sounds good, sounds good," Larson answered and hauled his great hulk to his feet.

Not handsome, Det. Hugh Larson had the kind of face that made you want to tell it everything. His was a comfortable face that would shine like a spotlight on your successes, one that would melt with compassion for you as a rape victim or as the victim's shattered husband. Larson's compassionate face was one reason his role in his church did not include counting the offering but visiting the sick and the bereaved.

Larson used the kitchen sink to splash cold water in his face while Bailey put the coffee on. Shortly the two men carried their steaming mugs out onto the office deck.

"Thanks again, Human Larson, friend *extraordinaire.*" Bailey clinked his mug to Larson's.

Larson just nodded with a tired smile and sipped the coffee before he said, "I'll turn in a report, put down the wording of the conversations, see if we have any known telephone cranks that have an engineering background."

"Okay," Bailey said with a nod. "Any way you can check on Nollan's background?"

"Through police records, of course. Doubtful there'll be anything. Most aircraft companies reject people with criminal records for jobs that can mean life and death, such as handling the parts directly."

Bailey nodded, and Larson went on, "While you haven't given me enough to justify putting a tap on Nollan's phone, I can pull a few shenanigans to get his voice on tape to see if you recognize it."

"Great! How?"

"How what?" Larson gave Bailey the look that had come to mean, *Don't ask.*

"Thanks, Hume."

"No problem. I'll also see if there are any similar reports mentioning the name your caller has chosen for himself."

"Is there any chance he's using his real name?"

"Crazies aren't stupid. Besides, from the conversation you related to me, he picked the name to describe the office he's assumed."

"Yeah, I was really confused about that part."

"'Cause I haven't made a church-goer out of you yet." The men exchanged comfortable smiles, Larson sipped and continued, "Levi's an Old Testament character whose descendants were called Levites. In the Jewish scheme of things, Levites held the office of priest."

"Thus he identified with that part of Ralph's make-up and thus the business about offering up sacrifice." Bailey shuddered, and he wasn't sure it was from the morning's coolness.

"You got it. Listen, Bailey, you'll have to come down and sign an authorization before we can put a tap on your line. I can't predict how soon it'll actually be accomplished, so I suggest you take everybody and stay gone all day for the sake of your nerves."

Bailey nodded heavily, hating the idea of being chased from his home by some nut. "I'll turn the voice mail off. I'd hate to come home and have one of the kids pick up some sick message."

"Leave the system on," Larson said firmly. "Just be sure they don't hear any playback." Bailey smirked at the idea, and Larson went on, "Bailey, if your caller is more than someone who gets his high from scaring people over the phone, we want his voice on tape."

Larson took a huge swig of coffee and rose from the deck chair. "On the other hand, it's most likely just what you suggested, some crank trying out a story idea on a recognized master of the genre."

"Flattery will get you another cup."

"Gotta go," he said with a shake of head and handing Bailey the empty cup.

As Bailey locked the deadbolt on the kitchen door after Larson, he wondered if he could get the family out of the house before any more threatening calls came. And what then? He would have to slip away from them long enough to sign the authorization for the tap. The simple thing would be to tell Sara the story.

Not so simple after all. You can read everything in Sara's face. If I tell her, I'll have to concoct some elaborate lie to explain her terrorized look to the kids.

Bailey suddenly had writer's block.

Though Bailey had slept little last night, the coffee and the recollection of the previous night's calls had him wired, and so he decided to take advantage of it. Just after seven, feigning enthusiasm, he went to the kids' rooms, clapping his hands and shouting for them to "Get up and at 'em! I'm taking the day off to party, so let's get partying!"

The kids got quickly into the spirit. Sara was less than enthusiastic. As a first-grade teacher who endured nine months of being at school before eight a.m., she cherished summers, when she sometimes got to sleep as late as nine. First-grade teachers had all legitimate cuss words expunged from their vocabularies prior to receiving their teaching credentials. Poor, cranky Sara Thurston was left to stumble sleepily around the house muttering, "Crud buckets!" as an unsatisfying substitute.

Marissa begged her dad to make his 'word-class French toes' for breakfast. Sara wanted nothing more than pure caffeine injected directly in her arm and groaned when Bailey declared that they were going to the International House of Pancakes east of the Marina for breakfast.

"Aw, Honey, why not something closer?"

Because I want to have distance enough to lose anybody following us, Sweetheart.

"I have a craving for their Swedish pancakes," he answered her.

Swooping the boys like a hen herding her chicks, he scurried them through the house and out into the van, their Reeboks in their hands and their hair unbrushed. He watched his rear view mirror frequently during the ten-minute drive down off the hill and to the restaurant. He was certain that no one had followed them, and so he relaxed enough to have a healthy appetite by the time they walked inside.

After her third cup of coffee, Sara said, "I guess the caffeine's finally kicked in. I'm wondering what prompted you to take a day off work? You usually reserve such aberrant behavior for when one of the kids is sick."

He shrugged. "I've been working hard lately. Besides, with the tour coming up, I'm kind of making up for my absence in advance."

"Making up in advance?" she said with a sly smile. "Is that an oxymoron?"

"Who's a moron?" Mike asked, blueberry syrup dripping from his chin.

"You are," Scott muttered.

"Mommy, I want some moron."

"What, Marissa?"

"Some more on my pancake," the girl said seriously, pointing at the maple syrup.

Family life as usual. Maybe I only imagined the calls last night.

After breakfast, Bailey picked up a couple of hundred dollars at the automatic teller from his bank on Lincoln. It was just after nine.

When he got back into the van, Sara said, "The malls didn't open till ten, theaters nearer noon. What's next on our dictatorial tour guide's agenda."

"Oh, don't be so negative," Bailey replied with a quick kiss to her strawberry-tasting lips.

Scott turned aside and muttered, "Oh, gag!"

Bailey thought a moment, knowing that he planned to leave them at the mall long enough to sign the authorization for the tap. "We could play some games till the mall opens and you can enjoy the arcade."

Sara looked aside disinterestedly. Mike said, "What kind of games?"

"Oh, I don't know, Mike. Word games maybe."

Scott muttered, "What a dorky…!"

Sara glared at him and he closed his eyes and threw his head back against the headrest. Mike said, "Aw, Dad, you know you always win."

"Not always, Mike. Remember a couple of months ago when you beat me?"

"Yeah, but you *let* me win. That doesn't count."

Marissa looked up at her dad with a serious, puzzled look. "Where dese words you gonna play wiff?"

"In our head, Sweetie," Bailey answered. Marissa cocked her head the other way with continued puzzlement.

Sara said quietly, "Surely there's something more entertaining than word games, Bailey."

"Magic Mountain!" Scott offered excitedly.

"Yuck!" Mike answered. "You know I get sick on those dumb rides. A Dodgers game. Could we, Dad?"

"They don't play at this hour, Son. What about you, Sara?"

"I'd just as soon go home and putter." The boys in the back groaned.

After fifteen minutes of everyone's sniping at everyone else, Bailey decided he would have to take a more direct approach to signing the paper.

"How'd you like to visit Uncle Human at the police station?"

"Whee!" Sara said sarcastically, waving her finger in the air in a circle.

"What for?" Scott asked.

"Can I try the handcuffs?" Mike asked.

"Okay," was Marissa's decision.

"Great, that's unanimous." Bailey started up the van. "I need to get some technical information from him for the book."

"Did you know Dad wrote about weird guys that sleep together in the hall, Mom?"

"I said I might not use that part, Mike. Hey, look! A truck full of tomatoes!"

"Whee!" Sara shook her head.

Pacific Division of the Los Angeles Police Department was just east of Playa del Rey and the Marina. A windowless concrete building with a brick facade that faced Culver Boulevard, the station was a frequent haunt of Bailey's. Hugh Larson and several other officers were happy to supply technical information on police procedures, vocabulary, ballistics, fingerprinting and countless other minutia that lent a great deal of authenticity to Bailey's mysteries.

He had always presented LAPD in a favorable light in his books, occasionally patterning a character after a particularly helpful officer. Of course one in a previous book was a ringer for Det. Hugh Larson's sterling character.

Bailey parked in the lot beside the station and offered everyone the chance to wait in the van if they weren't interested. The children were all interested. Wanting to keep them all together, Bailey asked Sara to come in to keep an eye on Marissa while he talked with Larson in private.

"Why can't we hear?" Mike asked.

"'Cause it's pretty icky stuff. I don't write for kids, you know, sport."

"Why not?"

"I don't know why not," he answered with a smile and ran his fingers through Mike's curly strawberry hair. "Maybe I'll try it someday."

Inside, walrus-mustached Irv Deacon was at the counter. "Yo, Bailey!" Deacon said, staggering backwards in mock surprise. "You guys taking over the station?" Mike dropped into his G.I. Joe stance and machine-gunned the lobby.

"Not this time anyway," Bailey replied cheerfully. I need to see Det. Larson with a technical question. You suppose you could show the kids your handcuffs while I'm at it?"

"Oh, sure."

Bailey visited frequently enough that nobody bothered to escort him anymore. He hurried from the lobby and through the busy interior room full of desks, toward the cramped office toward the rear.

Bailey felt a hard, friendly slap on his shoulder as the familiar voice of Duke Brown said, "Gotta admit, Bailey, you really know how to combine a marketing genius with suspense."

Puzzled, Bailey turned to respond to the chunky man in plainclothes, "Marketing? Me?"

"Yeah," Brown said with a wave of his meaty hand at the busy room, "every book that comes out, you got an automatic sale of everyone in the division, anxious to see if *this* time you used one of us as a dirty cop. I see I squeaked by again. *In the Shadows* is great!" The grinning man lumbered away toward the front, to the laughter of those within earshot.

Bailey shook his head, returned the smiles and reached for Larson's door. Through the glass top he could see that Larson was on the phone and waving him into the room. Bailey entered as always, coughing slightly and waving at the air thick with cigarette smoke. The office area was designated no-smoking and Hugh Larson had never smoked, but he expected to suffer the same lung diseases as the fellow officers who subjected him to their habit second hand.

He shoved the authorization in front of Bailey before he terminated the phone conversation and said, "My report's been filed."

Bailey sat down. "Anything on Nollan?"

Larson pulled a tape recorder from the bottom drawer and hit Rewind. "Nothing on him in the police records. Has, in fact, a Top Secret clearance in spite of his borderline attitudes. Got this just a couple of minutes ago."

The tape stopped, and both men listened to the playback. Nollan's taped voice was husky, the words crisply enunciated into the phone in the manner of a literate, extremely angry person making sure that neither the content nor the tone was missed.

"Well..., let...me...ask you...this. Why should someone with two masters degrees...squander the intelligence represented thereby...to answer the inane survey questions of you..., nameless telephone solicitor..., working for minimum wage?"

"Oh, I don't know," the young woman on the tape said pleasantly, "maybe because you once had to work for minimum wage yourself and know how humiliating it is for an intelligent person to...."

"I...*know*...that surveys aren't designed...with intelligent persons... in mind."

"Oh? I'd love to hear about that."

The patient, clever young woman played with Nollan's psyche for another two minutes before he realized he had never been in control of the conversation and he hung up with a curse.

At the end of the playback, Bailey squinted, shrugged, shook his head. "Can't be sure. Husky enough, but there's something I thought I would recognize, and it's not there?"

"An accent?"

"No, vocabulary, maybe? Can't put my finger on it. Hang onto it, okay?"

"Oh, you bet. If we get Levi on your tap, we can compare voice prints."

Bailey already knew that. It had been a key element in an earlier novel. "What about protection, Hume?"

"Captain's sympathetic, but it's like I told you last night. The department can't supply protection on the basis of a coupla crank calls."

Bailey swallowed before he nodded heavily and wiped his sweaty palms on his Bermuda shorts. He was signing the form as Larson continued, "But that doesn't mean we can't keep Nollan and the house pretty well covered on a volunteer basis. I've got six guys who'll carve the time out somewhere. Sara and the kids'll never know they're there."

"Thanks, Hume."

"No sweat. You stay gone like I told you, to give us time for the tap."

"Have you said anything to Cynthia about this?"

"No."

"Good. Don't. I'd hate for her to slip and let Sara or the kids know."

Bailey rose and laid the form in front of Larson, who was waving for someone behind Bailey to enter. Bailey moved aside to let two men in plainclothes enter.

Blond, wearing a sports shirt well cut to disguise his slight excess weight, Tony Victor was only vaguely familiar to Bailey as one of the police photographers. As he stepped into the room, fanning the smoky air with a handful of black and white prints, he went into a coughing fit.

Above the coughing, Larson asked, "Bailey, have you ever met Sgt. Ramon Rodriguez?" and nodded toward the stocky man with the black hair and mustache. A pack of cigarettes was peeking from the man's shirt pocket.

Bailey and the detective exchanged smiles and handshakes as Larson explained, "Ramon's an aspiring actor, and he flattered you the other day by saying he would like to play the part of the private investigator in *Shadows* if they ever do a movie."

"Really? Well, for your sake, then, I hope they do," Bailey answered politely.

Before Rodriguez could verbally express the enthusiasm that was on his face, Larson interrupted, "Gotta throw you out, now, Bailey, sorry. Whatcha got Tony?"

Bailey was glad to be leaving, especially since he had gotten a glimpse of the shooting victims in the glossies that Tony Victor was spreading across Larson's desk with his nicotine-stained fingers. He moved the tap authorization with the other. Rodriguez looked over the photographer's shoulder and began the gruesome narrative while the other man got his cough under control.

Bailey was always glad that *describing* police work was as close to serious crime as his work came. At least it was until yesterday.

He rejoined his family, to find that a female officer just going off duty had handcuffed Mike. He was delighted, and Scott was begging her to leave him that way. Bailey dragged the visit out for another fifteen minutes before his family began to get antsy. It was too early for the movies. When he suggested the video arcade, the kids all noisily seconded the motion.

Sara, however, said "Oh, come, now, honey. It's downright criminal to be indoors during such beautiful weather."

"Yeah, how about fishing?" Scott suggested.

The other two kids gave almost as noisy an assent as they had to the arcade. Bailey liked the idea of fishing even better than the arcade, since it further reduced the possibility that someone could follow and get close to them.

Before heading south to King Harbor in Redondo Beach, twenty-five minutes away, Bailey took them all to Gelson's in the Marina to pick up drinks and sandwiches from the deli and sun block.

Sara protested mildly, "Why Gelson's, Bailey? It's always more than Ralph's."

"I know," he answered, "but I might use the setting in the new book." She bought his completely plausible excuse, not knowing that the reason was that he wouldn't set foot inside a market named Ralph's until the question of the caller had been resolved.

*   *   *   *

At two-thirty, the boys were starting to get on each other's nerves—and Bailey's. He looked back across the deep green water toward the shore, where there were dozens of people milling about.

What kind of man am I to look out for?

He decided he would let the boys fish for another half-hour, maybe a little longer if Sara stayed asleep under the canopy. Then they would return the boat and pick a movie. He wondered if he could get away with two movies without Sara's becoming suspicious.

We'll have dinner out. That'll help. I hope.

He reached into the bag with the lunch leftovers and found the tube of sun block. He applied some to his own burnable skin, squeezed enough out to give Marissa next to him a fresh dose and tossed the tube to Mike.

"Do it again, Mike, and pass it on to Scott."

Marissa was looking over the side of the boat, intent on spotting Shamu and oblivious to Bailey's efforts to put the sun block on her cheeks without getting it in her eyes. He finished just as Scott tossed the tube to him. Bailey was holding the back of Marissa's life jacket with one hand and turned to put the sunscreen in the bag with the other when he saw Sara watching him, a contented smile on her face.

"No fair, Bailey," she said with a voice still husky from sleep.

"What's wrong?"

"Not only are you sexy as the dickens and intelligent to boot, but you make a better mother than I do."

*   *   *   *

They played two rounds of miniature golf, and the boys enjoyed the batting cage and automatic pitcher. After that, Bailey dragged dinner out by ordering an uncharacteristic pre-dinner glass of wine for himself and Sara, a Shirley Temple and two Darth Vaders for the kids, appetizers and dessert. Then followed the movie. It was nearly ten when the exhausted partiers pulled into the carport. Even Michael was staring dully off into space and had to be shaken by Sara. Bailey left her to deal with getting the sleeping Marissa from the car as he charged into the house claiming he heard the phone ringing.

He grabbed up the phone and hit the auto dial button for the voice mail system. The impersonal recording said that there were ten messages waiting. *Ten!* Dinner felt like a hot rock in Bailey's stomach. He laid the phone down on the desk and went hastily to close the door and lock it. He hoped he didn't have to make up a story about why.

He also prayed that nobody picked up an extension and heard the messages as he listened to the playback. His hand was shaking when he wrote down the details of the itinerary Mary Zada was arranging. Bailey hoped that the question mark of the caller had been resolved long before the tour, three weeks in the future. There was no way he was leaving the country with such a threat facing his family.

A friend of Sara's had wanted to chat. Mary had called a second time wanting Bailey to accept an offer for another TV talk show as well as another radio broadcast.

Hugh Larson's voice from the voice mail system made Bailey swallow with tension. "Hey, Bailey, Barely Human here." The greeting was Larson's embellishment of the nickname Bailey had assigned him. "Everything's on tap for that fishing expedition we talked about. See ya later."

So the tap's been installed.

The other six calls were for the boys, dumb messages like, "Hey, call me!" from some boy (or maybe it was a girl) who didn't say which of the boys was being addressed or by whom, and "Whatcha doin'?" again with no identified recipient or caller. They were the kinds of messages

Bailey would have left at that age, had voice mail and answering machines been as common.

The system didn't register those calls where the caller hung up before the beep, and so Bailey had to wonder if Levi had called during the day. When everyone was in bed, he checked the locks on doors and windows twice. He crawled in next to Sara where she lay on her stomach, sprawled in exhaustion from Bailey's day of partying. He rubbed her back until she was making the purring, snoring sound that confirmed she was asleep.

He waited fifteen minutes more before he crawled carefully out of bed, got a spare blanket from the upstairs linen closet, and went downstairs to sleep on the floor outside the children's rooms.

*   *   *   *

CHAPTER THREE

Over Sara's protests that they hadn't had a break-in on their street in the ten years they had lived there, Bailey had an alarm system installed the next day. Mike invited his best friend over to show off the sign out front.

"Armed response! That's guns, Joey! Cool, huh?"

Cool? I only hope Levi's more intimidated by the sign than Mike is.

Over the next several days, Bailey stayed near the phone at home, threatening to crack knuckles if anyone tried to out race him in answering it. Preparation for the tour was a good explanation. When any of the kids wanted to go somewhere, Bailey insisted that the whole family go or else the one child wouldn't go. Scott was sullenly trying to figure out what he had done to deserve this sadistic form of grounding. During Bailey's fourth night of sleeping outside the kids' rooms, Sara awoke and found him there.

"Honestly, Bailey, between the burglar alarm and finding you in the fetal position in the hall, I think your work's finally getting to you. Maybe you should take a break or write car repair books or something."

He began to wonder himself if he were paranoid, awakening numerous times each night, stalking downstairs in the darkness and checking on the children. Two weeks had gone by without so much as one call out of the ordinary. The only time the burglar alarm went off was when Bailey forgot the procedure and scared the daylights out of himself and the rest of the family.

The 26th of July was a Wednesday. Bailey was scheduled to leave for Tokyo Sunday, the 30th. His thoughts were only vaguely on the softball game unfolding disastrously in front of him as he watched Brad Nollan grind out another cigarette and curse at the umpire to polish his expletive glass eye. As carefully as Bailey had watched Nollan—and he knew Larson was watching Nollan also—the sullen man's behavior was as it always had been.

Mike and Scott had been warned to steer clear of him while remaining friendly with Dustin. The boys had shrugged non-understanding consent and had had no meaningful conversations to report beyond, "Dustin's got the hots for Julie Schroeder."

Just now, Bailey's glance went between the freckled blond boy at bat, squinting as if he needed glasses, and the angry father in the bleachers, squinting as if he needed a gun. Bailey wondered what kind of man-to-man advice Brad Nollan would offer his son, if any.

When Hugh Larson sighed and stood up from beside his petite wife next to Sara, Bailey noticed the scoreboard and suggested that maybe the dads shouldn't watch their sons go down in flames. The two men descended the bleachers and walked along parallel to the third-base line toward the cluster of palm trees. There they stood in silence for a moment, watching the ducks moving slowly about on the surface of the small lagoon below the field's grassy knoll.

Finally Larson heaved a sigh, turned and cast a painful glance the direction of the diamond. His gangly son was slumping up to bat. Larson gave his son a thumbs-up sign as he asked Bailey, "Any more calls from Levi?"

"No."

"That's good, that's good. He's had plenty of opportunity. We've had people checking Nollan out from close up, including on the job, and he hasn't mentioned you once. Seems like the same frustrated, unsuccessful writer he's been for the last fifteen years, from all we can tell." Bailey nodded noncommittally, and Larson gave him a quick smile.

"Sounds like you were just the victim of some crank. Probably got drunk and now doesn't even remember it." Larson's eyes went to the plate.

"Yeah, probably, but I'm thinking of canceling the tour."

"Bailey!" Larson's wrinkled face whirled toward Bailey. "You can't let one crank call run your life."

"It was two calls. And not forever, just right now. If you had heard him, Hume...."

Larson's face went toward the field again, and he winced as his son swung at a ball that was below the strike zone by a foot. Another thumbs-up.

"I thought of taking them all with me, but there's not enough time for passports and all the rest. Besides, it would clobber me financially."

"You'll be clobbered financially if you cancel. You've told me how your tours are what've helped keep you on the bestseller list."

"Which has higher priority with you, Human? Your job or your family?"

"You know the answer. Don't swing, son, don't swing!" the cringing man whispered. His son swung, missed, and his shoulders slumped just before he looked toward his dad. Larson smiled and moved his open palm up and down as if dribbling a basketball slowly, the sign for Stevie to slow down.

"Well, I can't go off and leave them without full-time protection. I know you can't assign anybody, and if I hired anybody, I'd have to tell Sara."

The pitch was on its way toward Stevie Larson. His father gathered up an anxious breath. Bailey could see that the boy was winding up to swing at what the umpire would call a ball if he left it alone.

The spectators in the bleachers screamed, "Yes!" almost as one at the *Ka-thunk!* of the ball's being hit hard. Stevie was so stunned he stood there for a half a second before he remembered to run.

The left fielder was backing up to catch the fly. "No!" Larson groaned. The outfielder backed into a gopher's mound and tripped. "Yes!"

Stevie was at second, pumping for third and watching the outfielder get to his feet and fumble for the ball. Everyone was screaming, "Run, Stevie, run!" from the stands. The outfielder had the ball, and the crowd's cries had changed to "Slide, slide!" The ball was thrown hard toward third, where the third baseman bobbed anxiously up and down, one toe on the plate and his mitt raised for the ball.

"Lord, Lord, Lord!" Larson was muttering. Bailey knew it was a prayer and not some absent complaint.

Stevie slid into third just as the third baseman made the mistake of looking down at him. His glove moved, he missed, half the crowd groaned, the other half took up, "Run, Stevie, run!" again. He got to his feet and scrambled safely home before the humiliated third baseman could get the ball started that direction. The crowd's screaming sounded as if he had just made the winning run. Even Brad Nollan was smiling through a cloud of smoke.

"Twelve to *one!* Thank you, Lord!" Larson then turned his attention toward Bailey. "Listen, I really, truly understand how frightening such a threat can be. I've had more than my share. But most of the time that's all they are—just threats. In two weeks there's been no repetition, no stalking or attempted intrusions.

Bailey tried not to look at Nollan and was clenching his jaw and working his moccasin's sole against the grass in frustration as Larson continued in a low voice, "After awhile, it becomes a matter of impracticality."

It was several seconds before Bailey looked up suddenly. "You've removed the tap?"

Larson shook his head. "Tomorrow. I can't justify it to my captain any longer. He's already ticked that whenever he tries to find anybody they're parked near your address." Bailey sighed and nodded.

"Listen," Larson continued, "Cynthia still doesn't know a thing about the calls or the tap, but she had a brilliant suggestion that just might make you happy."

"What's that?"

"That while you're globetrotting, Sara and the kids join her and our kids up at Running Springs for family church camp. The camp's well fenced, the entrance gated."

"I don't know, Hume...."

"I can't go, but there'll be two other cops from our church there—Ramon Rodriguez and another. They already know about the calls and know you don't want your family to know."

*   *   *   *

It was at breakfast the next morning when the phone rang. No one moved except Bailey, who darted to the kitchen wall phone.

"Hey, Bailey! Barely Human here."

"Mornin', Human. What's up?"

"Just thought I'd verify that our fishing expedition is no longer on tap. You think any more about the camp idea?"

"Yeah, they think it's a great idea. They're getting together with Cynthia today to go over the list of what to bring and all. In return for your brilliant suggestion, you'll get the honor of entertaining Bammer."

"Hey, no sweat, but this time he's sleeping in the garage. That tail of his doesn't stop even when he's asleep."

*   *   *   *

Friday evening there were about thirty-six hours left before Bailey would be on his Tokyo flight. Sara and the kids would be driving Cynthia, Stevie and five-year-old Jennifer Larson in a car caravan toward Running Springs. The phone had been kept busy with Mary Zada and Bailey making last-minute arrangements and with Sara and the kids finding out what to bring.

It was quiet now. Bailey was at his desk getting ready to print out copies of the detailed itinerary to give to Sara, Larson and a couple of neighbors who were going to water and keep an eye on the house. He was in the midst of a yawn when the phone rang. He glanced at the digital clock.

Just after eleven. Not Sister Mary with another change, I hope.

"Hello?"

"It's Levi, Thurston, and I want you to know I'm serious about exacting sacrifice from you for your portraying me all wrong."

Bailey lurched forward in his swivel chair. *Keep him talking! Give them time to trace.... No tap anymore!*

The gravely voice continued, "You'll hear in the morning news about someone on Oak Street. Read the details carefully. That's what I'm going to do to each of your children before I make you watch me do it to your wife. You'll be last—dead last." There was a deep laugh before the dial tone.

Bailey almost couldn't remember the Larsons' number, a number he dialed roughly every other day. Cynthia answered after the third ring.

"Cynthia, I need Human right now! Is he there?"

"No, Bailey. He was called in on some murder case."

"I've got to reach him. How do I do that?"

"Well, when he's on a case, Bailey, they don't usually...."

"It's about the case. How do I get him?"

"Oh, call the station. Ask for the dispatcher. Tell them to call Hugh and give him the password *Second Chronicles*."

"Uh...." Bailey replied, trying to understand the significance.

"I'll explain sometime. Anyway, it'll tell him that something is seriously wrong at home."

"Oh."

"I've never used it, but I'll have him call you right away."

It was nearly seven minutes after Bailey hung up with the police station before Bailey's phone rang.

"Human?"

"Yeah. Everybody there okay? Cynthia didn't know what...."

"Is your murder on Oak Street?"

There was a second's hesitation before, "Yeah. It make the news already?"

"No, Levi just called me and told me about it—says he did it to impress me with his seriousness. Damn it, Hume, I'm impressed! Help us!" Bailey's voice broke in a sob.

*   *   *   *

Bailey wouldn't have a gun in the house, where one of the kids might accidentally shoot themselves or someone else. After he hung up with Larson, he didn't even go upstairs to tell Sara what had happened. He went into the boys' darkened bedroom, found Scott's bat, and was sitting in the hall outside the kids' rooms when the approaching siren brought Sara scurrying downstairs and Bammer woofing toward the front door.

Ramon Rodriguez, the black-haired detective that Larson had introduced to Bailey as the aspiring actor, politely showed his badge and reintroduced himself to Bailey before being let in.

"Sorry about the bedroom slippers," he said with a smile. "I was home, and Det. Larson thought you could use a friendly face till he could get here himself. Let's check out security, then you can fill me in on what you know." He had an actor's naturally rich voice, with no accent to indicate he and his family weren't California natives for several generations.

But all Rodriguez' smoothness was lost on Sara. "Bailey? Bailey?" she asked breathlessly with frightened eyes.

"We're all okay, honey. Would you get some tea started while we check? I'll explain everything."

As Bailey and Rodriguez checked doors, windows and the burglar alarm, Bailey learned that the detective was already aware of the earlier threats and had been among those to periodically watch Nollan and the Thurston house. Bailey recalled that Rodriguez was also one of the men who would watch out for the Thurstons at church camp.

Sara boiled water for herb tea and listened as Bailey sat at the pine table with Rodriguez and gave him a report. Blessedly, none of the children awoke through any of the disturbance, but Bailey couldn't ignore the look of terror on Sara's face that he had tried so hard to avoid.

Hugh Larson arrived nearly two hours later, near one-thirty. When Sara and Bailey met him at the kitchen door, his greeting was a heavy sigh as he reached to gather them both to himself in a hug.

"Any leads?" Rodriguez asked.

"Zip," Larson answered with fatigue and nodded at the teapot Sara was gesturing toward. "We've got lab techs going inch by inch right behind the photographer. They're gonna take the place apart thread by thread if they have to."

"What about Nollan?" Bailey asked.

"I have someone checking."

In a delayed reaction, Sara asked Bailey, "Brad Nollan? What would he have to do with…with…?" She couldn't say murder and just waved her hand with futility and disgust.

Larson answered, "We don't know that he has anything to do with it, Sara."

She turned her dissatisfied look toward Bailey, who stammered, "He seemed so angry about the new book. I merely suggested to Hume…. I never actually accused…." She just stared at him, and his whole line of thinking concerning Brad Nollan suddenly sounded imbecilic to his own ears.

They all sat at the table, Sara and Bailey crammed side to side, with him clutching her as if she would be snatched away otherwise. "Status is this," Larson continued, directing his gaze between Rodriguez and the couple across from him. "Tap's going back on. And, since we've got reason to assume your caller did tonight's murder, you've been promoted from recipient of a threatening call to a material witness in a murder investigation."

"Some promotion!" Bailey snorted.

"I know, but it gets you the twenty-four-hour protection that we couldn't give you before."

Sara started crying, but the look on her face turned angry as did her tone. "We were in danger all that time and nobody told me!"

Bailey squeezed her though she was trying to pull away. "I was watching all of you the whole time, and Human had his guys watching most of the time."

"Most of the time!"

Even Rodriguez looked down in acknowledgment of the inadequacy. In a second, Bailey and Sara both jumped at the sound of the front doorbell. Rodriguez jogged to answer it.

Larson reached across to touch Sara's cold and shivering arm. "No doubt it's for me," he explained. "I told them to report in if my car was still here."

In a few seconds, Rodriguez returned, followed by Tony Victor. Black and white prints seemed a permanent fixture in his yellowed fingers. So did a cough.

He had a white handkerchief over his mouth and rasped, "If it's not throat cancer, it might be catching. Sorry!" He went into a coughing spasm as he held the stack of prints toward Larson.

A stranger wouldn't have seen the change in Larson's face, but Bailey could read clearly his friend's renewed revulsion. Without laying the pictures down, Larson said casually, "Sara, honey, would you see if all this commotion's awakened the kids."

"Oh, I don't think...."

"You'll feel better if you do," Larson said with a smile.

She arose slowly, her eyes on the back of the prints as wide as if she could see the horror on the other side. Tony Victor stepped aside and watched her go down the hall and into Marissa's room before his attention returned to the men at the table, and he nodded the all-clear.

Bailey couldn't get enough breath together to make either a request or a demand. He merely held out a hand, which he shook impatiently. Larson fanned the prints out on the table, and the four men huddled over them. Larson spoke in a clinical, detached tone.

"Tortured. Several hundred cigarette burns. Wrists, eyes, mouth taped. Throat cut...."

There was a squawk as Bailey shoved his chair back and raced to the sink to vomit. When he returned a few moments later with a damp dishtowel that he dabbed against his face, the talk stopped and Larson stacked the photos. "No need for you to torture yourself, Bailey. We'll just...."

He shook his head. "I'm all right now. Let me have a better look." He studied several prints, forcing himself to forget that this was a woman who was dead because his family lived well off his so-called commercial thrillers. Bailey tried to study the pictures with detachment, as if he were a police detective character in a yet-unwritten novel.

"Color hair?" he asked Larson after a moment.

"Red."

"I thought so."

The three others exchanged glances, and Bailey explained, "Ralph's first victim was a redhead. The other details are the same as in the book also—the taping, the burns, the final slash."

Larson nodded slowly and watched Bailey shuffle the pictures until he picked up one and examined it closely for a moment. He finally looked up and asked both Larson and Tony Victor, "Is this the only ashtray?"

Larson took the photo first and handed it to the photographer with the comment, "It's the only one I saw. Tony?"

"Same, why?" the man rasped and started coughing again into his hanky.

Bailey shrugged. "I'm awfully tired, but I thought you said the lab techs were going *behind* Tony."

"That's right. S.O.P." Larson cast an involuntary glance at the photo.

Bailey suspected there weren't too many times a civilian saw something that Det. Hugh Larson didn't. "I guess maybe Tony took more shots after the lab people came through."

Larson looked at the photographer, who paused a few seconds before shaking his head.

Rodriguez had been silently studying the photograph Bailey had focused on and said, "Who emptied the ashtray? Is that it, Mr. Thurston?"

"Bailey. Yes. Several hundred....Well, there should have been a mountain of cigarette butts."

Larson smiled at Bailey. "I'll check it out."

*   *   *   *

When the boys awoke, Bailey gave them the PG version of the story.

"There's some sick guy going around hurting people. And for some reason he's mad at me, so we're going to be super careful till they catch him and put him in jail. Friends of Hume's are gonna keep us company till they do."

Marissa toddled in. Being strictly a G-rated audience, she got: "We'll have company for awhile."

"What about camp?" Mike asked.

"No camp, Son. Can't take a chance. I'm canceling the tour, and we'll do our best to be happy campers here at home."

"Aw, guy!" Mike began to whine and ran from the kitchen as the tears of disappointment flooded his cheeks.

"That's what all the grounding was about?" Scott asked.

"Yeah, Son. I didn't want to worry you if there wasn't really any problem. Mom and I really need your cooperation on this, especially in getting along with Mike and helping us keep him entertained."

"How long's this gonna take?"

"I don't know, but Uncle Human's on the case, and he's good."

Scott nodded dejectedly and left his cereal, to go lie in front of the television and stroke Bammer. Only Marissa was content, in her state of ignorance and sitting in her mother's lap.

After several minutes of silence, Bailey refilled the bowl his milk-faced daughter was holding toward him and said, "Guess I'd better bite the bullet and call Mary." Sara was rocking back and forth in the chair. He wasn't sure she had heard him.

Mary Zada laughed when Bailey said, "Mary, I know it's a shock and I know you're not going to like it, but I'm canceling the tour."

"Suuure, Bailey. What's really up?"

"Have you read the morning paper?"

"I was looking at the Calendar section when you called, why?"

"Well, check Metro. There's an article on a murder last night."

"That's dreadful, Bails, but why call me to…?"

The killer thinks my *Shadows* was all about him, and he didn't like the way I portrayed him."

"How do you know this, Bailey?"

"Because he's been threatening me and my family. Last night he called to say the murder was to make an impression on me…." His voice trailed off and he had to take a breath and clear his throat before he could continue. Mary was silent the whole time. "I don't have a choice. I have to stay home."

There were several seconds of silence before Mary stammered, "What can I say, Bailey? Of course you have to stay home. I'll notify everyone. I'll have to tell them why. Yes, yes, of course! Bailey, we can turn this nightmare into a publicist's dream!"

"No!"

"Bails, Bails, we have to tell them something! Might as well just enjoy the fruits."

"Just cancel the stupid tour!" he said quietly and hung up.

*   *   *   *

Bailey had to wonder how many of the media vehicles along his street later were some of Mary Zada's 'fruits.' It was quite evident that she had gotten busy right after his phone call to her, since the late morning brought a phone call from Phil Hunter.

"Bailey, I'm very, very sympathetic with your family's situation. I wonder if it would be possible for our remote unit to interview your family."

"No!" he barked, then softened it. "No, Phil, it wouldn't."

"Well, Bailey, you know we don't go in for the Geraldo type interviews, and...."

"I know, but the answer's no. They're pretty shaken up and confused over it. Just, no."

"All right, but how about one with just yourself? You could make an appeal to the killer."

"You can't appeal to a crazy man."

"I suppose you're right. Well, couldn't you just spend two or three minutes telling our viewers how it feels to have one of the characters in your book more or less come to life? I know it isn't a laughing matter, Bailey, but it's ironic that something as awful as your endangered status just might make this book your biggest seller yet."

"You can tell your viewers for me that it's the last thought on my mind. Right now I'm wishing I'd never written the book."

And I stayed awake all night thinking that the victim's family probably feels the same way.

Hunter's professional voice cracked a bit, and Bailey thought he might be hearing the real man underneath the paid voice as Hunter said quietly, "Bailey, I've had a ton of calls already today, and I want you to know you have not only my own sympathy, but that of most of the public. I think it would be a big mistake for you to blame yourself for the murder."

Bailey let out a snort of rejection, but Hunter went on, "When you're able to calm down and look at the logic, I'm sure you'll see it makes no sense to blame a sane man for an insane man's actions."

Right now, I wonder which of those I am?

*   *   *   *

CHAPTER FOUR

Late in the day, Hugh Larson arrived, looking his perpetually weary self. Bailey had never known the man to get more than four hours' sleep at a stretch. If it wasn't some police emergency, it was one of the kids with an earache or someone from church whose father was dying or whose teenager was in trouble. Bailey had never been a Larson emergency call before, and he hated being one this time.

The two men talked in the soundproofed quiet of Bailey's office, sinking into opposite ends of the leather sofa as Larson commented, "Nothing helpful, I'm afraid, but it's a curiosity about the cigarette butts."

"Oh?"

"Gone missing, as the Brits say. There were two lab techs. Each of them assumed that the other one had collected the evidence."

Bailey threw his head back, gazed up at the ceiling, and considered the possibilities during the long moment in which Larson was silent, undoubtedly doing the same.

"Could be," Larson finally said, "somebody lost the piece of evidence. Our guys are good—almost obsessive about keeping and logging everything—but still, it happens."

"Could be," Bailey agreed and looked at Larson, "or it could be that Levi removed the most valuable piece of evidence because he knew it could positively ID him."

"Custom made cigarettes?"

"No."

"Okay, Detective Thurston," Larson said with a tired grin, "enlighten me."

"Saliva is one of the means of DNA testing."

"In the butts! Of course. Man, I must really be tired to miss that."

Bailey asked, "Any fingerprints on the tape?" Larson shook his head.

Bailey fell silent and chewed on the inside of his cheek for a long time before Larson said absently, "It's a very cool customer indeed who would have such presence of mind to avoid or remove fingerprints and then the cigarette butts."

And one very well informed, I'm thinking.

"The lab tests haven't turned up anything useful yet, and our investigation into Brad Nollan's whereabouts during the time of death was equally unsatisfying."

"Meaning what?"

"It was his night off, and he said he had been home, working on his novel since about noon. He was there, doing apparently that, when he was questioned. Dustin was at a friend's, so there's no one to corroborate. As I said, unsatisfying."

Bailey chewed the inside of his cheek again while Larson continued, "It's nothing conclusive, of course, but between Nollan's hot temper and the chaotic state of his housekeeping that the investigator described, he doesn't strike me as a man who would think to clean up after himself at a murder scene."

"Crazies do the most unexpected things."

Larson had no argument.

*   *   *   *

The days that followed stretched on endlessly, police officers relieving one another in guarding the Thurston household, Hugh Larson checking by phone and in person several times each day. The Thurston children were holding up far better than cither Bailey or Sara. Sara said almost nothing, moving in a daze around the house to fix the meals and straighten up. When she wasn't doing that, she would sit holding Marissa and staring at the boys while they watched TV or played a game.

Bailey tried to work, but he never got past turning on the computer and staring at the Delete key on his keyboard. *If only I could!*

Cynthia Larson had canceled the trip to Running Springs, and she visited every day with her kids to help relieve the routine. She was extremely glad to feel as if she was of even a tiny bit of help. Besides shopping for groceries and helping with the cooking while she was there, she brought casseroles and meal loafs plus board games and a handful of computer games that the Thurston kids didn't have. The newspapers were comparing Bailey's situation to that of Salman Rushdie.

"I hope to God it's not like that!" Bailey said to Larson outside the kitchen one evening. "He'll be in hiding the rest of his life."

"We'll get Levi, Bailey. I don't know how, but we'll get him."

Sleep was a sadistic tease to both Bailey and Sara. Night would find them lying in the dark, staring at the ceiling. Mornings, they stumbled around, drained. When they would try to occupy themselves in something useful—Sara mending a tear in a blouse or Bailey polishing the brass on a table lamp—they would be startled awake by one of the kids and surprised to realize that they had dozed.

One afternoon was like that. Bailey was sitting in the family room, the burlwood door to the Jaguar glove box lying on newspapers on the coffee table and Marissa sprawled on the rug, watching Sesame Street. The others were quiet in the various parts of the house.

Suddenly Bailey's head jerked, and he felt a jab of adrenaline. A Pepsi commercial was on low, and Marissa had disappeared.

From down the hall, a few yards away, Bailey heard the man's raspy voice threaten, "Open up, open up, or I'll break the door down!" Marissa's shriek was piercing.

Bailey's heart was squeezing furiously with fear as he lunged up off the sofa and tore out of the room, screaming, "No, no! You leave her alone, Levi!" The door to Marissa's room was open when Bailey grabbed the jamb and flung himself into the room toward the man beside Marissa's bed.

He was stopped in his tracks by the delight unexpectedly registered on Marissa's small face looking up at him. In an instant, delight melted into fear, and she cried out, "What's wrong, Daddy?!" before she clenched her eyes shut and pulled the covers over her crying head.

"Bailey, Bailey, it's okay, man! You must have been dreaming!" Rodriguez' smooth voice tried to calm Bailey, at the same time the officer smiled and squatted to gently peel the covers from Marissa.

Rodriguez? Not Levi? It was his voice.... At least I was so sure it was his voice. And Marissa screamed. Didn't she?

By now, Sara was standing in the doorway, looking as terrified as Bailey felt. "It's okay, Mrs. Thurston. Marissa and I were just acting out the Three Little Pigs, and I guess my Big Bad Wolf was too convincing. I'm awfully sorry."

Marissa recovered more quickly than either Bailey or Sara. Bailey was, in fact, still disoriented and shaky when Hugh Larson checked in two hours later. The men paced aimlessly in the small rear patio, near the carport.

"No calls today?" Larson asked.

"No. It's been nearly three weeks. Any more killings like the last one?" Larson shook his head, and Bailey continued, "I had an off-the-wall thought today while working on the Jag. Don't know whether you're interested in pursuing it."

"Let me decide."

"Well, I don't know the man at all. I only saw him once, talked with him for about thirty minutes. I can't imagine his motivation."

"The name?"

"Angelo Hayes."

There was a long moment in which Larson stared at Bailey before he combined a chuckle and exasperation as he said, "I thought you'd written enough of this stuff to know the questions the cop asks and the answers the subject gives. Give!"

Bailey answered in a singsong voice, "He's an auto body man, BJ's Body Shop on Grand in El Segundo, about fifty, has a reputation as a hard drinker and an ego that won't quit. He created that left fender from scratch."

Larson's eyebrows raised in admiration as he asked, "Any way of knowing whether he's read any of your books?"

"I don't have the answer, but Randy, a kid in the shop probably would."

"I'll check. Assuming this Angelo Hayes has read *Shadows* and identified with Ralph's mechanical and engineering genius, did you somehow set him off by criticizing his work on the fender?"

"No way! He wasn't even there when Randy installed it for me—home drunk, according to Randy. And I had only compliments to offer. I wouldn't put it past Randy, though, to try deflating his ego a tad by telling him I knocked the work."

Larson nodded and reiterated his promise to check into it. A new inside officer had arrived, and Rodriguez smiled at Larson and Bailey before he saluted and headed down the side driveway to his car out front.

"What can you tell me about Rodriguez?" Bailey asked quietly while picking at a nonexistent piece of lint on his shirt. When Larson didn't answer, Bailey finally looked up.

"Any problems with him, Bailey?"

"No, no, he seems very nice."

There was another pause, in which Larson studied Bailey before he said, "He has an impeccable record. Maybe it's his acting talent, but he has an amazing ability to adapt his behavior to suit the situation."

"Including adapting his voice?" Again Bailey's eyes went to his shirt.

"What're you suggesting?"

Bailey felt almost paralyzed with conflict. He had to weight the terror he had felt at the sound of the voice threatening Marissa against the fact he had not slept in two days. Finally he answered, "I'm suggesting that, as nice as he is, I'd like someone else guarding us."

Larson opened his mouth to speak, closed it, lowered his head and closed his eyes before he looked up and nodded.

"Thanks. Listen, school's supposed to start up in two weeks. Sara's told her school she's taking a leave. What'll we tell the kids?"

Larson nodded and drew circles on the patio bricks with his shoe before he answered, "Tell them they're going. With the faculty and staff alerted, nobody's going to bother them while they're on campus. We'll continue the surveillance here and taking them to and from."

"What kind of life is that?" Bailey asked with a frown.

"I know, but at least it has the advantage that they won't be restricted to the house and they can see their friends."

"I suppose so," Bailey said dispiritedly. "Yours is the only family brave enough to send their kids into a house targeted by a crazy man." Larson gave Bailey a bear hug before he left.

A couple of days after Bailey gave Larson the mechanic's name, Larson reported during his afternoon visit, again on the patio, "Nothing promising, Bailey. His wife said he was in bed drunk during the time of the murder. When I questioned her further, she admitted she only assumed he was there during the period in question"

"Oh?"

"According to her, he had passed out and was snoring loudly when she left around six for dinner and a movie with a girlfriend. Afterwards, she had a few drinks herself—which doesn't help her testimony—and says he was still snoring away when she got in at two-thirty."

"What if Ramon's not the only decent actor around?"

Larson nodded. "I checked with your fan Randy and with Hayes himself. Randy says Hayes has no idea who you are. He also says he told Hayes you were very flattering about the fender. Hayes seemed to corroborate it all. We'll keep an eye on him, though."

*   *   *   *

The children were all glad to be back at school, including Marissa at nursery school, where Sara was now a volunteer aide. The school day routine only heightened Bailey's anxiety, however. It meant that, from the time they left for school to the time they were returned to the house, he didn't know for certain that they were still alive. Every school day was a seven-hour hell for Bailey.

Mary Zada tried to convince him to take advantage of the dozens of requests for talk show appearances or tabloid interviews. He declined them all.

"Well, with all this time to go crazy thinking about how your family is, why don't you spend the time documenting the case. Surely you can see that you're living your next bestseller, Bails."

"I don't write horror stories, Mare."

He paced and stared at the videotapes of various comedy movies that Cynthia Larson supplied in a steady stream. He repaired the heater, washed windows, polished silver, tinkered with his Jag. The latter only made him wonder about Angelo Hayes' alibi.

Bailey would put his tools away, get them out to fix the sticky bathroom drawer, try to read a book—which brought Brad Nollan's angry face across the meaningless pages.

When Larson asked on a visit how Bailey was holding up, his answer was, "Ever try to hold your hand in a flame for seven hours?"

*   *   *   *

It seemed in the beginning that every blessed bit of pleasure had been stripped from Bailey and Sara. They ate because it was expected. When the plate was removed, neither of them could have told you what they had just eaten. It hadn't seemed possible that appetite would return, but this late November afternoon, there was the smell of sage mingled with that of pumpkin pie in the kitchen when Bailey returned from the library. Sara was smiling at the sight of her daughter squatted in front of the glass oven door.

"They look done, Mommy, really."

"I just put them in fifteen minutes ago, Marissa. You go on. I'll let you know when they're done. Then they have to cool before they're ready to eat."

"But they look done," the girl repeated seriously, "and I like hot pie."

Sara waved her daughter away from the room and kissed her husband after he had closed the kitchen door. It was a lingering kiss that hinted that tonight might lead to the same lingering lovemaking that they had enjoyed just last night.

Weeks had gone by in the beginning when they were too terrified to think of making love or else were so emotionally exhausted that they couldn't even go through the motions. But things had begun to feel nearly normal after almost three months with no calls and no more of the gruesome murders described in Bailey's book.

They finished the kiss and Sara said, "I didn't realize how inhibiting it was to have one cop or another inside with us all the time."

"Yeah, it felt sort of like having a thorn extracted from my big toe when they left." Bailey continued wolfishly, "The last three weeks have been terrific."

Sara swatted him playfully with a dishtowel and enjoyed a second lingering kiss.

As much as Sara enjoyed aiding in nursery school, she missed having her own classroom and had talked during the last week about trying to get back on staff in the January semester. Mary Zada was talking about rescheduling the Asia tour for February. Bailey told her to forget it. He was doing research for a book about classic cars in famous murder mysteries. She had gasped and labeled it a disastrous career move. He told her he didn't care a flying fig about his career at the moment.

It was dark at six-thirty that Wednesday evening when Hugh Larson came knocking on the kitchen door and calling out, "It's Barely Human!"

Sara was still in the kitchen and let him in just as Bailey walked in from the office.

"Oh, wow, Hugh!" Sara greeted him breathlessly with her eyes on the gelatin salad that he was presenting like a golden crown on a pillow. "You and Cynthia are definitely getting a raw deal."

"Never! I live all year just for a taste of your pumpkin chiffon pie."

She removed his pumpkin pie from the refrigerator, which made space for the salad, as Bailey commented, "I suppose your house will be overflowing with people again this Thanksgiving."

"Oh, you bet. We've got relatives plus some people from the church who would otherwise be alone. Cynthia has the gift of hospitality to the max. And you guys?"

Sara looked away and scrubbed the kitchen sink absently. Bailey answered, "Usually we're pretty full here, too. Sara's cousin and her family of six drive down from Bakersfield and two or three childless couples who miss family at the holidays are here.

Larson nodded and Bailey continued, "This year it's just the five of us. The cousin's pregnant again and at that green-faced icky stage." Bailey looked away as he said quietly, "The couples all made other plans, which is just fine by us."

He didn't have to remind Larson that his family was still the only one willing to visit their home. The kids had all gone to other houses to play, and even those invitations were few.

Sara dried her hands, commenting that she wanted to go change before she finished fixing dinner. She handed Larson the pie. "We're very thankful for good friends like you and Cynthia." She hugged him and went toward the bedroom.

Larson dragged his feet as he moved slowly toward the back door, which Bailey knew meant there was something else he wanted to say. "Anything new on Levi?" he asked the sad-faced man.

Larson stopped and smiled with fatigue. Always with fatigue. "Not really. Our surveillance on Nollan and Hayes hasn't turned up anything new. We've also scoured the records for any felons who are mechanics, engineers or scientists. The few we've come up with are either dead, doing time, or have some other airtight alibi. None had any records connected to murders similar to Levi's. None had any connection to you." He shrugged.

Bailey shrugged also after a moment, and Larson continued, "Listen, Bailey, I've pestered the captain to keep the tap on all this time, and surveillance. But with no new threats and no leads, this thing could go on…. It could go on indefinitely. He's finally pulled the plug on me. The tap's already off, and I'm to dismiss the surveillance out front on my way out."

Bailey nodded.

"Listen, I haven't stopped praying about this. And until we get him, the minute I have the faintest excuse, you'll get the full-time protection back. We'll provide what we can unofficially meantime."

Bailey merely nodded. He was glad Larson didn't wish him a happy Thanksgiving. It would have been a bit like his saying that to a cancer patient who was still waiting for the results of the latest crucial test. Bailey didn't tell Sara about the withdrawal of surveillance. He would let it come up naturally in conversation, if it did.

But Thanksgiving was happy, in spite of Bailey's gloomy anticipation of it. He and the boys threw the football in the back yard in the sunshine while the turkey roasted. Marissa ran around their legs trying to intercept the ball, which was always a good six feet over her head. They ate till they hurt and huddled together on the family room sofa to watch the football game.

The day and the long weekend couldn't have been nicer, and by the time school resumed on Monday and Bailey drove the boys to school, he was counting his blessings. Monday night in the dark, as he was running his hand over Sara's waiting body, the phone rang. Sara was reaching for it, and so he had to be quick to reach it first.

He had taken up praying of late and was right now praying that it was a wrong number when he answered, "Hello?"

"I'm a very patient man, Thurston, but I didn't want you to think I'd changed my mind or gone away. Another sacrifice was offered tonight. Next time, it'll be Marissa."

"No! God, no!" Bailey was shouting and crying at the whining phone in his hand.

*   *   *   *

CHAPTER FIVE

Cynthia Larson had to stay home with her sleeping children, but she had had the presence of mind to send the Valium left from a pulled back muscle several months earlier.

Larson held them out to Sara, and her hands were shaking so badly she almost dropped them. Once they were in her mouth, Larson asked to use the Thurston phone to check on the investigation at the new murder scene.

Bailey stood by watching Larson intently as he questioned the officer on the other end. He hung up with a long, sad breath and with his head down.

"Give!" Bailey said quietly.

Larson looked at Sara before he answered. "Maybe you should go lie down, Sara."

She looked almost as if she were having a seizure, she was shaking so badly, but she shook her head decisively and leaned against the kitchen counter. Larson began, "Okay, so the style of the murder is the same, except this time the victim was a man."

Bailey said, "Just like Ralph's second victim."

Larson nodded and added, "And with the same color hair as the character, blond."

A half an hour later, Sara's shaking was down to merely trembling. Larson sat forward in the kitchen chair, his big, dark hands clasped in the position of prayer as he responded to Bailey's angry suggestion, "No, Bailey, I don't believe he's a cop!"

"It seems like he knew the tap and surveillance had been removed."

"We were high profile about the surveillance after the first murder, on purpose. I'll bet anyone passing along your street knew who they were and noticed when they stopped coming. It's pretty S.O.P. to terminate a tap at the same time."

"I don't buy it," Bailey said. "Between the timing and the disappearance of the cigarette butts—again!—it points to someone with knowledge of police procedure and forensics."

"Well, sure, Bailey, but that in itself doesn't make him a cop."

"Why not?" he asked hotly.

"You have the same knowledge."

"As part of my work. How many people spend as much time reading and asking about such details?"

"How many copies of your books have been sold? At least that many. And, Bailey, frankly, as knowledgeable as you are about procedures, I don't think you have a realistic perspective on the details of the actual work."

Bailey's mouth dropped open, and he gasped for air several times before he flared, "Oh, so now I'm the one in the hot seat! I'm unrealistic, and my books might just have given Levi the blueprint for getting away with murder!"

"Heavens no, Bailey! All I meant was that writing about murder is a long way from...."

"I don't get you at all, Human. It sure as hell looks like you're more interested in protecting the reputation of your precious police buddies than in the flesh and blood of innocent civilians."

Sara's eyes were wide and her knuckles white from her clenching her fists. There was silence except for the rush of Bailey's angry breath through his nostrils, while Larson looked into the empty mug he turned in his hands.

Finally Larson looked up and said, "In spite of the fact I don't believe any of our officers is involved, I already asked someone from Internal Affairs to pursue that possibility without alerting anyone to his investigation. Beginning with Ramon Rodriguez, all our investigators came up squeaky clean."

Bailey glared at Larson a long moment before he heaved a frustrated sigh, looked away and absently stroked Sara's rigid back.

"I know it's hard for you and Sara to see it from your threatened position, but the protection of the flesh and blood of my dearest personal friends is uppermost on my agenda and always has been."

Bailey huffed and squirmed and snarled a few times before he said, still hotly, "Hume, understand I'm not really mad at you."

"I know that."

"But I'm frustrated, and I'm scared for my family. This on-again, off-again protection isn't going to do it. What can we do?" His voice was broken, and he tried to flash a smile at Sara next to him before he looked back at the tense man across from him. "How does the Federal Witness Protection Program work?"

"Forget it. I already knew it wouldn't help you, but I asked anyway. They told me what I already knew. They reserve it for witnesses who have been instrumental in breaking some really big case."

"I'm the only one to hear his voice. I've given them every scrap of information."

"It hasn't helped the case, unfortunately. Besides, murder is a state interest, not federal."

Bailey sat stonily clenching and unclenching his jaw. After a moment, Larson continued, "I know when it's happening to you it seems like a unique situation, and I know it's no comfort to know that there are *thousands* of innocent people in this city who have been threatened."

"Not by anybody this crazy."

"In some cases, Bailey, yes. My point is that there simply aren't enough officers to go around, not enough money to help hide every potential victim."

"Potential victim. We can't even go out of our own house."

Larson reached across the table and put one hand on Bailey's fist. "I'm on your side. While I can't get anybody to commit any bucks to stashing you all somewhere in a safe house at government expense for an indefinite period of time, I can offer you something I think will help. It's the only thing any of us can think to do to buy us some time." He sat back.

"What's that—put us in jail?"

"No, but I thought of it," Larson answered with a small smile. "I'm talking about borrowing from the Witness Protection Program's bag of tricks and having you drop out of sight as the Thurston family and resurface somewhere else as the Smiths or Joneses."

"What about protection in our new location?"

"No can do."

"But, why?" Sara asked, speaking for the first time since Larson had been there.

Larson answered her, "For one thing, it would mean letting someone else know where you are. I can vouch for our guys, but I don't know every police officer in the country. For another reason, the best surveillance in the world gets spotted eventually. A neighbor or school chum would start asking questions, word would get around, and your cover'd be blown."

Bailey sat motionless for a moment mulling the idea. It seemed a pitifully small solution in light of the horrendous danger to his family. He had had bloody nightmares since the first phone call. Finally he said, "Any opinions, Sara?" with a stroking of her cheek. It was like ice.

"I want the man dead!" she whispered with a trembling chin. "I want him dead."

"So," Bailey said, holding his arm around her and turning back to Larson, "the options are being prisoners in our own house or semi-free people somewhere else as somebody else. That the bottom line?"

"'Fraid so. If it were me, Bailey, I'd opt for the change of scenery. Mind you, we'll get this guy, and you can come back home."

Home!

Bailey and Sara had designed most of the remodeling to the house themselves. It had been a tiny, single-story cracker box before they had knocked out walls and added the upper floor. Sara had done all the papering and had painted the flowering garlands that framed several of the interior doorways. The boys had chosen their own paper and window blinds, as had Marissa just last year.

Sara stared into space and said in a near whisper, "I expected to raise our family in this house, to see them through college, married, and bringing their own kids to visit on Thanksgiving and Christmas." She looked at Bailey when she finished, "It's a lot to walk away from. Even temporarily."

Bailey nodded and after a moment turned toward Larson. "How much do we take with us?"

Larson looked across at Bailey then Sara, swallowed, looked down before he answered Bailey, "Cash."

"Okay, but I meant, clothes for how long? And of course the kids'll want to bring a bunch of their toys and the Christmas stuff...." Bailey stopped at the sight of Larson's repeated swallowing.

"Just cash, Bailey."

Bailey began to turn as cold as Sara had felt as he listened to the procedure that was about to strip them all of themselves.

"No wallets, purses, credit cards, driver's licenses, inoculation cards. No birth or marriage certificates, no passports, address books, scrapbooks, or books you were working on."

The list of things that they might be tempted to bring along was recited to Bailey and an uncomprehending Sara for several minutes before he stopped and Bailey asked, "What happens to all our things?"

"They go into storage. With your help, we make it look like you packed up and moved and then put your house on the market before you disappeared."

Sara looked at Bailey, herself terrified, as he cried, "I don't want to sell it!"

"All I'm talking about is having you list it for rent."

"He could trace us through the renters. They'll have to know where to send the rent."

Larson smiled through his fatigue. "I have my own money-laundering tricks."

"Sounds to me like you've been working on this idea awhile."

Larson nodded. "There's no way he'll get to you or even know your new name. I'm going to work alone on this, Bailey, so you won't have to worry about a leak in the department. Cynthia won't even know how to connect with you all."

* * * *

Though Larson worked alone in the horrendous undertaking, he had his captain's authorization to aid the Thurstons in relocating. The authorization carried the proviso that the department wasn't picking up the tab for such things as the moving van, the cost of storing their belongings, the cost of getting established in a new location. The department would cover the cost of getting basic new papers: birth certificates, Social Security cards, inoculation and school records for all of them, driver's licenses.

The city would also pick up the small tab for seeing that Thurston's substantial credit line evaporated in the Experian file and materialized under the new name, with cards to match. Background checks on the three Experian people in a position to accomplish such a feat were as thorough as for those people guarding the President.

Hugh Larson thanked the Lord that he had been forced into making similar arrangements once before. He had learned a lot that time, and so he anticipated less than a week's time before he could send the

Thurstons on their way to safety and breathing space, while he conducted the murder investigation.

Many times in the past Larson had been the one to search for holes in Bailey's plots. It felt odd to both men for their roles to be reversed, with Larson doing all the inventing, revising, and manipulating, while Bailey was left to search for flaws—and to be one of the characters being manipulated.

*   *   *   *

The morning after Larson's visit, Bailey and the boys were at the kitchen table, Sara at the stove making pancakes. Marissa was still in dreamland. Bailey had just finished explaining the proposed arrangement.

"So what do you think, guys? Think you can live with this new-identity idea better than going back to being grounded by the cops? Think you can treat it like one very long game?"

Sara swallowed at the use of *very long* to describe the hiding out, and Scott asked her unspoken question, "What's *very long* mean?"

"A couple of months maybe." Bailey answered without looking at Sara. He didn't dare. The guilt for triggering all this horror was tearing him apart inside.

Mike said, "Piece o' cake."

Scott shrugged, and Bailey asked, "Okay, then, what names should we use while we're playing the game?" He went and got the phone book from the kitchen drawer.

"What's the phone book for?" Scott asked.

"Sometimes I get stuck trying to come up with a name for a minor character, so I browse through here. Usually something strikes my fancy. We need a new last name."

Mike was looking over Bailey's shoulder as Bailey thumbed through the pages. Scott's attention was focused on the plate of pancakes Sara was setting down in front of him.

"Suzuki!" Mike shouted.

"What about it?" Bailey asked.

"It's a really cool car, and there's this really cool kid at school named Suzuki."

"He's Japanese, dummy." Scott's response got a scowl from both his parents.

"So?" Mike asked seriously. Scott rolled his eyes and began the destruction of his pancakes.

Bailey answered, "Since none of us look Japanese, Mike, it would make people curious about a name like that. We don't want to attract attention, remember?"

"Oh, yeah." Now Mike's attention was on the steaming pancakes set down before him.

Bailey suggested several names from the phone book, all of which got the thumbs-down, then Mike said, "I'd have trouble remembering names like that. I'd rather just use my own name."

Bailey shook his head, "Mike...,"

"How about our middle names for our first names?" Scott asked Mike. "Think you could remember those?"

"Yeah, that's cool!" he mumbled through a mouthful.

"Terrific," Bailey said with relief and pushed the phone book aside to make room for his plate of pancakes.

Scott looked at his mother as she put a pancake on a plate for herself. "You're not in on this, Mom. That's not fair."

"Well, then, how about I toss my maiden name in as a last name."

Mike's forehead wrinkled. "When were you a maid?"

Scott rolled his eyes before answering, "It means her last name before she was married, dum...."

"Oh, cool!" Mike answered. "Woods. Totally cool, Mom."

So first and last names were decided. Next came choice of new location. They were in the middle of this discussion when Marissa toddled in.

"I wanna live in Disneyland," she offered.

Sara tousled her daughter's hair and answered with a smile, "That's a charming idea, Sweetie, but Disneyland's a play place, not a house place."

Scott wanted some remote mountain location, one where he could guard the entrance with a shotgun. Mike thought Hawaii would be cool.

During his career, Bailey had created several characters who needed to disappear. He had chosen for them to hide in the crush of New York City or London. One stranger in a tiny town was too noticeable. Five would never get away with it. But Bailey also knew that neither the kids nor Sara would adapt well to something as metropolitan as New York City or closer downtown San Francisco.

And since he wanted to spare himself some expense, he considered several moderately large California cities or their suburbs before he felt comfortable with the San Diego area. Being the second largest city in California, it would allow them to get lost. Being spread out over a very large area, they could avoid the big-city atmosphere quite easily. He knew that once they were there, the kids would start lobbying for a visit to Sea World and the zoo.

*   *   *   *

When Bailey and Sara had prepared to move into the house ten years ago, packing had been a labor of love. This time it felt like a burial detail. He broke down in tears twice as he boxed the boys' baby shoes and then Marissa's baby book. After that, he steeled himself and tried to blank out what it was he was holding in his hand as he grabbed and stuffed.

They hadn't told Marissa she couldn't bring anything with her. Of the boys, only Scott seemed to understand that they could take absolutely nothing with them. Even the clothes they would wear would be burned as soon as they had replacements. There was no way of knowing what familiar thing the killer might notice about them if he were to cross paths with them accidentally at their new location.

It was December fifth, a fittingly cold and grey Tuesday, when the huge Bekins van pulled up in front of the Thurston house. Several neighbors came running when the first load of furniture started toward the street.

"Only temporary, Ed. Just till they ID the nut."

"Only temporary, Diane."

Only temporary, Bailey.

"Where're you going, Bailey?"

"The other side of the world."

By two in the afternoon, even Sara's van and the Jag had been loaded into the Bekins van. It was on its way to Kansas City, where its contents would remain in storage. Anyone tracing the shipment would only find it a confusing dead end.

The children were having an adventure exploring the house, searching in closets and cupboards for any scraps that needed to be tossed. Bailey and Sara were in the living room, the sound of their slow steps echoing on the bare wood floor of the hollow space.

Sara was rigid, her arms hugging herself as if she would crack and crumble otherwise. Her breathing was in the desperate, gasping way of someone trying to gain control. Bailey reached for her, and she shrugged him off with a hard jerk of her shoulders.

"I'm had as hell, Bailey Thurston!"

"Me, too, honey. If I hadn't written that particular story in that particular way...." He couldn't finish.

"I'm mad, mad, mad!" she said harshly, stomping one foot and with the tears saturating her face.

The three children burst into the room. "You gonna get a divorce?" Mike asked, looking between his parents with fear. Scott also looked fearful, and Marissa was trying to climb up her mother's skirt.

"No!" Bailey said and stepped quickly over to put his arm around Sara.

She was still crying, but she had forced an uneasy smile and picked up Marissa. "I'm not mad at your dad, Mike. I'm mad at your old friend, San Andreas. Let's just say this is all his fault, okay?"

*   *   *   *

CHAPTER SIX

Bammer was 'vacationing' at the Larsons'. Bailey had signed the papers authorizing Coastline Realty to act as rental agent for the house. For a commission, of course, they were to see that rents were collected and donated to the First Christian Church in Culver City.

Their chairman of the board of elders, one Hugh Larson, had alerted the board to a pending donation. The persuasive chairman had convinced them to use the windfall to grant additional monthly funds to five church-supported missionaries in widely scattered locations. The chairman of the elders of their sponsoring church had in turn, contacted each of the missionaries.

Privately Hugh Larson told each that, while the church elders had approved an increase for them, as chairman of the elders he was urging them to recognize the need for help in the church's own back yard. Larson convinced all five of the urgency of donating the extra funds to The Beacon, a Culver City organization aiding the homeless throughout California.

The chairman of the elders had, of course, informed The Beacon of yet another family needing their help, a family from Redondo Beach whose every belonging had been destroyed by a fire. They were emotionally devastated and trying to find work and relocate in San Diego, where they wouldn't be reminded of what they had lost quite so intensely as in Redondo Beach.

The Beacon's Christian administrator, Carl Moe, had always supported Larson and his church's needy families. He was happy to forward a monthly support check to the family at an address which Larson would supply. Larson had said nothing about monies to come from any missionaries. He and Moe had always operated on faith. Where there was a need, God would supply.

Larson expected Moe to notice later that the amount he was sending to the needy family was the same as the increased giving received unexpectedly by The Beacon from five apparently unrelated donors. But instead of raising a question with Moe, it would only cause him to praise the Lord one more time.

Funneling the money through an organization for the homeless and to which Bailey was a regular contributor, was a solution fraught with so much irony that Bailey told Hugh Larson he had the makings of a writer of satire. Or bookkeeper for the mob.

*   *   *   *

The taxi was waiting at the curb, Sara and the children already in, when Bailey swallowed hard, pulled the front door shut, then shoved the key ring inside through the mail slot. He shoved his hands into his pants pockets and hunched his jacketed shoulders against the cold breeze as he hurried toward the taxi. Without the weight of the keys, the small amount of change in his pocket felt out of balance. What felt like the familiar lump of his wallet in his hip pocket was the plain white envelope containing nearly five thousand dollars in folded bills.

To help the kids remain untalkative during the ride, Sara had violated her no-candy rule and supplied them each with a Sugar Daddy on a stick. She and Bailey had no trouble remaining silent. During the ten-minute ride to LAX, the driver talked about nothing more personal than whether it was going to rain or not. Bailey watched the cab's side mirror to verify that they weren't followed.

None of the children knew of the ultimate destination, and the boys had been drilled about not making any remarks about wherever Bailey took them or what odd things he might ask them to do. Taking a cue from Mary Zada, Bailey had told them he wanted to enlist their aid in living out a suspense story that he would turn into a bestseller. They liked the idea that their names would appear on the cover as co-authors.

Only Marissa spoke as they got out of the taxi at the international terminal. "Where we goin', Daddy?"

"Up, up and away!" he said and tossed her into the air as he swooped her from the car.

The cabby commented as he accepted payment, "I thought no luggage meant you were meeting somebody. Did you forget your things?"

"Sent everything ahead," Bailey answered casually. The taxi pulled away, and the foursome accompanied Bailey inside the busy terminal.

The boys are taking in all the foreign dress and language, probably wondering which exotic, faraway destination I have in mind. San Diego—what a rat!

He steered every one along the length of the building and herded them back outside to the shuttle stop. During the brief ride to Parking Lot C, off airport property, the suckers continued doing their magic. Sara was dutifully dabbing at Marissa's face with a tissue, to keep the sticky runover from getting on her jacket or T-shirt. Since they were going to be burned, Sara had picked a jacket Marissa had nearly outgrown and a shirt that she didn't particularly like. Nonetheless, they had to last until they got to their new location and shopped.

In with the folded bills was the parking receipt and ignition key for the car Hugh Larson had parked in the C lot this morning after signing it out of the police impound yard. The record said it was needed for a sting operation. Larson's verbal directions to Bailey were good, and they had no trouble finding the red Blazer in the numbered space that was written on the ticket. They got into the car, and the kids exploded with talk—nothing important or even about where they were going, just the talk that had not been expended in their half-hour of imposed silence.

Bailey let them vent for the twenty-minute drive north along the San Diego Freeway and then the streets of Santa Monica. When they pulled up in front of the large apartment on Lincoln, just south of Idaho, he told them to resume the adventure. Suckers went back into the mouths.

Human would be pleased that "Thank the Lord!" just popped into my head.

Sara wiped the surfaces in the back, where the kids had sat, and Bailey did the front where he and Sara had sat, before they got out. He quickly wiped the keys, dropped them on the floor in the front, locked and closed the car and wiped the handle before joining his family walking briskly across the street and toward the lobby of the apartment building. Larson would see that the car was picked up in a few hours and returned to the impound lot.

The lobby was several steps below street level. Bailey used the security keypad beside the double wood doors to gain access. As he turned to close the door, he didn't see anyone watching from the street. He was glad for that and that the lobby was empty as he took a handful of letters from his jacket pocket and shoved them into the mail slot.

Within forty-eight hours, Mary Zada would discover that she was temporarily out of work as Bailey's publicity agent. He had acquired an anonymity agent—Hugh Larson. Bailey's letter gave Mary no clue as to how to reach him. There wasn't, in fact, anyone who would know how to reach him except eventually Larson. Not even Cynthia.

Larson had promised Bailey he would never write down their new address or phone number anywhere. Of course The Beacon would have the address, but even they wouldn't know its significance. They would have no way to know it was connected with the killer or the disappearance of a writer of best-selling murder mysteries and his family.

A letter had also been written to Bailey's agent in New York. Bailey said he was having all his mail forwarded to him and was trusting him to use the royalties that would be received, to pay all the bills that would continue. Sara wrote to her pregnant cousin and various close friends.

The boys wrote to a couple of their friends. Bailey had read all the letters to be certain there were no hints of their intention to change identities temporarily. The boys' at least were simple and honest: *We're going to have to go away and hide out till they get the creep. I hope we're back in time for Christmas.*

Bailey didn't like thinking about that part at all. Larson hadn't been encouraging, and Christmas at home had always been the highlight of the year in the Thurston household. If they caught the guy tomorrow, Bailey could never put things back in order in time to have it feel right.

Damn that old San Andreas anyway!

From the lobby of the apartment, Bailey and his family went through a door to the parking garage. He was grateful it was also empty of people and was not visible from the street. Larson hadn't told him about the black window glass, which Bailey was glad to see throughout the shiny black BMW sedan three spaces from the elevator. It, too, was from the impound yard, confiscated in a coke bust in Venice.

Bailey pulled the last key he'd been given from the envelope and unlocked the car. The boys were breathing heavily, grins on their faces and eyes running over the body of the car. They looked the same drooling, sappy way he expected they would look the first time they noticed a sexy girl—*really* noticed.

Everyone was quickly in, the doors locked and the car started. The boys were jabbering away in the back, feeling the upholstery, reading all the labels, speculating over how fast the car would go. Bailey found the flat box under the driver's seat and tossed it to Sara next to him as he backed out and headed toward the exit.

The secured garage exited in the rear alley. The heavy iron gate rumbled to one side when the car approached, then Bailey pulled forward and checked traffic. A Toyota driven by a woman of about seventy crept by, toward Idaho, and then the alley was empty.

There was no one parked in either direction, and Bailey quickly turned left and worked his way toward Broadway. He spent fifteen minutes creating a dizzying trail through streets, mall parking lots and alleys. Finally, convinced they were not being followed, he worked his way to the San Diego Freeway and headed south.

Sara was looking through the box of paperwork and didn't notice when they passed the turnoff they usually took toward Playa del Rey. Bailey thought about putting his foot to the floor to get past it quicker. He managed to leave it in cruise control at sixty.

Twenty minutes later, at the outskirts of north Long Beach, Sara looked up from the box and took a deep breath. She smiled briefly, and ran her hand under Bailey's ponytail to give his tense neck a quick massage as she said, "You've been doing a great job. It's time I did mine."

She turned toward the back seat. Marissa had fallen asleep, and the sucker was glued to the seat belt across her chest. "Okay, listen up, guys. Class is now in session. What's your name, young man, you on the right?"

There was a half a second during which Scott's eyes darted around before he answered, "Holden Woods."

"No middle name, young man?" Sara asked with a sly smile.

"No ma'am. Family tradition."

"Very nice, Mr. Holden Woods. And You?" she asked of Mike.

"Joseph Woods, but I hate that."

"Would G.I. Joe suit you better?"

"Yeah!" He slew everybody in the car with his imaginary machine gun before Sara could bring him back to the task at hand.

"What's your mother's name?" she asked.

"Mrs. Woods," he answered, firing at the truck passing on the left.

"Her first name, G.I.?"

"I forget."

"It's Ann, dummy!" his elder brother said with an elbow to his ribs. "Ann Woods. It's important!"

"Okay, okay!" Bailey called from the front seat. "It's important, but it's going to take a little time to get used to."

For the next hour, Sara and Bailey took turns drilling the boys and each other on important facts about their manufactured history, making up games to motivate the boys. Marissa stayed asleep. She was going to be the toughest one to retrain. Though they had been calling her Jane for days, she only rarely responded to it and still called the boys their original names. Larson had urged them to keep her as isolated as possible until everyone's names were second nature to her. He hoped the killer was found long before then. Additional lab experts had been called in to try to find any clue to the killer's identity.

A little more than an hour below Long Beach, as they approached Carlsbad, the boys were lobbying for food and drink. "Is that in the plan, Bai…Stone?" Sara asked, feeling awkward with his middle name.

"Guess so. We need to stop for some supplies anyway."

Taking his cue from the highway sign indicating restaurants, he pulled off the freeway at Elm Avenue. A Carl's Jr. was on the right, across the street from a Big Bear store, which looked to Bailey like a convenience store. He pulled into the restaurant's lot and parked near the street and restaurant entrance.

He turned in his seat to address Sara then the boys. "I'll stay with Sleepyhead. You know what we need from the store. Boys, I want to see you doing an award-winning imitation of Siamese twins while you pick out some food for all of us. I'll be watching out, but you both be on the alert for any advances from strangers, okay?"

"G.I. Joe is on the job!" Mike said with a salute. Scott heaved a martyred sigh and stuck his hand out for money from his dad.

Bailey and Sara were certainly realizing the crippling reality of their cover story. By 'losing everything to the Redondo Beach fire,' they had nothing as basic as pen or pencil with which to make a shopping list— as if they had notepaper to write on.

Larson had warned them about not buying their customary brands of things, of not buying too much of what they needed in one place, and particularly of not presenting a five-some to the world any more than they had to. So Sara would buy here only part of what they needed for overnight. They would have to make several other stops for everything they needed.

Marissa Jane stayed asleep for the fifteen minutes it took the boys to return with the food and drinks. The smell of food woke her, and she began complaining about needing the potty. Bailey had almost decided he would have to let Scott take her, when Sara returned. She left the bag of things and hurried toward the restaurant with the child.

Bailey sipped his iced tea and rifled through the bag for what he needed immediately: scissors and a tool for home haircuts. There was also a hair coloring kit.

"Mom gonna dye her hair?" Scott asked with a mouthful.

"Yes, maybe mine, too."

"Rad! Me, too?" Mike asked.

"G.I. Joe would never dye his hair. He'd get a buzz. How 'bout it?"

"Rad!"

Bailey addressed his elder son, "And how would Holden wear his hair?"

"In a ponytail?" the boy asked hopefully.

"Why not?" Bailey answered.

"Rad!"

"Somebody has to carry on the tradition," Bailey replied as Sara helped Marissa get into the car.

"What're you talking about?" Sara asked.

"Cutting and dying our hair. Are you going to dye Marissa Jane's the same as yours?"

"I suppose."

The child screamed and put her arms over her head. "I don't want my hairs to die!"

It took several minutes for Sara to calm Marissa by showing her the pretty lady on the Miss Clairol box and explaining what dye with a Y meant. Then she asked if Jane wanted to hold the empty restaurant bag to catch her daddy's hair as her mommy trimmed it, first with scissors, then with the trimmer to a shorter style of thick auburn hair.

"Ralph Lauren clothes would suit you, I think," Sara said, admiring her handiwork and brushing stray hairs off the car's headrest several minutes later.

"I'm not the horsy-set type."

"You are now," she said with a smile as he saw himself in the rear view mirror. "We'll see if that's still true when the beard fills in."

The bag of supplies contained disposable razors, but those were for Sara's legs and underarms. Bailey hadn't shaved since yesterday, and the stubble was already darkening his chin. He tossed the black rubber band to his elder son. Though Scott was overdue for a haircut by a week, he tried in vain to gather up enough hair for a ponytail before he put it into his pocket.

They drove on to Encinitas, a few miles to the south, before stopping at a shopping center for Sara to pick up more supplies, then again in Del Mar. Beyond some generous donations to the same pet charity for the homeless that was about to "support" him, Bailey had thought little about the realities of being in that position. Now, as he handed yet another two hundred dollars to Sara for basic necessities, he wondered what someone did who really had lost everything to a fire.

*   *   *   *

It was after six p.m., cold, windy and dark in San Diego when Bailey drove past the used car lot on Rosecrans and parked the BMW a couple of blocks farther on, at the front door of a Burger King.

"You boys pick up some more food while I keep an eye on Jane."

"Marissa!" the child insisted with a glare and her chin pulled in.

"Play the game with us, honey," Sara coaxed, as she had countless times in the past few days.

"Where're you gonna be, Mom?" Scott asked.

"Getting another car."

"For yourself?"

"'Fraid not, Son."

Bailey elaborated, "It's been fun while it lasted, but we have to ditch this one." There was verbal protest from all three children as Bailey went on, "Uncle Human's going to report it stolen while he was supposedly using it on a case. There'll be nothing to connect it to us after we wipe it clean."

The boys were groaning and complaining as Sara walked with them as far as the restaurant's door. The cheap plastic purse she had purchased earlier looked very out of place on the shoulder of the woman who loved natural, quality things. Since the car had a good view of the entire restaurant from the curb, and since Bailey knew considerably more about cars, he would have preferred that Sara wait with Marissa while he went for a different car. But Larson had emphasized how important it was for nobody to see him until his beard had grown in.

The boys were back long before Sara, and Bailey was debating about moving the car to where he could watch the car lot. It was more than half an hour longer before Sara came walking up to the BMW.

Bailey's question of, "Where's the car?" was drowned by the boys' eager question of, "Whadja get?"

"For five hundred dollars, not another BMW, I can guarantee you. A '71 Camaro."

"Was there any hassle?" Bailey asked.

"None. I stuck with the story about the fire, gave him the address of a real estate company we'll be using till we get settled. And thanks for reminding me to pick one from the phone book at our last stop. With all these details and nothing written down, it's scary."

"You're telling me! So where's the car?"

"At the far end of the block, near the Pic 'N' Save."

"Why there?" Scott asked before Bailey could.

"So that any passersby won't wonder why five people are abandoning a gorgeous BMW to ride off in a heap. Nobody will think a thing about our meandering over toward that string of stores there as if we were going to do a little shopping."

"You're really getting into the swing of this," Bailey said with a tired grin.

They spent ten minutes wiping down the interior of the car for fingerprints. Bailey wrapped the car keys in the piece of paper that had held his burger, put that inside the empty burger box, added garbage from the kids' dinners, before he smashed it all down to carry it to the outside trash can.

Sara crammed the supplies she had accumulated over the afternoon into two huge blue backpacks she had purchased and gave one to each of the boys to carry. The plastic bags that everything had been in were also in the backpack, to be disposed of at their motel.

Since it was dark, Bailey would have been conspicuous in the dark glasses Sara had purchased. He would just have to hope that no one passing him on his way to the car was a fan or recognized him from recent news pictures. He was regretting the modest fame Mary Zada had worked so hard to achieve for him.

In opening and then closing the car's doors, Sara and Bailey wiped them with tissues they palmed. As the boys and Sara started ahead across the lot, he hung back by a couple dozen yards, carrying Marissa. About halfway along the lot, a couple came striding his direction. Before they were close enough to see him clearly, he tossed Marissa to his other arm and raised her so that she completely blocked his face until the chatting couple's conversation and footsteps had faded completely.

Bailey and Marissa caught up with the others at the Camaro. It was clean, and Bailey pronounced that things under the hood seemed in reasonable order. His mechanical skills would see that things stayed that way. Sara had looked up motels at the same time she looked up a realtor's address to give the car dealer. She had also purchased a local map, which she used to direct Bailey to a Motel Six on Hotel Circle in the Mission Valley area. A vacancy sign was lit.

Sara went in and registered, showing both her new driver's license and credit card. Since there were quite a lot of vacancies, the woman clerk, who had two rowdy boys of her own, was happy to assign the Woods family a room that was removed from other occupied rooms. The boys carried the backpacks into the ground-floor room after Sara unlocked it. At that point, Bailey went quickly from the car into the room.

The children were fascinated with the fact that their mother had a key that opened a second room adjoining theirs. "Rad!" they all declared and claimed the one that had been revealed like a treasure vault.

Bailey looked automatically at his wrist for the time. His Rolex had been left behind, but he and Sara had refused to leave their wedding rings. Larson agreed that two plain gold bands were probably common enough that it wouldn't be a problem.

The room's clock radio showed nine-twenty. As he entered the bathroom, he jerked with the shock of the stranger in the mirror. Short, precisely trimmed hair wasn't Bailey Thurston. Neither was five o'clock shadow on a man who loved necking with his wife.

"Hello, Stone Woods," he said with a smirk and began to undress.

*   *   *   *

CHAPTER SEVEN

Bailey had fallen asleep telling himself that today's sterling performance on the part of his children wouldn't last. He awoke before sunup to Marissa's crying because she had wet the bed next to theirs and was scared to find herself in some strange, dark place. Bailey took her to the bathroom to clean her up and settle her down while Sara dragged herself out of bed to remove the wet sheets before they soaked through the mattress protector. Marissa was very disturbed over the accident, because she had been toilet trained since before she was three.

"I know you're a big girl, Jane...."

"Marissa!" she said and hit her father's arm with her doughy fist.

"We're still playing the game, big girl Jane. And don't worry, this little accident doesn't mean you aren't grown up enough for nursery school. As soon as you play the game all the time and call the boys by their middle names, we'll find a really nice school."

When the boys awoke near seven, they began fighting over the television channel and complaining about wanting breakfast. There was no room service, and Bailey and Sara decided that, since Marissa was now pacified with the cartoons on their television, Sara would take the two boys. Bailey was a mass of tense muscles until she and the boys returned more than an hour later.

"What took so long?" he asked as she put the deadbolt back on the door.

"I let them blow off some steam running around in a little park near McDonald's before we picked up the food." She handed one of the warm bags to him. The boys were already demolishing the several Egg McMuffins they had carried to their room.

"There's no mention of us or Levi in the local paper. I'll have to find some place to get the *Times* later."

Bailey nodded. Since the first murder, Bailey had forbidden any of them to watch the television news, for fear one of the announcers would give details of the bloody slayings.

Being restricted to their Playa del Rey house had been bad enough. A hotel room with three active kids was impossible for any length of time. Obviously they wouldn't last the week or more that it would take for Bailey's beard to fill in. Sara made a foray to a nearby shopping center just after ten, to pick up several board games, crayons, coloring books and books of rainy day games. She also picked up a black and white velour whale. With it being only three weeks until Christmas and with shoppers throughout the store with baskets piled high, her purchases were not in the least conspicuous.

With the emergency supplies delivered, she left the four of them while she went in pursuit of a furnished house to rent. She would begin by checking in with the real estate agent whose address she had given the car dealer for purposes of mailing the registration. Besides seeking the advice of the agent in locating a rental, Sara intended to pursue rentals advertised independently.

But the ads had not been the lengthy list she had expected, and she had deliberately distracted Bailey from getting a look at the classifieds. He was feeling bad enough without his discovering that there were only four furnished houses listed for all of San Diego. If none of them would do, she would bite the bullet and take an unfurnished one, keeping purchased furniture to a minimum.

*   *   *   *

"It's as near perfect as we're going to get, guys," Sara related as she handed Scott a Burger King bag and one to Bailey just after two in the afternoon. "There's no yard unless you count the steep hill out back, but there's a very large deck."

"We can send for Bammer!"

"No, G.I. Joe, sorry."

He slumped, and Scott also sagged and turned away. In a second, Bailey said quietly, "I wouldn't mind adopting some mutt from the pound."

The kids squealed with excitement and carried the food into their room to argue over breed and size and name of their new pet. Sara and Bailey sat in the two side chairs at the lamp table and ate as she described the house.

"The hill drops off very steeply behind the house and on one side. On the other side, there's a solid wall of trees about eight feet from the house. The front is entirely fenced in. Besides all those security features, you almost can't find the house. It's along a driveway, behind another house that's also almost hidden behind an eight-foot hedge."

"Sounds like an ideal 'rock house.'" He said and rubbed his itching beard.

"Furniture's not to my taste or yours, pretty beaten up stuff for the most part, but for a family who lost everything to a fire, it looks like heaven."

"What's the garage situation like?"

"It'll only hold one car, but at least it connects at the front, to the kitchen."

"Garage door opener?"

"'Fraid not."

"Add that to the shopping list. Sears is probably the best place. I can install it."

She nodded heavily. "Bail...uh, Stone, what do people do that have no money? Thank you for being so smart!"

He shook his head. "Thank you for loving the dummy that caused all this."

"It's the saint's fault, remember?"

"Hey, Mom!" their middle child said, racing into their room. "Sc…uh, Holden's barfing in the bathroom!"

Bailey beat Sara to the boy, on his knees at the toilet. When the boy had emptied his stomach and Bailey was holding a cold washcloth to his forehead, he asked his concerned wife to check the half-eaten burger that Scott had left on the bed.

"It smells okay," she said. "The others, too."

"I'm sorry, Dad," the shaky boy said and took the cloth from his father.

Bailey didn't have to ask his son what he was sorry about. The perpetual knot in Bailey's stomach reminded him how much alike he and his firstborn were.

*   *   *   *

Sara spent much of the remaining afternoon buying still more supplies, some of which she left in the new house, including the garage door opener. In the early evening, she brought everyone pizza, green salad, and cheese toast. Then, just before eight, she paid their hotel bill in cash and unlocked the car for everyone to pile in. Bailey was the last, after Sara told him the coast was clear.

It was a five-minute drive to the rented house in the Mission Hills district, above the Mission Valley area that their motel occupied. Sara had left lights on in the front room, garage and kitchen, to make it look more welcoming to the children. G.I. Joe hopped out of the car and threw the garage door up with a flourish before he invaded the empty space, spraying invisible enemies with his equally invisible machine gun fire.

After Sara had turned off the motor, she closed the garage door. As Bailey was getting out, he turned to check on the two quiet children in the back. Marissa was asleep, her face resting on the cuddled Shamu. Scott was huddled in the opposite corner, the stomachache he had complained about after dinner evident on his face.

Compared to the space they had in Playa del Rey, this house was very small. Its best feature (besides the security aspects they sought) was the spectacular view of the city and ocean below from the master bedroom and deck at the rear. It was evidently not the house of anyone who loved to entertain, since there was no dining room. The kitchen appliances were all economy class, but at least they were clean, as were the cupboards that were standing open.

"I miss my Jenn-Aire already," Sara said with a sigh.

"Let's be happy with thrift shop stuff, okay? We've gone through a bundle already."

Except for the garage door opener, she had already concluded that used things made more sense, and she had Bailey and the boys carry in the trunk load of kitchen supplies, towels, and used clothing from several church thrift shops.

"What's with the sleeping bags, Mom?" Mike asked when he looked into the room he would share with his older brother.

"It would have cost four times as much to get linens and blankets for everybody."

"Us, too?" Bailey asked her.

She looked exhausted, but she smiled as she put her hand to his rough cheek. "Just pretend we're back honeymooning at Arrowhead."

Marissa stayed asleep even after being carried by Bailey from the car to the bedroom next to the boys' and tucked into her Rainbow Brite sleeping bag with Shamu. Sara had purchased a night-light, and Bailey plugged it in and turned it on before coming out and partially closing the door.

"Hey!" G.I. Joe announced with indignation, "There's no TV in this tacky joint!"

"Well, crud buckets, soldier!" Bailey responded. "We'll see what we can do tomorrow. Meanwhile, just consider yourself on a dirty field mission where conditions are haaard!" Bailey rubbed his boy's curly hair. "You ready for a haircut?"

"Cool!"

Sara loved her son's hair, so much like her own, and couldn't watch as Bailey used the tool to trim his strawberry blond curls nearly to his scalp. They had decided that they wouldn't attempt to enroll either of the boys in school until after the new year. It would give them a chance to become used to their new names and surroundings, for Scott's hair to show three weeks of growth, and for Bailey's beard to be well established.

By ten-thirty the boys were both asleep, and Bailey turned off their light before going to his and Sara's room at the rear. The sparking lights of the city below were filtered through the loosely woven drapes. He turned toward the interior bathroom and could see Sara's outline through the glass shower door. He closed the bedroom door to the hall.

No lock—something I will remedy tomorrow.

When the shower was turned off, everything became very quiet. Hortencia Street was a short horseshoe, and Bailey guessed it was quiet most of the time. With their house set back from the street by sixty feet, with no radio or television, no telephone, Bailey felt blessedly cut off from a world that had grown progressively more threatening with every call or news report.

Sara came to the bed in a flannel nightgown Bailey had never seen before. "Can I help you out of that?" he asked her quietly and turned out the light.

"There's no lock. Besides, I already feel like I'm having an affair, sleeping with an unshaven man with short hair and a different name from my husband's." Nonetheless, she allowed him to slip the gown off over her head and drop it beside the bed before she crawled into the cocoon of the dark blue sleeping bag.

"I'll take my chances about the lock," he said, reaching for her damp, creamy body. "Come let me show you a few things your husband never learned."

*   *   *   *

The Lucky Market's parking lot was ordinarily quite busy. Today, the shoppers and employees were home celebrating Christmas. Even though the sun was shining brightly, it was very cold at the phone outside the market as Bailey waited. His cheap digital watch said it was ten-twelve, two minutes past the time that Hugh Larson was to call. It rang ten seconds later, startling Bailey, as it had the other two times he had heard from Larson, even though he had been expecting it.

He snatched it up and said nothing. "Barely Human here," came the caller's greeting.

Bailey sagged with relief and answered, "Hey, Human, how goes the battle?"

"Slowly, I'm afraid. I was hoping to have a Christmas present for you, but the new lab test came back empty. How're your troops holding up?"

"Only okay," Bailey answered.

He pictured his friend standing at some equally cold pay phone in Los Angeles as Bailey spent the next several minutes describing the changes they had all undergone.

"Marissa's still wetting the bed, and now she's added thumb-sucking and baby talk. It was been charming when she was two. Right now I'm scared she might suffer serious, permanent psychological damage."

"Kids are extremely resilient, Bailey."

"I hope so. It's potentially worse with Scott, because he keeps so much inside. I'm glad we got the dog. At least in the daytime it seems to help him to sit and stroke it. Mike seems unaffected, actually enjoying the role-playing."

"And Sara?"

"Better than I expected. I think all the work she's had to do to make this seem like home has kept her pretty well together." He didn't tell Larson that both Sara and Scott had been discovered in the middle of the night several times sick in the bathroom.

"We both feel like we're cheating on each other. I can't wait for her to go back to her own hair color and perfume. I can't believe she likes the beard, though," he said with a tired chuckle. "She says it makes her feel like she's living out some trashy bondage fantasy she never knew she had."

"At last—a shred of silver lining." Larson said with a deep chuckle of his own.

There was a long moment of silence before both men sighed and cleared their throats. Bailey was about ready to say goodbye when Larson got around to the part Bailey didn't want to hear.

"Listen, Bailey, I won't insult you with a trite 'Merry Christmas.'"

"Thank you."

"And you're probably tired of hearing me say we're still praying."

"Pretty much." Bailey was looking down at his second-hand Nikes as they shuffled on the gritty sidewalk.

"Well, besides praying, we haven't relaxed the investigation. I've never seen our guys go after evidence the way they're doing on this case, putting in loads of overtime."

"Good," Bailey answered, disheartened rather than encouraged.

"Listen, Bailey, I know you and Sara probably don't care about your Christmas presents, but tell the kids we have theirs. We'll celebrate as soon as we get the guy."

After another moment of idle chitchat, Bailey hung up and went to the Camaro for the two-minute drive to the rented house. As he passed a deserted Christmas tree lot, the sickening thought entered his mind: *I wonder where Hume will find a Christmas tree if this drags on till summer?*

Neither Bailey nor Sara had believed their desperate circumstances would continue beyond a month or two. Somehow they had each locked on two months in their minds, though they had never discussed it. That is, until the deadline passed, and Larson's weekly phone call had nothing more encouraging than any of the previous ones.

Immediately after their disappearance, there had been a flurry of news items about the missing family, including rumors in some of the more tasteless publications, bordering on the sensationalized Elvis sightings. A month later, there was not a mention of them in print, and hope had sprung up that they could slip home and quietly resume their lives.

That hope had lived for two weeks before another killing in Los Angeles in Levi's style fanned the rumor mills afresh. The police said it looked like a copycat and not Levi. There were only about fifty cigarette burns, a half-dozen butts ground out in the carpet, the victim's eyes left untaped. Unfortunately for the Thurstons, the incident still resulted in pictures of Bailey all over the papers once again.

Two weeks after that killing marked two months since the Thurstons' disappearance. Sara and Bailey were in their sleeping bag that February night. She was as stiff as a mannequin in his arms as he held her and stroked her.

"I never thought it would go on this long," he finally whispered.

"I know."

"It's not safe to go home yet."

"I know," she said through a choking sob and turned to cling to him until they had both cried themselves to sleep.

*   *   *   *

CHAPTER EIGHT

The air in the house was almost warm enough to justify an air-conditioner, Stone Woods realized when a rivulet of sweat ran down the middle of his back underneath his second-hand, faded Sea World tank top. He was at the computer table he had constructed from a kit and placed in one corner of their bedroom, editing a chapter of the book he had been developing about classic cars in famous mysteries.

He was glad the boys were outside in the more pleasant air of the side deck. Holden and G.I. had just walked home from school with a bunch of neighborhood kids and were pitching a softball among them. Ann Woods was at the nursery school with her daughter Jane. The two of them usually returned home from school before three. Today they weren't expected home till near five, since Ann had volunteered to stay and help repaper the nap room before the open house June first, two weeks away.

It was always a relief to Stone to hear the garage door open and the Camaro's deep hum as it pulled inside. He hit the macro keys to save the file and call up the text on auto mechanics, just in case one of the neighbor kids came in and wanted to see what kind of work he did. Then he went to see if his wife had forgotten her promise to stay at school and help. It was only three-thirty.

The five-year-old Jane raced to hug her bearded daddy. She let him run his hands through her chocolate curls that matched her mommy's, before she raced to join the boys. When Stone turned toward the door to the garage, he recognized the look of terror on his wife's pale face.

"What's happened?" he demanded in a frightened whisper.

Her lower lip started trembling. She bit it, looked down, and started toward their bedroom. "Maybe nothing. Maybe nothing at all."

He jogged the few paces necessary to catch up to her and to turn her toward himself. "Tell me anyway," he said and laid a hand gently on the side of her tense face. Her eyes were darting around as if she thought the tears wouldn't spill if she could just keep her eyes moving.

"Well, there was all this noise and the commotion of the kids playing and screaming while we were trying to work. I was up on this cheap old rickety ladder trying to concentrate on not falling, and…."

"Did somebody get hurt?"

She shook her head and swallowed several times before she said in a choking voice, "Everything was so distracting that I couldn't concentrate on what Cindy was saying, and when she asked me what kind of work you did, I blurted out that you wrote murder mysteries."

"Oh, God!" he said in a breath before he realized that his wife looked as if she were about to self-destruct from panic and guilt. He pulled her to himself, and she went on in a broken voice, "I think I covered it up by laughing and then telling her it must have been a Freudian slip, that you write textbooks for auto mechanics but you spend an inordinate amount of time reading murder mysteries."

"Good," he said shakily, though he wasn't completely relieved. Neither he nor Ann had to remind each other that new nursery worker Cindy Brown was married to an aspiring writer who was funding his university writing classes by submitting sensationalized news items to various national tabloids.

"I tried to change the subject, and I tried to settle down and go on with the papering, but I was so upset I had to come home."

"What did you tell her was the reason?"

"That I had forgotten you had a dental appointment and needed the car."

"That's good. I'm certainly glad you didn't try to take her into your confidence or anything."

She groaned. "That would have been the worst thing to do. But what *should* we do? Anything?"

He walked into the bedroom with her, where she put her plastic purse on the battered dresser. "From what you've said, Honey, I suspect Cindy bought your story. Don't bring it up again, but be on the alert for any probing questions about us, me, our background. You know what to watch out for."

*   *   *   *

Chatty, cheery Cindy Brown seemed her normal self the next day and in the days that followed. On days when Ann was an aide, she carefully assessed Cindy's questions and the directions the worker's conversations took. The questions centered mostly on the nursery children and on Jane's status in the thumb-sucking and bed-wetting departments.

Ann and Stone both thought that, if Cindy had told her husband of the slip and he had a suspicion of who Ann's husband really was, he might have asked Cindy to test the story of the Redondo Beach fire. Ann had given Cindy the fire as the basis for their moving to the area and for Jane's infantile behavior.

But Cindy didn't test. Conversation stayed on the neutral ground of what TV or movies Cindy or the Woods family had enjoyed recently or of what restaurants they liked or whether the family had visited the zoo or Sea World yet. They had been to those places, though Ann didn't point out that, while there, the family remained split into two groups, continuing to follow Hugh Larson's admonition of not presenting their five-member family profile any more than necessary.

*   *   *   *

The man waved a hand to clear the heavy cloud of smoke that had settled in front of his eyes that were squinted and staring at the two pictures and the brief article in the paper on his kitchen table. He had almost overlooked it at the AM/PM checkout a few minutes ago.

He had a habit of talking to himself when alone. Just now, his heart was pounding with excitement as he said, "Well, now, I thank you, Mr. Rick Brown. San Diego, is it? No sweat. Got all kinds of buddies down there that'll get the address for me."

He rose heavily and went to the badly stained coffeepot and poured himself his third cup of morning coffee. "You think you're so damn smart, Thurston, trashing my image in your lovely little novel." He swore and went on, "I'm smarter, and now you're cornered in unfamiliar territory. Yes, indeed, Mr. Brown, I thank you."

*   *   *   *

It was June 22nd, a Friday. Stone Woods' depressing premonition about the case's dragging on into the summer had become reality. It was, no doubt, a contributing cause to the blinding headache that had awakened Ann this morning. Though school was out and the boys were home, they were mature enough to remain quiet when inside the house. Jane was a walking noisemaker, however, and so Stone thought he'd better take her to preschool as usual.

He had been to the Mission Hills Preschool a half dozen times before, picking up or delivering Jane and, three weeks ago, to attend the open house for families. He parked on Lewis Street and accompanied his skipping daughter through the gate. "There's my pet tuna, Daddy," Jane said and squatted to point at a blue flower.

Every cluster of petunias had a three-by-five card stapled to a Popsicle stick, the card bearing a child's name in his or her own printing. The 'e' on Jane was backwards, but he wouldn't point it out any more than he would point out her misunderstanding of the flower's name.

No problem. It's enough that she's finally adopted Jane as her name.

He congratulated her on her green thumb, which promptly had her denying any such thing and thrusting her decidedly flesh-colored thumbs toward him before one went into her mouth. He was chuckling over it as he followed her up the two shallow steps and into the big room with the numerous tables and chairs that looked as if they were designed for a large dollhouse.

Making contact with a nursery worker and then signing the child in were requirements of the school, and Stone looked around for an adult. Most were outside in the play yard, where all the children had congregated. Only Cindy Brown was inside, standing at the counter where the sign-in sheet was kept on a clipboard.

Jane hugged her father quickly once then called, "I'm here now, Mrs. Brown! Did you see me?" She raced through the room toward the door opened to the noisy play yard.

Cindy nodded. Stone recognized the look on the woman's face: barely controlled terror, the same as he had seen on his wife's a few weeks ago after the slip. He hoped there wasn't a connection. Cindy's chubby chin began to tremble as he approached the sign-in sheet. She cleared her throat and began in a nervous, raspy voice that told him there was indeed a connection.

"I'm so very, very sorry...." She stopped. Her head was jerking, and the tears began running down her freckled face.

"What's happened?!" he demanded and grabbed her arm to shake her slightly before he released her.

"I didn't know who you were. I only mentioned Mrs. Woods' comment about you being a mystery *writer* when she meant *reader* to Rick because he reads so many himself. I didn't know!" she said and wiped her face with her hand.

"So who does Rick think I am?"

"He *knows* you're Bailey Thurston."

Bailey slumped and his head rotated toward the children playing outside before he turned back to Cindy. "I suppose he plans to submit an article somewhere."

The way a groan slipped from her at the same instant her forehead wrinkled in even more pain told him he had the tense wrong. "I didn't know!" she insisted. "He showed me the article at breakfast. I was going to call you, but I lost my nerve."

"What paper or magazine?!" he demanded and started toward the door to the play yard.

"*Weekly World News.*"

Bailey snatched his startled daughter off the play yard swing and told her he had forgotten he had plans for her.

"Sea World?" she asked with hope in her eyes.

"Probably not. I'll tell you all about it later. First I need to run by the grocery store."

Lucky Market wasn't far from the nursery. He carried his daughter in his arms and hurried in to the check stand. Two pictures of himself stared accusingly at him from the black and white paper's front page. He had the panicked impulse to buy up every copy in the store. Head down, he paid for the one copy and a Hershey bar from the rack above the magazines before he hurried out. Inside the locked car, he tore open the candy for the drooling child then huddled over the article.

The picture on the left was one he recognized as a publicity photo. Rick Brown could easily have gotten a copy from Mary Zada or Bailey's publisher. The other shot, the one with bearded Stone Woods, took a moment of study before Bailey recognized the metal structure faintly visible in the background as the nursery school swing. Since he never would have allowed his picture to be taken, it had obviously been taken with a telephoto during the noisy chaos of the nursery's open house some three weeks ago—not too long after the disastrous slip of the tongue.

Bailey had never read the rag, but it lived up to his expectations for sleaze in the article: all innuendo. Someone had explained to Bailey once that, by doing that, the writer and the publication avoided lawsuits. He could just hear the defense this time: "We never *said* he was Bailey Thurston. We only asked the question."

The article asked, *What are the odds of some unrelated family of five having the same last name as the missing wife's maiden name and all five family members having the same first names as the missing family's middle names?*

The article went on to point out that the appearance of the Woods family in the San Diego area coincided with the disappearance of the Thurston family; the ages of the children were right. Stone Woods was passing as the writer of auto mechanic textbooks, a subject on which Bailey Thurston was an expert. Bailey put the paper down.

Cowardly, but still a damn convincing article!

Feeling as if he had been kicked in the stomach, he started the car and headed home.

Home! That crummy little house has come to feel like home, and now we're going to have to leave it, too. But where can we go? How can we hide? And for how long?

Yes, God, for how long?

Sara had taken a pain pill in his absence, and the headache was under control when Bailey returned. The minute he turned the newspaper toward her, she whirled and ran to the bathroom. Bailey was at his work desk, on the phone to Hugh Larson, when she came out into the bedroom with a cold wash cloth on her pale forehead.

"No, it doesn't give our address or phone number, but it wouldn't be too hard for a clever crazy like Levi to track us down now that he has our name—possibly through the Experian file or DMV. What do we do, Hume?"

"Number one, change your phone number."

"This one's unlisted."

"But you've given it out to schools, doctors, the owner of the house…."

"Okay, okay."

"And get another burglar alarm."

"We don't want to stay here! I feel like a sitting duck now."

"Just till I can set up a new ID and new location."

"Where?! Where on God's earth can we go that somebody won't eventually recognize us?"

"I know you don't like the idea, but you could split up. You'd be less obvious."

"Forget it! We're staying together." Sara had come to stand beside him, and she nodded as he reached to stroke her back. "Can you try the Federal Witness Protection Program again?"

Larson's voice was soft when he answered, "The rules haven't changed, Bailey. Listen, we haven't dropped our surveillance on Brad Nollan and Angelo Hayes, but we'll make it 24-hours now." Bailey made no verbal response before Larson continued, "I'll phone the San Diego PD and prod them to provide some protection even though no new threats have been made."

Larson reported later in the day, "They weren't encouraging. Assume you're unguarded, Bailey, and watch out. I wish you'd change your mind and get a pistol or a shotgun."

"If I locked up everything to make it safe for the kids, it would be just as inaccessible to Sara or myself. That's not an option."

*   *   *   *

The third security company Bailey talked to said they could have a system installed before nightfall. While Marissa Jane napped, the boys were shown the article and told of their new danger. Mike expressed his anger by crying and escaping into the garage to kick the Camaro's tires. Scott wordlessly found Rags and huddled with the dog on his bed. Bailey unplugged both telephones so that no chilling threats could be received. He would plug them back in at the time Larson had told him he would call to check on things.

Then life stopped for the people in the rented house off Hortencia Street. Waiting for the security company to come wasn't really living. Waiting to learn what new names they would carry and where they would attempt to hide out again wasn't really living. Waiting for Levi to strike wasn't living.

At the moment, Bailey couldn't even imagine what the living did with their time.

Bailey checked the driver's license against the laminated ID badge of the security company's installer before allowing the small man inside the house. Still, Bailey stayed with him every moment.

Larson had explained to Bailey that most of the time when a burglar alarm was triggered, there was no intrusion, and Bailey had recalled his own accidental triggering of the system in his Playa del Rey house. Knowing this, the police in most areas used the less-urgent approach of sending the first available unit. Sometimes units weren't available for fifteen minutes or more. The average burglary took under eight minutes.

Fortunately, at Larson's request, the San Diego police had agreed to Red Flag Bailey's address. It meant that any report of a disturbance at the address would be treated as a 'righteous call,' and police would immediately dispatch a patrol car Code Three without waiting to confirm circumstances. The term 'disturbance' included both a triggered alarm or one unexpectedly terminated.

It was all small comfort to Bailey.

The warm summer night was as quiet as the first night they had moved into the house. Only an occasional neighborhood dog could be heard barking once or twice. But this night, instead of feeling safely insulated in the house, with a new burglar alarm and no possibility of a ringing phone, Bailey felt cornered and exposed. When he wasn't lying in the dark next to his tense, wakeful wife, he was pacing the house, checking the doors and windows and the red lights on the new keypads by the door to the garage and outside his bedroom that said the alarm was active.

Over the next several days, the boys whined about being grounded again. This time was worse since there weren't the Larson kids to break the monotony. Neither was there Cynthia Larson to do the grocery shopping. Sara had deliberately kept her distance from all her neighbors, and so there was no one she could ask for help with any confidence. Bailey wouldn't let her go, and so she resorted to having the Fiori Deli deliver pizza, sandwiches and fresh milk.

Television news was still off-limits in the house, even to the adults, and Bailey and Sara were dependent on the local paper that was delivered every morning for news of their situation. From the paper's accounts, legitimate news sources across the country had gotten wind of his new identity and the area in which he was hiding. San Diego police acknowledged that they were aware of the Thurston family's location but refused to release it.

When asked if the police were providing special protection, the answer was, "Not at this time." When queried as to the reason, the response was, "It has always been the Department's policy to provide special protection for those individuals who are legitimately endangered while in our jurisdiction."

Asked if that meant that the police captain didn't consider the Thurstons in any 'legitimate danger,' the response in the paper was, "As far as we can tell, the killer has no knowledge of their exact whereabouts. We cannot justify the manpower in the absence of so much as a threatening phone call, but we are watching the situation closely, I can assure you."

Situations don't get killed! Bailey thought as he slapped the paper down on the kitchen table.

Bailey also thought it was ironic that no threatening phone call that might result in protection could be received. Even though the phone number had been changed within twenty-four hours of his request, still Bailey continued to keep the phone unplugged when he wasn't using it or scheduled to receive a call from Larson. He didn't think his shattered nerves could take another threat from Levi.

Once again Hugh Larson was working alone in establishing a new identity for the Thurstons and in locating housing for them, this time at some very distant location. Bailey had always depended on publicity to boost his book sales. He had paid big bucks to Mary Zada to assure that he got lots of it. Now the very thing that had put him at the top of the bestseller lists endangered his entire family.

Thinking of the cause of the renewed danger, Rick Brown, Bailey wasn't sure he could ever look at another reporter without putting his fist in their face.

*   *   *   *

It seemed as if it had been a year since Brown's article was printed. It was one week. A hundred sixty-eight hours. Ten thousand eighty minutes. Six hundred four thousand, eight hundred seconds. Bailey had counted them all.

Larson had said he thought he'd be ready to meet with the Thurstons in three or four more days, to brief them on the move he had planned. The boys had gotten over the initial shock of being endangered and were looking forward to a move that Uncle Human said would allow them to get out of this confining house and give each of them some personal space.

Their pattern of spotty sleep had returned to nearly normal. At two-thirty in the morning, they were all asleep, in fact, except Bailey. As he lay in the dark, grateful to hear the sound of Sara's breathing evenly in sleep, he couldn't help wondering how much worse Marissa's bed-wetting and thumb-sucking would get when they made her resume the game with some new set of names and history.

He threw back the sheet and blanket and rose from his bed hastily, wondering which had come first just now: his thoughts of Marissa or her cry of surprise? It was the same every time she awoke to find she had had another nighttime accident—a small cry of disbelief, a second of silence, then the louder crying of shame and frustration.

Tonight's different, though. This is terror I'm hearing!

"Marissa!" Bailey hurried barefoot from his bed toward the door and the dark hallway leading toward the front of the house. He heard Sara's footsteps behind him.

"Bailey, that's not coming from her room! Where is she?"

"I don't know. Toward the front of the house." He didn't mention that the screaming was moving rapidly away from them. Neither did he mention that his glance toward the security keypad in the hall revealed that the system was dead. Somebody was inside and had Marissa.

Levi!

In the distance, above the child's screaming and his and Sara's cries of "Marissa, Marissa! We're coming!" was a siren.

Oh, God, please make them hurry!

As fast as Bailey thought he was running, Sara was hitting him on the back, punching him forward in her panic. As they both reached the end of the hall and made the turn into the kitchen, Bailey hit the light switch. The kitchen was empty, the door to the garage standing open. The sound of Marissa's terrified screams were overlaid with the rumble of the garage door as it went up.

Bailey tore into the lighted garage as a blur of black ducked under the rising garage door and disappeared to the left. Bailey bumped into the side of the Camaro in his haste to reach the fleeing figure. He regained his footing and ran past the car and outside several paces before he realized he had run past the child on the garage floor. She was silent for the several seconds it took her to gather up the next stream of terrified cries. He returned to her, and she clutched at the violently shaking parents who had scooped her up off the floor together.

Two patrol cars arrived only seconds apart. Bailey screamed, "It's Levi! The killer, in black, that way!"

Three of the four officers raced that direction, fanning out as they did. The fourth officer, a tall blond man hurried over to check on the family. It was he who noticed the cigarette burn on Marissa's bare right arm.

*   *   *   *

CHAPTER NINE

It was all a blur to Bailey, but it was only a couple of minutes before additional units arrived and established how the intruder had gained entry to the house. A slender Latino man with white beginning to show in his heavy moustache and at his temples explained to Bailey, "As you can see, the padlock to the front gate was broken with a bolt cutter, which is nowhere to be found."

"I didn't see anything like that as he ran out."

"No, he would have wanted his hands free and probably stashed it in his car before he invaded. You can see here that he cut the alarm, then moved down this narrow strip between the house and trees to the kids' rooms. Their curtains were open. Did he do that?"

"No," Bailey replied. "Because the trees are so high and thick, there was no reason for the kids to close them."

"I see," the officer answered. "It would have been easy, then, for him to shine a flashlight in to be certain he had the right room before he used a glass cutter to unlock the window and climb in."

"But he didn't open the window to Marissa's room. That's the boys' bedroom."

The officer looked puzzled for a moment than said with recognition, "Ah, the dog!"

"What about the dog?"

"Officer Tuttle said your boys woke up when they heard all the sirens and the screams of you and your wife racing through the house, and they were further freaked when they tripped over their dog's body on the floor."

"Rags?!" Bailey said with fear. Oh, what would this do to Scott?

"Relax, sir, Tuttle says Rags didn't act poisoned, only tranquilized. There were bits of raw hamburger around the dog's mouth. An old, old, burglar trick."

"I know," Bailey mumbled in response. He had used it on one book.

While Bailey and the boys gathered up clothes for everybody, and a few toys, another officer took Sara and her hysterical daughter to the nearby emergency room of the University of San Diego Medical Center. Bailey hated not being able to accompany Sara and Marissa, but he was comforted by the thought that, at the moment, Levi was more interested in getting away than in making another try for one of the Thurstons.

Nearly an hour after the incident, feeling stupid doing it, Bailey locked up the house and went with the boys to an unmarked police car down the block. Bailey was so worried over his family that he barely noticed the jam of police traffic on his street or the helicopter that was still directing its blue-white searchlight into neighborhood back yards.

It was nearly four a.m., still dark, when they pulled up into the driveway of a small house just off Ingraham in the Pacific Beach area and parked near the rear door. Scott had the silent, limp dog on his lap.

"This is a safe house," the detective said as he turned off the engine. "You'll have plenty of protection to see it lives up to its name."

They went inside the small, fifty-year-old stucco, and the boys went to the bedroom where the detective's partner told them they could stash their things. They were too wired to sleep. So, after dumping everything in the middle of the floor, they turned on the small television on the bookshelf and lay on the two twin beds watching the Japanese monster movie while Scott rubbed the sleeping dog.

An unshaven man whose pajama top showed from under his open windbreaker was waiting in the living room to question Bailey. Worried about Marissa's status, Bailey answered the man's questions with only half attention.

"No, I didn't get a look at him. If I hadn't been expecting this particular creep, I wouldn't even have been positive it was a man—just a black blur."

"How tall, would you say?"

"I've no idea. He was ducking because the garage door wasn't all the way up yet. All I saw was his back, not even his head." *It could have been either of them—Nollan or Hayes. Or Rodriguez.*

The detective who had driven them to the safe house gave the investigator a report on the breaking-and-entering evidence. A team had descended on the house before Bailey had left with the boys and had dusted for fingerprints as well as looked for a usable footprint outside.

The investigator asked the detective, "You're sure it was a cigarette burn on her arm and not just a scrape?"

"Damn sure!" Bailey answered over the detective's simple, "Yes."

There was the sound of car doors closing outside. The detective used the peephole on the wooden front door to check. "It's them," he said and opened it to receive the uniformed officer carrying the dazed-looking Marissa. Sara was behind him.

Bailey took Marissa and asked Sara as he carried the child to the sofa to sit holding her, "Did they give her something to make her like this?"

"Yeah." Sara's voice showed the emotional strain of recent days. "Me, too. I think we should ask for our money back. I don't *feel* tranquil!" Her chin wrinkled up and the tears flooded her eyes. Bailey raised one arm to beckon her, and she stumbled to the sofa and clung to him and Marissa.

Marissa was in no condition to answer any questions. Even the next day when she awoke, she was too confused and frightened over what had happened. It didn't help either that the wound to her arm hurt badly. "A bad man!" was the only description they could get from her.

"I wouldn't count on her being any help," Bailey commented. "It was dark in the house to begin with, and her typical reaction to anything scary is to close her eyes."

Word of the incident had gone out over all the police communication networks as well as over all media channels. In the early morning after the incident, Hugh Larson had contacted the San Diego police and told them he wanted to visit the Thurstons. Not only did he want to comfort them, he wanted to cooperate in any way he could. The message was relayed to Bailey, and he and Sara both eagerly consented to a visit.

The three fell on each other about noon that day when Larson lumbered through the door being opened by a plainclothes officer with a holster under his arm. The children were glad to see him, especially since he had brought their much-belated Christmas presents.

"Thought it might perk things up a bit," he said as the children raced back to the boys' rooms to tear their packages open while the adults talked in the kitchen over iced tea.

Larson sat heavily and sighed. From the way he leaned forward and rested his clasped hands between his thighs, Bailey knew that Larson was asking the Lord to help him deliver bad news.

"Out with it, Human! My nerves are so fried that they can't feel anything at all anymore." He sat next to Sara and held her ever thinner, shaking body next to his.

Larson sat up straight and nodded. "Well, the good news is you're gonna have protection for as long as it takes."

"Good news?" Bailey said with a smirk. *Don't tell Sara, but it sounds to me like we just joined the Rushdie Confined Condemned Society.*

"It's just that everybody concurs that another move and change of identity—with or without protection—won't work. There's been too much media hype."

"Swell."

"I know it's hard, Bailey. We've scoured the country for any open cases of murders matching Levi's, thinking Levi was already at work before your book hit." Bailey looked at him hopefully, but Larson said quietly, "When that didn't pan out, we didn't give up. We've expanded the investigation way beyond the original handful of suspects and beyond known felons. We've checked into every name you gave us of people you know with any mechanical or engineering background—and all their connections. It takes time."

"Time!" Bailey said, throwing his head back in frustration.

"But try to take encouragement from the evidence the case last night gave us."

"What evidence? The burn on Marissa's arm?"

"A very clear footprint right outside the boys' room, they tell me. Size eleven."

"Eleven? That's pretty big," Bailey said, settling down.

"Nothing compared to my thirteen, but big enough. And big feet are usually associated with a big man."

"Will you check on the original names I gave you?"

"Nollan and Hayes? Sure."

"And Rodriguez. He's big enough."

"He doesn't even smoke."

"Maybe not around you, but I saw a pack of cigarettes in his pocket the day I met him and a couple of times at our house." Bailey's body tensed as he prepared to do verbal battle with Larson again over one of his police buddies.

"All right, then," Larson answered matter-of-factly. "Meanwhile, the local investigators wanted me to ask you if it could belong to some recent legitimate visitor, say a gardener?"

"No, we don't have one. There hasn't been anybody around—except the security company installer."

"The local guys'll check him out. Do you remember the name?"

"I made such a big deal of checking his ID, that his name's stuck in my memory. Duncan Bellwether. But he was at least two inches shorter than me, Hume. I think I would have noted if he had size eleven feet."

"Most likely, but we'll check anyway."

A footprint. Such a tiny glimmer.

*   *   *   *

Over the next several days in the safe house, reports of the investigation carried no progress in identifying the owner of the left shoe that had made the print. The pattern from the sole told them the shoe was a Nike brand. Stores sold them by the tens of thousands. Hugh Larson's telephone report to Bailey was as unsatisfying as all the previous reports.

"Your body man, Hayes, has no alibi, claims he had a blackout. He wears a nine."

"Which leaves the possibility that he was wearing larger shoes."

"Ramon Rodriguez wears 10-1/2..."

"Same possibility."

"...and was on an all-night stakeout with Greg Lipp."

"Greg Lipp. Why do I know that name?"

"Probably from that time he was investigated on charges of taking bribes, but...."

"Well, Hume, that certainly makes him questionable as an alibi."

"Oh, Bailey," Larson responded with a sigh, "he was exonerated. I'll check further if it'll relieve your mind, I but I think our time's better spent tracking down Brad Nollan."

"What do you mean 'tracking down'?"

"A few weeks ago, he left Dustin at his ex's and said he was going down to Mexico for some research on his novel. Didn't know when he'd be back, and he hasn't been heard from since. We're checking.... Oh, and he wears a size eleven. We've issued an APB."

Bailey was feeling nervous excitement when he said, "You know the border's only minutes away from here. And if thousands of illegal aliens have no trouble routinely slipping in and out, an American citizen with ID would have no trouble crossing legally whenever he wanted."

"I know."

*   *   *   *

Bailey watched as his family's physical and mental health neared collapse. He and Sara continued to lose weight and to find sleep nearly impossible. Marissa had nightmares—when she was able to sleep. Scott had also lost weight, nearly unable to keep anything down. Rice seemed to be one of the few things his and Bailey's nervous stomachs could tolerate. Even Mike, who had been the least affected by the whole ordeal, began to have nightmares. The two boys had always fought less than the average siblings. Now they poked and jabbed at each other and fabricated lies. Bailey didn't know where it all would lead if it continued much longer.

Independence Day slipped in like a bad joke to the people confined in the safe house. With no solution to the crimes in sight, the San Diego police concurred with Bailey that everyone might feel better if they 'served their time' under their own roof in Playa del Rey. Hugh Larson was delighted to hear the idea and said he would arrange for their belongings to be brought back from storage in Kansas City. He said he would also try to talk the renters into waiving the thirty-day notice and vacating early.

A week after the attack on Marissa, July 8th, Bailey was counting the days until the truck would arrive in Playa del Rey from Kansas City. Human Larson had worked his magic on the couple who had rented the house, and they would move into another one nearby in just about a week from now. Ten men from First Christian would do all the packing and the moving for them. Sara and the children actually perked up at the news. Scott was anxious to introduce Rags to Bammer.

The stocky plainclothes officer, Bill Mosher, had been a great help at the safe house, teaching the boys card games and magic tricks and reading stories to Marissa. His smiling, mustached face had become a welcome sight each time he came on duty. This morning as Bailey sat at the kitchen table nursing a cup of weak tea, the tense look on Mosher's face told him something had happened.

"Don't let 'em turn on the news today, Mr. Thurston. Levi's hit again. Here."

That he had hit and that it was here, where Bailey was, were no surprises to Bailey. All he could do was nod. Shortly he asked Mosher not to say anything to Sara, and they got through the day without any further mention of it.

The next morning, however, as Scott was flipping the channels in search of a comedy, he hit the morning news channel just as the announcer said Levi had killed in San Diego for the second time. Scott started screaming hysterically and shaking so badly that Bailey thought he was having a seizure. It triggered hysteria throughout the house for more than fifteen minutes, with Bailey, Mosher and the other officer stationed in the house holding and stroking the four screaming, crying people.

Mosher offered quietly, "I'll get a doctor in to give them all something."

"No!" Bailey barked. "They're already on stuff! Besides," he said, calming himself, "they have a right to be afraid."

When everything was finally quiet and Bailey was alone in the living room with Mosher, he said, "There'll be a third one here, tonight."

Mosher's tan forehead wrinkled. "Why do you say that?"

"Because I have three children." Bailey rose and went to see which one needed holding the most.

*   *   *   *

Bailey had never considered himself masochistic. This night, after the rest of his family was in bed, he sat in the living room playing chess with dark-haired Stu Lenz, the officer who had relieved Mosher. The television was on the local channel, the volume down low. Still, when the announcement broke in, they both heard what Bailey had been listening for: the report of the third local Levi victim. Terrified locals were flooding the station switchboard, wanting details.

Bailey nodded and motioned with a listless wave for Lenz to take the chess game away, just as the phone rang in the kitchen, making Bailey jump. Lenz ran quickly toward it.

"I'm sorry, Thurston. They're not supposed to call so late."

Bailey followed slowly, bringing his cold tea to dump into the sink. Lenz snatched the phone off the hook in the midst of the second ring, shaking his head. "Lenz. What is it?" He was silent, listening for a second before he said, "Yeah, he's still up. Who wants him?"

Lenz's face jerked at the response, and the muscles in his arm stood out as he gripped the phone. "Okay, okay, he's in the john. Just let me get him!" He put one hand over the mouthpiece and held the phone toward Bailey. "He says he's Levi. I don't know how he'd get this number, but nobody in our department would play such a sick joke. Count to sixty before you answer, and try to keep him talking."

Bailey took the phone with a cold, shaking hand, and Lenz ran toward the back door where his car was parked. After the agonizing sixty seconds, Bailey uncovered the mouthpiece and said, "Levi?"

There was the same sound Bailey had heard at the beginning of the first call. Levi was smoking, and Bailey clenched the phone in anger at the thought of a glowing red tip being ground into his daughter's arm.

"Yeah," the raspy voice said. "Heard the news just now?"

"How'd you get this number?"

"Easy. There's not a place on earth you can hide that I can't find you, Thurston."

A dial tone buzzed in Bailey's ear like the sound of a heart monitor registering flatline.

Levi had terminated the conversation about the time Stu Lenz had gotten on his car radio to ask for a trace. Security at the safe house was doubled within ten minutes of Lenz's report to the station. The San Diego detective lieutenant handling the investigation was at a loss to explain how the phone number had gotten out. He swore up and down that the handful of his men who had it were all long-term, trustworthy individuals. None of it helped Bailey or his family.

When Hugh Larson heard of the third killing, he called Bailey at the safe house near ten the next morning. He was astonished to learn that Levi had gotten the number.

Bailey's tone was demanding: "He had our number! Where in the hell was your buddy Rodriguez this time?!"

Larson's answer was quiet and businesslike. "On stage, in front of several hundred people in the auditorium at El Camino College. Cynthia was there, and a photo of him in the cast made the *Times* Calendar section. By the way, she said he looked out of place with a cigarette in his mouth. Guess the cigs you saw were for the part."

A flash of guilt crossed Bailey's mind at the realization that he had wanted the nice officer with the impeccable record to be guilty as sin, just to put his own suffering to an end. "I'm sorry for wasting your time with it."

"No problem. Angelo Hayes has an equally ironclad alibi this time, I'm afraid. He was flunking the Breathalyzer test in Ventura at the time of last night's murder. Our only remaining question mark with a name is Brad Nollan, whereabouts still unknown."

At that realization, Bailey mentally raked himself over the coals for not seizing the opportunity to test Levi during their brief phone conversation, with something like, *What will Dustin think of you when he finds out what you've done?*

"Human, innocent people are dying because that psycho wants to torture me. There's gotta be a way to find him, to stop him, gotta be somewhere we can go that he can't get to us!" Fatigue and fear had caught up with Bailey, and he was no longer able to keep the tears from flooding his haggard, bearded face.

Larson arrived at the safe house near one in the afternoon. He spent a few minutes with the children, giving them each a Polaroid shot of Bammer before asking if he could talk with Bailey alone. The two men went out the back door and sat in Larson's Ford Taurus, parked in the rear driveway behind an unmarked police van.

"The stress is gonna kill us if Levi doesn't. We've gotta have some relief!"

"I won't mess around with words of encouragement. Frankly, Bailey, we're running out of options."

"Do we actually have any?"

"None you'll like. There's still the option of heavy security around your house. It's confining, I know, but it's safe."

"So was *this* place supposed to be."

"I have more confidence in my own department, Bailey." He shifted and rearranged his long legs in the small space. "If it drags on and you just can't cope with the confinement, then you're faced with the option of changing identities again, and I don't...."

"No! There's been so much publicity on this thing that it'll be years and years before people will forget."

"I agree."

"And meanwhile more and more innocent people will be killed just so he can remind me of what he plans to do." There was silence between the men except for several separate sighs of frustration before Bailey asked hotly, "How do the feds make a witness disappear—permanently?"

"They do more radical things than anything we've done."

"Like what?"

"Like plastic surgery to the face, removing scars or adding them and birthmarks, even surgically altering fingerprints. Frankly, Bailey, I don't think you want to go that route with your family, particularly the kids."

Bailey swallowed several times, rubbed his hands on his legs a few times as he looked out the side window before he looked back at Larson and said, "If I decide I do want to go that route and I'm willing to pay for all of it, can you help me arrange it so we really could disappear?"

"I could," Larson said with a slow nod, "but I think you should know about the ramifications of doing that."

"Go ahead."

"I've spent a lot of time discussing this case—Levi, you guys, everything—with the several police psychologists involved in the case. They tell me that deep cover such as I was describing is reserved for only the most extreme cases since it almost always results in serious psychological damage, particularly to children."

"What do you think we're suffering now?"

"I know it's bad, Bailey, but not as bad as what almost invariably happens when children change not only their name and their appearance but their history and their very personality."

Larson shifted in the seat again and continued, "In order to avoid somebody slipping up in conversation later, surgery is accompanied by hypnosis and brainwashing. Every recollection of the old life is blotted out—every first word, every home run, every special anniversary, every endearing little saying. A new, fabricated history is substituted, a new, fabricated *personality*."

Bailey was chewing his lower lip hard as Larson continued, "Very, very frequently it has resulted in the most extreme personality disorders such as psychotic breaks with reality—very frequently, suicide."

Bailey turned his face quickly away. Larson had obviously seen the tears coming, because he handed Bailey a cotton handkerchief. After a moment, Bailey had control and turned to Larson.

"Any more dazzling options?"

Larson took a deep breath, and his hands went into his typical prayer position between his spread thighs.

*   *   *   *

CHAPTER TEN

It had been five days since Hugh Larson's last, cheerless visit. Arrangements were moving along for the transfer from the San Diego safe house to Playa del Rey. In discussing the move with Sara and Bailey during that visit, Larson had said that, for the sake of Bailey's shattered confidence, he wanted Bailey to inspect security arrangements before the rest of the family was moved. The San Diego investigator offered to have one of his officers drive Bailey up. Larson thanked him but said he wanted the time during the drive to visit with Bailey.

It was just before noon on the hot Monday, July 16th, when Larson pulled into the San Diego driveway in a silver Hyundai. The Thurstons' belongings weren't expected to arrive from Kansas City until tomorrow, and so Bailey had packed a bag for his overnight stay with the Larsons in Culver City.

"Hang in there, guys," he said to the three children at the lunch table. Rags was looking up expectantly, and Bailey absently scratched his head as he continued, "If Uncle Human's done his homework, day after tomorrow you'll be unpacking your stuff in your rooms."

They had all brightened at the prospect of going home. He hugged and kissed each of the children. They remained at the table, talking about the toys and friends they had missed. Sara walked to the back door holding Bailey's hand.

"I'll be in the car," Larson said and went out. The officer guarding the back door excused himself and moved down the hall, out of earshot.

"First thing I'll check," Bailey said with his hand on Sara's pale cheek, "is the lock on the bedroom door." Her smile showed her exhaustion, but her share in the kiss that followed held as much energy as Bailey's.

*   *   *   *

It was dark outside in San Diego. The children were lying tumbled on the boys' twin beds. Marissa was sprawled nearly on top of Mike, and Scott was lying with one arm around Rags. Sara sighed. She heard the exhaustion in it, but there was a hint of anticipation also. She knew how important the children's own things were to them. It would help, too, to have the Larsons to brighten the confinement.

She turned and walked toward the living room, to sit in front of the television that was running some comedy that Stu Lenz was chuckling over. His black hair shimmered in the light of the lamp on the table by the sofa, and Sara thought how nice it would be for all of them to return to their own natural hair color and style.

With another sigh of fatigue and anticipation, she sat down thinking of Bailey's shiny auburn hair. She wondered whether she would ask him to keep the beard or not. He did look terrific in it, and it was too soft to be uncomfortable when they kissed.

A moment later there was the sound of car doors being closed out front. While Lenz was checking the peephole and opening the door, Sara was pleasantly recalling the parting kiss she had exchanged with Bailey. The thought was so pleasant, bringing such a sense of peace that she hadn't felt in days, that she only reluctantly turned to see who had called her name from the doorway.

Lenz had opened the door to a plainclothes officer whom Sara recognized. Next to him stood Cynthia Larson. There was only one explanation for Cynthia's visit and for the devastated look on her face. Sara shot to her feet. "They're dead! Something's happened, and they're dead!"

"Just Bailey," Cynthia answered in a broken whisper and rushed with Lenz to catch Sara before she collapsed in a faint.

"Good God, what more, what more?!" Sara cried out for a long time after she had come out of the faint. Her bewildered cries generated the long, chaotic moments that followed, in which the children screamed and cried. It was after eleven and after the crying children had been brought under control when Cynthia related the details again. She knew that Sara had not heard when she had said it all several times before in the presence of the children. Sara sat on the sofa staring dumbly into space. Scott was on one side, Cynthia the other. The other two children were with Lenz in the boys' bedroom.

Cynthia's face was as wet with tears as Sara's had been. Her voice was squeaky.

"It was a blow-out, Hugh said. He tried to keep control of the car, but there was this curve and there was oil on the road, and he clipped a bridge upright. Bailey was thrown out."

"He always wore a seatbelt," Sara said dully. "How could that be?"

"I guess both men's minds were just somewhere else. Hugh is tearing himself apart over not noticing Bailey hadn't put it on."

"Where is Uncle Human?" Scott asked in a ragged voice.

"He wanted to come, Scott," the tiny woman answered and reached toward the boy who was leaning on his mother. "His cuts and bruises didn't look too major, but he was complaining of a headache. I think he has a concussion, so I wouldn't let him."

"Can I see Bailey?" Sara said, suddenly agitated. "I have to see him!"

"Mom?" Scott said with worry.

"No," Cynthia answered and took Sara's hand. "There's no need to torture yourself that way."

"I'll have to identify the body."

"No, Hon. Hugh already did that."

"But I want to see him!"

Cynthia told Scott to go check on Mike and Marissa before she held Sara tightly and said in a choking whisper, "Sara, Hon, the body was so bad they had to use his fingerprints as the official means of ID."

*   *   *   *

Cynthia had flown down, and she stayed overnight at the safe house, holding Sara and each of the children in turn as they would take up crying again. Their grief came in waves until finally, near five in the morning, Sara fell asleep. Cynthia followed suit next to her on the bed shortly after that. Late in the morning the phone was busy between the safe house and the Larson home, where Hugh Larson was recovering from his concussion and coordinating funeral arrangements.

Horrified sympathy poured toward the Thurstons, from the officers still guarding them in San Diego, to the investigators there and in Los Angeles, to the media internationally. After all the family had been through, this seemed just the cruelest crowning touch.

The San Diego police were very kind about keeping the Thurstons' whereabouts undisclosed and about transporting them and Cynthia Larson up to Playa del Rey on Wednesday. Though police psychologists at both police jurisdictions concurred that Levi was probably no longer a threat to the Thurstons, LAPD was taking no chances. There would be heavy protection 'for awhile.'

The Thurstons' belongings had arrived Tuesday. Sara and the children had, at Cynthia's suggestion, delayed the drive up by one day, to allow members of the church to attend to the monumental task of moving Sara and the children back in. Those boxes with Bailey's name on them were stacked up in his office. The congregation also provided an endless stream of food.

Sara moved about in a daze. So many traumas had been suffered in recent months that this one was almost impossible to absorb. When she wasn't totally numb, she was collapsed with grief, sobbing on Cynthia's shoulder or Hugh's chest as they cried with her.

Sara and Bailey had never talked about dying. It had always seemed like something that happened to other people. She chose a closed-casket service rather than cremation, for the sake of the children more than herself. First Christian was packed on Thursday, with people standing in the side aisles, outside on the sidewalk and in folding chairs in the church play yard, where speakers had been set up. Newspaper and media reporters were out in force.

Sara didn't remember one word of the service delivered by the Larsons' minister, not one song, nor one of the hundreds of condolences offered at the church or at the cemetery in Inglewood. She was oblivious to most of the sea of people around her, oblivious to the microphones and cameras flashing and clicking.

Only vaguely, a few faces registered: her cousin, some neighbors, Rodriguez and two other officers who had guarded the Thurstons before they ran, the cough-plagued police photographer and of course the Larsons. Mary Zada clung to the arm of Bailey's devastated agent.

Some of the mourners were grieving over Sara's pain and the children's more than for the loss of Bailey. Some were strangers, fans of Bailey's work. Many were unfamiliar with his books, merely family people who had followed the Thurston plight with fearful sympathy, asking themselves, *What if it had happened to us?*

At the end of that endless day, Sara went through her house turning off lights. The red lights were glowing on the keypads of the system that she had told Bailey they didn't need. She knew that the plumber's van out front contained an undercover police officer. There was another officer inside, in the family room. Furniture was in place, as were many of the smaller items like books and statues. The children's rooms were a clutter of rediscovered toys and books, now idle as the children lay in their beds, asleep.

Things were very much as they had been before their move more than seven months ago, but when she reached upstairs and saw the lock on the bedroom door, she felt the stab of Bailey's absence. She fell on the bed sobbing—and wishing she and her children had died with him.

* * * *

Hugh Larson rubbed at the aching, itching wounds on his wrinkled forehead as he drove. The several bruises underlying the scabs were still quite tender. It was just getting dark when he pulled his Ford Taurus into the parking lot of the Bayside Motel in Santa Monica. He parked and got the large brown envelope from the seat next to him to carry to the end room on the ground floor of the two-story string of rooms that faced the ocean. The Do Not Disturb sign was on the door.

Larson checked to see that there was no one around before he knocked three times and hollered, "Barely Human here!"

After several seconds, there was the sound of the deadbolt being turned, then the door opened a crack, exposing a chain. Looking out over the chain was a man with strawberry blond hair and mustache, several inches shorter than Larson and wearing slightly tinted glasses with tortoise shell frames.

"Your paperwork, Mr. Black," Larson said, raising the heavy envelope.

The chain was quickly removed and the door opened to receive Larson before the blond closed and locked it again.

"Mr. Black?" the man said, as if Larson had the wrong man.

"As I frequently remind my children, the world can never have too many intelligent blacks." A fatigued grin spread across his face before it faded and Larson asked seriously, "How're you holding up, Bailey?"

As far as the two men in the motel room knew, only one other person on the face of the earth knew that Bailey Thurston had not died in an auto accident: Dr. Peter Younger, a coroner with Los Angeles County. Larson had worked for years with Younger and had found him to be one of the most honest, trustworthy people Larson knew—strange characteristics to look for in a man you were depending on in executing a deception. It would, in fact, never have entered Larson's mind to ask such a thing of Younger. Younger had brought the idea to Larson.

The coroner had followed the Thurston/Levi case closely, not only because the two L.A. victims had come through his lab and not only because he was an admirer of Hugh Larson's highly professional work—he was an avid fan of Bailey Thurston's.

Larson had initially resisted Younger's idea, but he began to consider it seriously when Younger told him he had done it successfully twice before at the request of the FBI. Both times the FBI had succeeded in getting the killer, and both times the supposed dead men resumed their identities and normal lives.

The third killing in San Diego and Levi's getting the safe house phone number had sold Larson on the plan. He had suggested it to Bailey that day in the car outside the San Diego safe house. The initial reaction was a hasty, "No! My family's been through enough!"

But as the two men had sat that hot day unspeaking for the next twenty minutes, Bailey again examined the options. The disastrous picture of taking the 'deep cover' route for himself and his family had quickly eliminated that as an option.

As if in answer to his question of how well they could survive being confined to the Playa del Rey house for weeks or months, from inside the San Diego house he could hear the sounds of Mike and Scott screaming at one another and Marissa crying. Rags started barking, which had Sara screaming through tears for some order. Through the back screen door Bailey watched as Scott raced down the hallway toward the door. The large shadow of the officer inside the door stepped in the way and held the boy for a moment before he shrugged off the officer and ran crying toward the bedroom.

Finally Bailey had asked in a whisper, "Do you suppose they could cope with grief better than the endless torture of not being allowed to go on with their lives?"

"They'll have a whole church seeing that they do."

There had been no accident. Bailey had been safely delivered to the motel room that Larson had secured and stocked with food as well as a hair-coloring kit, glasses, clothes and everything else for the change of appearance. The accident had been manufactured on paper.

Anyone interested in examining the totaled car would find it in the police impound yard. The front windshield was shattered and completely missing on the passenger side. Although that particular silver Hyundai had been in that condition for two weeks, the paperwork identifying it as the fatal car had been skillfully arranged by Larson.

While the accident had been faked, Larson's injuries, on the other hand, were real. He had held an ice pack to his head for several minutes, to deaden it somewhat, before he had allowed Younger to first bruise his forehead with a rubber hammer and then inflict several cuts with the edge of some broken window glass. It was only a half a step up from a poke in the eye with a sharp stick.

There was a body to view, if anyone came looking to see the grisly result for themselves. It was the right size and build for Bailey—the necessary ingredient which had prompted Younger to make his suggestion to Larson. The extensive injuries to the body, particularly to the head, assured that no one could dispute the identity of the victim through visual means. Bailey's fingerprints had been taken by Larson and were in the coroner's file with Bailey's name on it.

Los Angeles County John Doe Number 119 had received an elaborate funeral witnessed by the nation, instead of the ignominious *disposal* that the coroner's office afforded unclaimed bodies after the allotted time.

Larson lowered his bulk onto the end of the sagging bed and watched as Bailey opened the brown envelope at the desk. "I feel obligated to remind you, Bailey that it's a non-negotiable point that you leave the area. Otherwise, I know you. You'll be tempted to check up on the family."

"I understand."

"Even if no one recognizes you, you'll be running the risk of arousing the suspicion of our surveillance team. They might just run you in for questioning, thinking you could be Levi."

Bailey gave an angry look as he sat down. "I promise I'll be a good boy. At least I won't have to worry about how Sara will manage finances. The royalty checks will continue to come in, and there's my million-dollar life policy."

"That's a tidy sum," Larson said.

"Actually, they'll pay double because it was accidental death. Knowing Sara, she'll sock it away to guarantee the children's education."

Larson cocked his head and said with a half-smile, "You sure you'll be willing to give it back when we get Levi?"

"Sounds tempting, I know. Resurface in a new identity and marry the wealthy, grieving widow. But no thanks, I'll be delighted to be Bailey Thurston again and to return the money with generous interest."

"Well, let's hope that's real soon. With the three San Diego killings in such rapid succession, all the investigators agree that Levi must have slipped up somewhere in his haste. Certainly the footprint was a slip-up."

Larson had too much compassion for Bailey to tell him that the men who had played dead with Younger's help had been in hiding for two years in one case, four in the other.

Larson said, "Meanwhile, you're not in Sara's cushy position financially. You're gonna have to scour up a job pretty fast. The emergency donation squeezed out of the congregation 'for another homeless family' is gonna be quickly eaten up by your need for transportation, clothes and a place to live."

"I already thought of that," Bailey replied and spread out numerous black and white photos taken at the previous day's funeral and included in the envelope from Larson.

Larson rose to look over Bailey's shoulder, commenting, "Tony Victor assures me he made it a point to get absolutely everyone there, even those who appeared to be passing by accidentally."

Larson gestured to telephoto close-ups of drivers passing the church grounds and staring with curiosity. Bailey was studying them as Larson continued, "Our detectives have been over them several times, looking for Brad Nollan in particular and any known felons. We'll go over them again, but take the time to let me know if *you* recognize anybody we should be checking into."

Bailey spent more than half an hour with the magnifying glass that Larson pulled from his inside pocket, stopping to consider every familiar face as a possible suspect. The grief on their faces was too real to suggest that any of them could be Levi.

"That one mean something special?" Larson asked when Bailey studied one man's bearded face a long while.

"Just wondering whether it was Brad Nollan with a beard and a Mexican tan."

Larson was as familiar with Nollan as Bailey from softball, but he was no more successful in deciding whether the man in the picture with the serious, deeply furrowed brow was Dustin's frustrated father.

"I had two men watching for him besides myself, thinking he would be there. It's possible he got past us with a new beard and dark skin, but it's doubtful. We're still covering Dustin with surveillance and a tap in case Nollan tries to make contact."

Bailey nodded dispiritedly. After another ten minutes of checking the photos, deliberately speeding past the pictures of his family and the Larsons, Bailey returned the pictures and magnifying glass to Larson with a shake of his head.

"How're they doing today, Hume?" he asked in a raspy voice.

"Pretty normal in their reactions, the counselor tells me."

"Good," Bailey replied. "Just don't let them stop the sessions too soon. They've been through so much." His voice broke, and he looked through a blur of sudden tears at the pile of papers on the desk before him. He was in need of counseling himself.

When Bailey's vision cleared in a few seconds, he studied the resume showing his experience as James Paul Black, teacher of English at West Los Angeles College.

"I'm not a teacher! And this says I have a master's!"

"You sure coulda fooled me, the way you brought Stevie's grade up from a D to a B-plus in one semester."

"What if someone phones one of these references?"

"They'll get a glowing recommendation. James Paul Black is the name of a real man who taught English in Los Angeles for ten years before he quit to sail with a friend around the world."

"Okay, so say I convince some California school system that I'm him and that I'm back after my adventure. They hire me, and through a teacher's union or some such thing, the jig is up when the real guy turns up and goes back to teaching."

"So little faith!" Larson said with a sly smile. "The guy's in prison in Egypt, along with his buddy, for trying to smuggle valuable antiquities out of the country on the boat. That's life imprisonment over there."

"Well, wouldn't his former employer know that?"

"Nobody on that list of references does. To check it out, I phoned as head of the English Department at Chico State to say that Mr. Black had applied for a position. West L.A. College loves ya, Jim Black!"

"How do you know all this about him?"

Larson slumped back down onto the bed as he answered, "I don't know how they became aware of Jim Black, but our undercover cops look for situations just like his, so they can use someone's identity safely. That's a real Social Security card, a certified birth certificate. I just lifted Jim Black's file from one of our guys while he was out. I thought you could handle teaching English better than the other choices—brain surgery or nuclear physics."

"You got that much right, anyway, but won't your undercover cop miss it?"

"Not from among the fifty others. And if he does, he won't say anything. He'll assume an undercover buddy needed it."

Bailey was shaking his head. "You know, Human, for a Christian, a cop and a pillar of society, you sure do a convincing con man."

Larson's shoulders bounced with the man's slight chuckle as he said, "Maybe it's from reading too many of your mysteries. Can you find any holes in this plot?" he asked with a wave toward the paperwork.

The blond man sighed, wriggled his mustache in contemplation a moment before he asked, "You're sure you didn't tell anybody else what we're doing? Not even Cynthia?"

"No, she wouldn't have been able to hide the knowledge that you're alive any better than Sara. Just me. Not even Dr. Younger knows of your I.D. I've made no duplicates of any of that, kept no notes. When you leave here, not even I will know where you are unless you let me know."

"Oh, I'll let you know. I want you to be able to get in touch with me the minute you've got Levi. Or if anything happens with Sara or the kids...." His voice trailed off again.

*   *   *   *

Damn him to everlasting hell! A freakin' accident! Idiot didn't have a seatbelt on, and his sloppiness cost me my satisfaction.

The man's shaking slowed and he considered all the news he had gathered in the last few days concerning the fatal accident involving the target of his vengeance. He used his half-burned cigarette to start another before he ground out the first in the overflowing ashtray. As he gathered the equipment he needed for that day's first task, his thinking took another tack.

But Thurston's not a sloppy man. Lots of research in his books, attention to accuracy in the details. Most of the time, anyway! How dare he portray me like....

What if he's not dead at all? What if the accident was faked? He's got that damn Bible-thumper as his best crony. He could do it. He could fake the papers on the car. He could have used a substitute body for the one I saw in the morgue.

Sure as hell was the right size, though, right build. Hair color wasn't his, though.

Hmmm, but he had colored it, and nobody mentioned what color. They had his fingerprints, but that's easy enough to fake.

The man stuck his cigarette between his lips so he could gather his equipment and open the door to leave. He was weighing all the possibilities and was frustrated that there were so many.

Damn, but Larson's head was sure clobbered, and I'm the pope if he was faking his grief at the funeral. No way his kids or Thurston's could have been faking. Damn!

I won't rest till I know for sure. Guess I'll have to watch the Thurstons some more. He's a damn devoted family man, so my bet is he'll come sneakin' around to check up on them before two weeks are out.

Yes, that's just what he'll do.

If he's still alive.

*   *   *   *

CHAPTER ELEVEN

San Luis Obispo sits in the San Luis Valley, on California's Highway 101, about four hours north of Los Angeles. A small city of just over forty thousand, it is the hub in a wheel whose spokes lead to dramatically contrasting terrain. To the south and west, the highways lead through rolling countryside to the Pacific Ocean. To the north, Highway 101 snakes up the treacherous Cuesta Grade and deposits you in the south end of the Salinas Valley; whereas to the east, beyond the Santa Lucia Range, lies wilderness.

Although the San Luis campus of Cal Poly had a bigger faculty, they did not have the opening for an English teacher that Cuesta College did. The regular teacher had become pregnant and was having difficulties that required her to stay in bed.

Professor Jim Black felt rather guilty when he signed on in early August, thinking of leaving them in the lurch again when Larson's call came saying they had Levi. He knew he wouldn't even bother going back to the cheap, furnished apartment he had rented on Brizzolaro, facing the ceaseless freeway traffic. He wouldn't want any of the used clothing Larson had supplied. He certainly wouldn't want the papers identifying him as Jim Black.

In order to take the incredibly drastic step of making his family believe he was dead, he had had to convince himself that this time they would get a lead on Levi and have him in a matter of a few weeks, if that. He hadn't been prepared for the racking up of bi-weekly calls to Larson reporting no progress.

Watching with desolation as the sycamore leaves dropped outside his office window, he wasn't prepared for that to be so quickly followed by the Christmas decorations cropping up all over town. He recalled the sadness registered in his aged grandmother's face one day when he had visited her in the convalescent home not long before she died.

"I don't understand it," she had said, sitting in her wheelchair and shaking her feeble head. "The years *fly* by! It's the days that last forever."

It was very cold in the phone booth outside the San Luis liquor store, and he hunched the shoulders of his parka up around his blond head. He recalled the previous cold Christmas Day when he had stood at a pay phone waiting for a call.

It had seemed impossibly hard that time, hiding out with his family in an unfamiliar little house in San Diego, when they should have been ripping open packages and making a joyful mess in their own living room. Today it was so hard that his chest almost couldn't move for the next breath. Breathing was, he told himself, incongruous. *Dead men don't breathe.*

Though he was expecting it, he let the phone ring four times before he decided to pick it up. He knew he couldn't help but ask the questions, and he knew the answers would only deepen his grave.

"Barely Human here," came the caller's quiet greeting.

"Same here," he replied with despondency. "Any progress?"

A pause before, "No, no leads on Nollan yet. Whoever Levi is, he's a very smart, very careful crazy."

There was a moment of silence before the dead man asked in a whisper, "What are they doing today, Hume?"

"Coming over to our place for turkey in the early afternoon. I called this morning, and they were okay—feeling your absence, of course." The dead man nodded to the emptiness, and Larson went on, "Santa made his visit in the night, so the kids got everything you had on the list."

"Sara?" he asked in a choking whisper.

"She's okay. The counselor tells me that her involvement with the church has been good for her. I know it's been good for the kids now that everybody's not confined to the house. Marissa's over the bed-wetting even, and Sara says she almost never sucks her thumb anymore. Scott's quiet, but his grades say he's recovering. Nothing below a C-plus."

The dead man recalled the D's and F's his elder, A-student son had gotten in the San Diego school. "And Mike?" he asked.

There was a deep, tired chuckle. "G.I. Joe? 'Totally awesome,' to quote him."

The Thurston family was home, unguarded, unendangered, using their right names and sleeping nights. Although that is exactly what the husband and father had wanted for them, today picturing them like that, the dead man wished he were just that.

*   *   *   *

Damn, but I was sure he'd show up in some disguise or other. Nobody even close to his description for Thanksgiving or Christmas. Really dead, damn his ugly, stupid hide!

Oh, but what if he figured I'd be watching and he'll wait a couple of weeks before he puts in an appearance? That would be shrewd, damn shrewd. And he knows I can't watch them twenty-four and seven. Damn!

But then, maybe he's really dead.

Maybe, but maybe he's a genuinely sacrificial husband and father. Hah! What does he know about sacrifices?! No, he's really dead.

On the other hand, if I've misjudged and he faked his death without letting anyone but Larson know, then I know what'll bring him out somewhere or other. His work. The man's got to have some reason to stay alive while he waits for me to slip up.

I'll bet my life he's the one to blink first, so I'll just keep an eye on murder/suspense books, till I come across one in his unique style but with somebody else's name on it.

*   *   *   *

Living through the long school holiday seemed like six months' hard labor to Jim Black. He tinkered with the ancient VW beetle that he managed to keep running, cleaned the tiny apartment and repaired its garbage disposal and a kitchen chair that was ready to collapse. Out of years of habit, he prowled the numerous bookstores of the small city. The mystery sections were lined with titles by the late Bailey Thurston.

The eyes of the author on the book jackets followed the blond English teacher as he tried to find something that would keep his interest, something to make the time pass more quickly while he waited for the police to identify Levi. He worked on his lesson plans for the upcoming semester, praying that it was wasted time. He prayed that Levi would be caught today and that he could rush home and be Bailey Thurston.

The effort on the lesson plans was not wasted. Winter passed, then spring. The calls every other week from Hugh Larson to various public phones were the same: "No progress." In June, standing in the heat of a gas station phone booth, Bailey finally exploded in angry tears.

"Don't call me anymore like this! I can't handle it! Just don't call me till there's something positive to report! You know the apartment number."

All the bi-weekly calls from Larson had been tough, but today's had conveyed to Bailey Thurston just how radically his children were changing. While his life was on hold, Scott had acquired braces, pimples and a girlfriend. His voice was changing.

Who will explain to him that it's all normal, that he's okay? Sara, sure, but what do women know about how it feels? Scott needs to hear it from a man—his father.

And Marissa was losing teeth left and right. Bailey had always been the Tooth Fairy. Mike had learned to windsurf through some man from church that Bailey had never heard of. He had also fallen out of a tree and broken his arm. Bailey had wanted to teach both boys to windsurf, and he hated that he hadn't been there to pick Mike up and comfort him when he had hurt himself.

And Sara. Sara was going right on with her life, aiding at Marissa's kindergarten twice a week and Sundays and Wednesdays at the Larson's church—which had become her church and the children's.

They're all acting as if I were dead.

*   *   *   *

Summer school was about all that saved Black's sanity. Still, the evenings were unending. When he was home in the balmy evenings, he ignored the freeway traffic rumbling in the background, stared at the telephone and fingered the back door key to the house on Trask. He had kept it without a word to anyone, as an unspoken promise to himself that he would get them all home safely.

But the phone rang rarely, and the occasional calls from other faculty or from students with a question about their writing assignments were always a disappointing substitute for one from Larson saying they had Levi.

'Secret anniversaries of the heart' had always been an expression that Bailey and Sara Thurston had appreciated together. They had had lots of them. So had Jim Black, but his were not the joyous occasions for intimate celebration that theirs were. He marked the December day the movers had emptied the house on Trask, the day in June when Rick Brown's article had exploded across the country, the day soon after that when Bailey and Sara had run screaming through the San Diego house to find their terrified daughter. He marked the anniversaries of each of Levi's victims.

The July 16th date of Bailey Thurston's death, however, had weighed on him more heavily than any of the others. One year later, he still remembered how it felt for every muscle in his body to be so tight it felt as if they would snap. He had had to control every word, every look, every gesture so that the four people he was leaving in San Diego would not know the significance of his departure.

And now one year later, he played over and over in his mind his last moment with Sara at the back door. Each time, he saw it clearly in his mind—the feel of her small hand in his, his hand against her face, the last, passionate kiss. Each time, he told himself that he could rewrite it. He told himself that he could explain to her what he was about to do, convince her that she, at least, could be in on the secret.

The script remained the same, however, no matter how frequently the writer tried to edit it.

By late August, Black wondered if Hugh Larson had lost his number, and he used a new phone booth to venture a call to Larson's office. "You change your mind, Mr. Black? I thought you only wanted me to call if there was progress." It was said kindly by the detective, still the discouragement of it cut through Mr. Black like a sword.

*   *   *   *

School had just resumed. Whenever Jim Black thought about the new crop of writing students he had, he couldn't help wondering about his own children, who their teachers were, how the children liked them, what new subjects they had, what changes had occurred in their behavior that he would have to get used to when he resurfaced.

Such thoughts were pressed toward the back of his mind this evening, though, as he sat at the rickety kitchen table, sorting through the pieces of the window air-conditioner that he had disassembled for repair. He had asked Herb Weiss for a bit of wire earlier. Black assumed that the knocking at the door meant that his next door neighbor had found some after all.

Hugh Larson's huge frame filled the doorway. At the look of grief on Larson's face, the frightened man inside asked in a whisper, "Who's dead?"

Larson shook his head and stepped inside. The door was closed, and both men moved toward the center of the small space. "Damn it, Human! What's wrong? Are the kids all right?"

"Yes," was the croaking answer.

"Sara, then. Is she sick, hurt?"

Larson shook his head before he threw it back. A great sigh and a groan came out together. "Oh, God, oh, God!" His chin was trembling, and his black and wrinkled face, saturated with tears, looked like a bad section of wet pavement that was a record of every calamity that had ever careened across its surface.

"I didn't see it coming, Bailey. I swear to God in heaven, I didn't see it coming!"

Sara isn't sick or hurt. What else is there...?

"Another man?" Bailey demanded.

Larson nodded as he chewed his upper lip. His huge hands were working against each other. Bailey's own chin had begun to tremble, and he turned to go flop on the end of the sofa. Larson came more slowly, like a beaten dog, and sat down on the other end.

"Lord, Bailey, I feel like I just backed a truck over my own family."

Bailey knew that he should have seen this coming, too. He had managed to block the possibility out of his mind by focusing on thoughts of the children. He had so blocked sexual thoughts of Sara from his mind that he had not so much as thought of *any* woman in such terms.

"Well," he said with a nervous laugh, "any chance you can convince her that he has AIDS or is a child-abuser or anything else that'll turn off the romance?"

Larson swallowed. When he leaned forward in his prayer pose, the blood drained from Bailey's head. He knew that Sara Thurston had already remarried.

Larson wiped his face with his big, bare hand and explained in a broken voice, "Larry Turnbow's a single man in our church—or, rather, he was. Nobody knew they'd gotten close."

"How could that happen?!" Bailey's chest was pumping up and down. His hands were knotted fists on his thighs.

"Well, they saw each other at church, of course, but they kept their personal get-togethers private from everybody—even the children—until the day they had the private ceremony, two days ago. Cynthia didn't know, I didn't…" He shook his big, dark head.

"How?! and Why?!"

"Well, Bailey, you know all the grief Sara's been through. Larry lost his wife to cancer two years ago. They were both looking for comfort as much as anything. The rest…? Bailey, I honestly don't think either one of them expected to fall in love."

Bailey jerked up from the sofa and went to the kitchen sink to run cold water over his face. He carried the damp kitchen towel back to the living room with him, where Larson was still sitting on the sofa, slumped in obvious prayer.

After a few seconds, Larson sighed, raised his head and said in a shaky voice, "Bailey any court in the land would annul that marriage in a minute if you were to go home…."

The inflection told Bailey that there was a 'but' omitted from the end. He supplied the rest himself: *But, besides the 'minor' issues of shocking the life out of my family and breaking a nice guy's heart—and possibly Sara's, too!—the killings would start up again. What's more, I'd be putting my family right back in danger to a psychotic killer.*

"Is there any glimmer of progress in the case, Hume?"

The answer was a slow shake of the suffering man's head.

"How could this happen?! How in God's name did the life of one pretty decent, family-loving man get so utterly destroyed?! The life we built seemed so solid, permanent, Sara's and my bond unbreakable!"

His tear-blurred eyes glanced absently around the cheap apartment. There were cracks in the plaster over two of the interior doors, damage from the last five-point quake along the San Andreas. The fault was capable of quakes up to 8.3 on the Richter scale. A quake of that magnitude could take the strongest building and flatten it if it hit just right.

Quakes could take a rocky piece of ground and apply so much force that pure rock would actually bend back on itself.

Right now, Bailey Thurston felt like a man standing at the edge of a jagged tear in the earth as it was rent in two. *Everyone, everything* that he loved was on the other side of the chasm that had opened at his feet and which kept widening and widening and widening.

He fell to his knees and cried out with agony into the hollowness that went to the center of the earth.

* * * *

Part II

AFTERSHOCK

Chapter Twelve

The sycamore trees outside the language arts office building window were bare, and they stretched their huge trunks up toward the January morning sky, where gathering clouds suggested another rainstorm.

"Hey, Jimbo! Congratulations!"

Jim Black looked up from his work to see Grayson Anders saluting him from the doorway through a cloud of his cigarette smoke. Bailey responded, "Uh, thanks, I think—unless you've just cast me in your latest production." Black removed his tortoise shell glasses and laid them on his desk.

"Sorry, no, old chap!" the drama instructor teased as he slid naturally into an English accent. "Merely doing the civil thing and acknowledging your anniversary."

"Oh," Black said with a half-smile, "thanks."

Anders moved aside at the nudging of the slim, dark-haired woman who was bulldozing her way into Professor Jim Black's small office. As rude as she was being, Anders' eyes followed her like those of a hungry lion tracking a gazelle.

"Anniversary?! Don't tell me the man I've got the hots for is married!"

"Good grief, Lacey! You want to get me fired or something?"

Now Anders' accent was French. "Monsieur Black! I challenge you to a duel at sunrise!"

"You know you're never up before ten," Lacey said with faint disdain.

"For the fair hand of Mademoiselle Bonner, I would arise in the dark and cold night and…."

"Yeah, yeah!" Lacey said and waved him away impatiently. "Don't forget to close the door."

Anders raised his handsome chin with mock pride and closed the door. Black was scowling at his student when he said, "Between the two of you, always thinking life's one big stage...,"

The woman smiled wickedly. "I just love to rattle the cage of an old maid like you."

"I am not an old maid!"

"Prove it," she said, taunting him with her cat-like body that was swaying slightly in front of his desk.

He smiled, shook his head and sighed with futility. "You're impossible."

"You'll never know till you try, will you? Seriously, though," she said, sitting down, "what was the business about congratulations and anniversary and all?"

Black reached across to tap the back of her hand with a ruler, where she was shuffling the various student papers and trying to read them upside down. "Yours isn't in that pile, so mind your own business. I started here as a temp at the tail end of summer school, but today's my third anniversary of regular status."

"Oh. How dull."

He lowered his head and tried to sound nonchalant as he said, "I thought for a second that Grayson had found out about my selling a manuscript to a publisher—Wyman Press."

"J.P., that's great! I've got the hots for an author—a real, published author! Oh, it makes me feel so intellectual!" She snatched the eyeglasses off his desk and jammed them onto her well-sculpted face. "Do I look intellectual?"

"Never. Give them back."

"Are these prescription lenses? Nothing looks different." She was looking around the room, raising the glasses up and down.

"You found me out," he said, waving his hand impatiently for them. "I had an eye injury as a kid, so I'm paranoid about protecting my eyes."

She handed him the glasses. "Do you wear them to bed?"

"Cool it, Lacey!" His stern look quickly melted into a tolerant smile.

"I came to invite you to lunch so you can provide succor to my shredded ego after that last lousy grade you gave me, but I'd rather have you tell me all about the book deal." She reached across the desk and grabbed his hand.

Most schools frowned on teacher/student relationships that became more than that outside the classroom. But frowning was as far as prevention could go at the college level, where you were dealing with adult students. Lacey Bonner was twenty-three, sixteen years younger than Professor Jim Black. She had an inheritance that local papers referred to as 'substantial.'

Though she apparently didn't have to work, she did, for the phone company as an operator. Anyone knowing flamboyant Lacey would have thought it an impossible choice for her—until they learned she used it to indulge her taste for drama, as she tried out various voices on the customers.

Besides that job and occasional roles in local stage plays, she took various night courses. One of the classes Lacey took was in the recently added drama program, under the direction of Grayson Anders. Professor Black's new course on character development was the other class Lacey took.

She had signed up for Black's course because someone at the phone company had, in a moment of being overwhelmed by Lacey, told her she needed to mature, to, 'Develop some character!' Upon discovering that it was a *writing* class, she had stayed because she had, as she so delicately put it, gotten the hots for the professor.

Michael's Deli in the heart of San Luis was busy as usual, in spite of the cold, blustery weather. Lacey led the way to a booth toward the rear, where she slithered in. She was nearly Black's height. Though she was extremely thin, her large, flat bones and fluid grace always gave Black the impression of a cat woman. She certainly wanted to pounce!

"So tell me everything!" She leaned forward in the booth with her arms stretched toward him on the table, the cat studying the goldfish in the bowl. Her short, dark brown hair was cut into sections of different lengths. Every time Black saw her in class it amazed him how she had used some sort of goo to make the sections stand at attention in ever-changing patterns.

He ran one hand through his own short, blond, un-gooed hair as he laid down his menu. "Wyman Press is a small publishing house just getting established, so the advance isn't much."

"How much, how much?" she asked, rubbing her fingers together greedily.

"A thousand bucks."

She pouted as she whined, "Does this mean we're not spending the winter in the south of France?"

"You really should stick with drama, Lacey."

"Okay, so I'm not a writer. At a thousand bucks a book, who needs it?"

He shrugged. "It's a start. It takes awhile for an unknown to build up the size of readership that commands the big advances. I'm not even sure I want to do that. I'd rather you didn't spread it around about the book just yet. The contract hasn't arrived, and anything could hang it up."

The waitress stepped up to take their orders. Lacey went first. "I'll have pastrami on white with extra mayo, an extra pickle, large Coke, and the chocolate cheesecake for dessert." She handed the waitress the menu.

"Gads!" Black said with a shake of his head. "That overdose of sodium, fat, and sugar ought to have a name on the menu! Slow Suicide Special, maybe."

"If we ever make a kid together, J.P., I'll let you be mother. You'd be better at it than me," she replied with a smile.

Like a knife stabbing into him came Sara Thurston's voice, *No fair, Bailey…you make a better mother than I do.* Jim Black almost couldn't contain the choking sob that wanted to break from his throat.

There was sometimes an entire week at a time when Jim Black did not think of the Thurston family. He had worked hard to convince himself that they were dead—all of them, starting with Bailey. Before Black had broken off contact with Hugh Larson more than four years ago, Larson had spent countless hours reminding him that by remaining as Jim Black, he was doing the most loving thing he could possibly do. It was, according to Larson, a sacrificial act of Christ-like proportions.

Bull! Christ went willingly to the cross. And enduring all that pain and humiliation, he actually asked God to forgive those responsible. No way, brother! I'm mad as hell at Levi—whoever and wherever he is!

The one thing that Jim Black had managed to retain from the life lost to him across the great, impassable chasm was the ability to write. There had to be some reason to live, and writing was it. It had taken Black a while to decide what style and subject he could adopt. He definitely couldn't write a contemporary murder mystery, definitely not a book about classic cars in famous mysteries, either.

Det. Hugh Larson had always teased Bailey Thurston that he had the mind of a crook. There was a great deal of interest in local history among the San Luis residents. And so had evolved, rather naturally, Jim Black's interest in criminal activities during the late part of the 1800s. Cattle thieves and bank robbers escaping on horseback, Morse code over the telegraph lines and fugitives escaping posses along rutted mountain roads were definitely not marks of the late Bailey Thurston's contemporary murder mysteries.

What's more, in writing about people long since dead, he wasn't running the risk of offending the living.

The first manuscript from J.P. Black was "Trespass Against Us," the fictitious, suspenseful story of a landowner war in San Luis Obispo County in the 1870s. After Black had sent out copies of the story synopsis and a sample chapter to half a dozen agents in New York, he was as nervous as Bailey Thurston had been while awaiting a response to his inquiries in search of his first agent.

It had actually surprised Black that five of the six wanted to represent him after reading the complete manuscript. The sixth was complimentary about the material but was too busy. Black was familiar with the agents' reputations, and so he signed with Rita Armstrong, an aggressive woman with a reputation for getting material seen by lots of publishers in a short time.

In only two weeks after she had received the full manuscript, a note from Armstrong had come via Federal Express, bugging Black for his phone number and saying there was an offer from Wyman Press for a thousand dollars. The letter had gone on to say that Armstrong was certain she could get five or maybe ten times that from one of the bigger houses that hadn't yet responded.

Ignoring her request to talk to him by phone, Black had written back for her to take the offer. That had been about a week ago. He had vacillated between telling everyone at school and saying nothing, until today when Lacey had unwittingly coaxed it out of him. He had decided later that it was because he knew she would respond with proper enthusiasm.

That evening, parking in his apartment space and with the lunch somewhere in the back of his mind, Black was plotting out an idea he had been toying with for a second book. The conflict this time was over water rights. Making a mental note to check on the rainfall records for that time period, he stopped at the mailbox just outside his first-floor apartment facing quiet Palm Street.

There was a bill from the insurance company for the VW and a postcard reminding him to schedule a teeth cleaning. Last was an envelope from Armstrong, heavy enough to suggest it contained the contract with Wyman. He kicked off his shoes and carried the mail to the small wood table in the kitchen, grabbing a bottle of Calistoga water before sitting at the table to open the envelope.

Rifling through the pages, he confirmed that it was the contract. The tone of Rita Armstrong's cover letter was quite excited, as she related how she hadn't wanted to say anything in earlier correspondence in case she hadn't pulled it off. What she had pulled off was virtually unheard of with a first novel, particularly one with such a small advance: the publisher had agreed to a modest promotional budget.

The words sent an electrical charge of fear down Jim Black's spine.

*   *   *   *

None of Bailey Thurston's hundreds of successful personal appearances, interviews and book-signings came to mind. Instead, it was the knot in the gut and the shaking hand holding the phone that came to mind with the memory of Phil Hunter.

Would it be possible for our remote unit to interview your family?
No!
You could make an appeal to the killer.
You can't appeal to a crazy man.

Because he could never be Bailey Thurston again, Jim Black wanted with all his heart at least to be able to write full time. He had quickly regretted his decision to sell the manuscript for so little. He had realized that he had jumped at it out of the deep-seated fear that there wouldn't *be* any other offers. He had to write. Everything else had been stripped from him.

Legally he could still reject this offer. He could tell Rita Armstrong he had been too hasty and for her to wait to hear from one of the publishers she thought would pay considerably more. But Jim Black didn't go back on his word any more than the late Bailey Thurston ever had. What's more, taking it to a larger publisher might only result in a bigger promotional budget! The words *personal appearance* and *book-signings* sat on the page like scorpions.

Then there was the accompanying rattlesnake, the author information sheets that called for all that education and work history that Det.

Hugh Larson had handed the dead Bailey Thurston in an envelope. He threw the letter down with a snarl.

This James Paul Black doesn't dare become too successful—someone might see through the changed appearance.

He went to stand in the shower until all the hot water had been used up. After dressing, he heated some frozen lasagna in the tiny microwave sitting on the counter, ate it and a small salad he made, before heading back to the school for his night class on character development.

The college was about eight miles outside of town, through mostly farm country, though there were several large institutions along the way. The entrance to the Cal Poly campus was on the right, then the prison (California Men's Colony) and the military base of Camp San Luis Obispo just before the unpretentious college campus. The rain hadn't arrived, and when Black parked in the lot next to the language arts classrooms and got out, he noticed the cold wind that was holding the rain at bay.

Of the fifteen adults in the class, probably only two had any writing talent, in Black's judgment. One was a grandmother in Ben Franklin glasses who always sat in the back row. She was a natural-born observer of life and, trick of all magic tricks, was able to transform those whom she observed into written words that breathed. The other was a man of about thirty. Black hoped that the tension and seriousness of that student's demeanor didn't mean he was going to burn out early.

Most of the other students were merely entertaining themselves through the class—which generally proved to be very entertaining indeed, thanks to Lacey Bonner's gift for dramatization. She was almost always the first to raise her hand when the professor requested character descriptions from real-life encounters during the past week. Her description this Tuesday night reflected how her job limited her means of assessing a caller's character.

She had risen from her customary seat in the front row and had turned to address the class. "...so you know the guy's in bad shape. He's huffin' and puffin' like he smokes too much—which is miles away from heavy breathing, I can guarantee you." Giggles from the class.

"And he's probably wide as a barn and has the manners of a goat to match, smacking and chomping and belching through the whole thing." Squirms and groans. "You know there's not much between the horns…," She taps her head. "…because he's called me to report a supposed case of fraud."

"Fraud?" the professor asked from the side of the room, with vague interest.

"Yeah, get this—he says he needed some supplies, so he looks up a couple of places in the Yellow Pages and goes to one on Higuera Street. 'What the bleep kind of deal is it,' he says to me, 'when some guy's art supply house doesn't have paints or brushes or canvas?'"

Black was squinting in concentration along with the rest of the class as Lacey continued, "All they had, according to Mr. Wonderful, was a bunch of short canvas jackets, colored rags to wrap around your head, and exercise mats."

A small smile began to grow on Black's face, and he nodded as Lacey gave the punch line. "The place was *Martial Arts* Supplies of San Luis. This guy was calling to find out what '*Martial's*' last name was so he could report him to the D.A."

The class laughed loudly for a couple of minutes. Black would have laughed harder if the example hadn't reminded him of a few phone calls in which he had tried to picture the smoker on the other end—the smoker who had ground his cigarette into a tiny arm.

After the conclusion of the class, students were filing out, pulling on their coats and talking about the assignment for the next class, Thursday. Black erased the whiteboard and turned to gather up his books and note pages from the lectern when he saw Lacey standing there in her bright red leather coat, uncharacteristically serious.

"Thanks again for lunch, Lacey. Did you have a question?"

She nodded. "I'm wondering where the man went who toasted to his first book at lunch. This guy," she said with a wave of her hand toward him, "looks like he just came from a funeral."

He shrugged nervously and fumbled with the papers on the lectern, turned to wipe the empty board again while he composed himself. *It's dangerous—dangerous!—to be so transparent to someone like Lacey who wants to get very, very personal.*

But he knew she would probe until he said something, and so telling her as much of the truth as he could safely do seemed prudent. He pulled on his dark blue parka and motioned for her to go with him, and they walked together toward the building's exit to the adjoining parking lot and out into the cold night air. The earlier wind had blown the rain clouds away before dying down and leaving the air quiet and crisp.

"It's just that I got the publishing contract, and it includes an unexpected promotional budget."

"That's great! So where's the problem—getting time off?"

"Of course that's a problem, but even if I could get time off, personal appearances and book-signings have as much appeal to me as an amputation without anesthetic. I'll have to refuse."

"Oh, come now, J.P., you put on a performance every class, standing up there talking, answering the questions getting fired at you."

"It's not the same—trust me!" He looked down and away, thinking, *Just don't ask me why you should trust me on this particular subject.*

"I'd love it, if it were me," she said with a shrug as they stepped from the sidewalk onto the lot's asphalt. Their breaths were clouds in the still night air. "What'll happen to the book sales if you don't promote it yourself?"

They stopped beside his blue VW beetle. "It'll probably sell pretty well in this county where they'll concentrate their advertising. What happens in the rest of the country's anybody's guess."

"What if it becomes a runaway bestseller?" she asked with a bold sweep of her hand. "You'd *have* to do the talk shows then."

"It's extremely doubtful with a first novel. And if it did happen, then they wouldn't need me to promote it, would they?" He opened his car and tossed the books and folders of notes across to the empty seat. "Should I walk you to your car?"

"Why, suh!" she said in her Scarlett O'Hara voice. "Truly a gentlemanly offer, I'm shoo-uh, but unnecessary." Her voice and stance changed until she could have been playing Popeye. "Anybody messes with me, I pop 'em in the chops!" He laughed, and in a moment Lacey had soften to her cat-woman self and purred, "Anybody but you, that is."

"Good night, Lacey," he said shaking his head and getting into his car. *Maybe I should think of her as a chameleon instead of a cat.*

              *   *   *   *

Jim Black had been home fifteen minutes. He had accidentally left the thermostat up when he had left, and so the apartment was stifling by comparison to the outside chill. He had kicked off his shoes, pulled off his shirt and changed into sweat pants before heating a mug of water in the microwave. He sat at the computer desk in the living room, where a steaming mug of tea was now holding down the corner of Rita Armstrong's letter that stubbornly wanted to curl up.

He had gotten no further in his attempt at composing a response than the greeting. His struggle was over how to be tactful about getting off the hook for personal appearances while retaining the advertising budget mentioned. The doorbell rang.

It was nearly nine-thirty. His bell rarely rang after dark. Black felt as if his chest were made of stone as he went toward the door. He had good reason to hate having an unexpected caller in the night.

"Who is it?" he called and strained to see through the peephole.

"Lacey Bonner. Open up!"

Relieved and then suddenly tense again, he hollered, "Just a sec!" and reached for the jacket he had tossed on the sofa by the door when he had come in from class. He slipped it on and opened the door. "What're you doing here?" He stood in the doorway, blocking her entry as he zipped the jacket.

"Hubba, hubba!" she said, raising her eyebrows up and down, Groucho style. "Let me in or I'll scream rape and tear my clothes."

He sighed with annoyance as she pushed him aside and came in surveying the living room and the kitchen in view through the doorway. "How did you know where I lived?"

"I followed you home one night," she answered, turning toward him.

Her blatant way with the truth always rattled him, and he stammered, "Lacey, if you have anything of a…a…personal…social…uh…intimate nature in mind…,"

"Sex," she stated flatly.

"Yes, that," he answered, feeling stupidly lost. "Then you should leave. Please don't take it as an insult. You're not exactly unattractive."

"Why, Professor! I heard your sermon on double negatives as noncommittal expressions. 'Not unattractive'? Was that a wimpy way of avoiding saying I *am* attractive?"

He laughed, shook his head then answered, "Yes."

"Good! The man can see after all—fake eyeglasses and all. Listen, I didn't come to seduce you. Next time maybe. I had an idea. Would you let me read your manuscript?"

"I don't know. I suppose so, but what for?"

"Well, letting my creative imagination off the leash when I started home from class, I got thinking about what it would be like for me to promote a book I'd written. I love being center stage, in the limelight, and all that show-biz stuff."

"I know you do," he said with a smile. "So why don't you write your own book so you can do just that?"

"Because I'm not a writer, as you have so frequently pointed out. No, I was thinking I'd like to promote the one J.P. Black wrote, *Trespass Against Us.*"

"Be my spokesperson, you mean?"

"Nope—be you! Who knows that J.P. Black's a man besides people at school? The publisher? Your agent?"

He found himself backing nervously away from her. He was dizzy with the ironic image of a woman playing the role of a new male writer who was a dead man playing the role of a writing teacher. Lie upon lie. *Dizzying!*

Lacey Bonner playing Lacey Bonner never entered a room, she *invaded* it, and tonight every defense Black raised went down in flames.

"No problem at all," she said and snatched the blank author information sheets from him across the kitchen table, where they were sitting with their mugs of tea. "We just put my history on here. Lovely J.P. here gets all the public glory. Mr. Mustache there gets all the royalties."

"Why would you want to do something crazy like that? I'd have to really hit it big before I could pay you anything."

"Money's not my motivator. The way I figure it, between now and when the book's in print, you and I will have to spend all our free time together getting me ready to pass as the writer of the manuscript." Her sly, sideways smile and glance teased him over the rim of the mug she touched to his in a toast.

Why in the world, he wondered, *is she so attracted to me? I've tried my best to stay low-key, to be very professional in my student and faculty relationships. Why in the world don't she and Grayson Anders have a thing going? Anders is certainly eager enough—and he certainly beats me out in the competition for blatant sex appeal!*

Anders was a year or so older than Black, forty-one Black thought. Several inches taller than Black, Anders had a dancer's fluid grace and strength. He spoke several languages fluently and had a world traveler's experience to accompany them. While Black could never feel close with Anders—because he never knew who the real Grayson Anders was among all the characters the man played—Black enjoyed the stimulating discussions the two of them frequently had. Anders had, in fact, asked for Black's opinion on how several characters should be played to be consistent with the writer's intention.

In spite of all those things about Anders that comprised a dating service's dream profile, Lacey Bonner was attracted enough to quiet J.P. Black to propose an outrageous charade. That evening, all he agreed to was to postpone writing his agent for several days while he thought over the options.

The simplest option would be to refuse Lacey's suggestion and to strike the portions of the contract concerning personal appearances and just let the book succeed or fail on its own, with the limited help of the advertising mentioned in the contract.

But he really, *really* wanted to stop teaching and to return to writing, and novels by unknowns died an early death without promotion. This was particularly true of novels lacking glamorous contemporary settings and lifestyles. It could take years for him to build a reputation, years to get the kinds of advances and royalties he needed in order to quit teaching.

Black had been startled to learn he was actually jealous of the continuing success of the late Bailey Thurston! How long would it take this unknown English teacher to gain even a fraction of Thurston's success? he wondered.

He looked for flaws in the idea of letting Lacey pose as J.P. Black, using her own history when people asked about where she went to school and so on. He certainly couldn't see any of Jailbird Black's friends coming to any events expecting to see him if the ads carried Lacey's picture.

The flaw he saw was that the book would be most heavily promoted right here in San Luis Obispo County, where dozens of people knew who J.P. Black was: faculty, students, neighbors, plumbers, dentists.... An even larger number knew who Lacey Bonner was. She didn't exactly keep a low profile. There would surely be media interested in why a rather well off local amateur actress would be pretending to be the writer of a book bearing a local teacher's name. Jim Black couldn't stand too much scrutiny.

It seemed that the flaw in the scenario was in having Lacey use his name. The dizzying image suddenly came into focus: With Lacey Bonner's name on the book, all that the locals would be curious about was how she had learned to write that well.

Black carried the empty mugs to the kitchen sink chuckling to himself. *The simple answer to that is the brilliant teaching of one Professor Jim Black.*

*   *   *   *

Chapter Thirteen

Black explained his plan to Lacey, who accepted it readily.

"Step one in the creation of Lacey Bonner, writer of western suspense," he said, "is changing the names on the publishing contract and in the agent's records. Let's get a cover letter to Rita Armstrong started."

"Oh, this should be good," Lacey said, pulling up a chair next to Black at his computer desk. "A work of fiction will appear before my very eyes."

"Okay, so we start by apologizing for any inconvenience required to change the contract. The reason is that, I, Lacey, put the name of my business manager, J.P. Black, on the manuscript because Black and I both thought a tougher-sounding name might help in selling the manuscript."

"Ooh, I like it. Makes sense."

"Yes," Black went on, tapping away at his keyboard, "but, when the manuscript was accepted so quickly, my friends and manager urged me use my own name."

Lacey and J.P. Black both initialed the change to the publishing contract saying the author's name was Lacey Bonner instead of J.P. Black. Lacey's letter indicated that the advance check and any subsequent royalty checks were to be made out to her manager, J.P. Black, just the way the contract between author and agent stated. Lacey's letter still showed J.P. Black's address, but this time it included a phone number—Lacey Bonner's house on Binns Court.

Lacey was happy to provide the publicity photos requested. She had plenty from various plays and brought them to Black's apartment Saturday afternoon. There, as he banged away at the computer and called for background information about Lacey, she sat beside him posing and gesturing as if she were a celebrity and he an interviewer. It was late in the afternoon when they finished getting all the paperwork and photos ready to send to Armstrong.

"This calls for a dinner celebration, don't you think?" Lacey asked and rose from the chair to stretch her body unashamedly.

"A little premature, is what I think. Let's see whether we're able to get past first base."

"Okay, party pooper. What happens next after you mail that?"

"Assuming Ms. Armstrong buys 'your' letter, she'll deliver the contract to Wyman Press. Assuming that they buy it, they then owe the promised thousand-dollar advance. After that, they do any minor editing of the manuscript like correcting typos and unclear sentences before they'll send it to typesetting. We'll get galleys to proofread before final printing."

"Boooring! When do we get to the fun part, the talk shows and the autograph parties?"

"That will depend on the publisher and you. You can count on being contacted in a few months, when they have a fairly firm release date, to work out the appearance dates. The contract says they have to have the book out in no more than eighteen months."

"You talk like, ho-hum, you've been through this a dozen times already."

Black's stomach tightened, and he answered, "I have to know all this because many of my students ask about such details. That now includes you, in case you haven't thought about it. You'll have to pay attention to all those boring details, because friends will ask you when they find out you've gotten yourself published."

"Oh, I love it!" she said with a wide grin that exposed her perfect teeth. "Listen, we don't have to make a celebration of it. How about a simple dinner at my place while you start on the making of a new author?"

"Your choice of words tells me I'd better take a rain check on anything at your place. But would you have time tomorrow to go somewhere for awhile?"

"Only the whole day."

He smiled and plucked her jacket off the kitchen chair before escorting her to the front door. All the while, he was thinking that an afternoon walking around Morro Bay, talking writing with the cat-woman, would accomplish more than a candle-lit evening at her place. Well, at least accomplish more of what *he* had in mind.

*　　*　　*　　*

While Black's apartment near the end of Palm Street was a giant step up from the first one facing the noisy freeway, he felt a bit intimidated Sunday morning as he followed Lacey's directions and turned up the hill and into the Buena Vista development, a collection of small homes. A modest bit of land—modest by California standards, anyway—separated each of the Mediterranean style structures that overlooked the small city. He parked in one of the open visitor spaces next to Lacey's address. As he got out and looked back down the drive, he enjoyed the view of the city and the two chaparral-covered sandstone peaks to the west and north of the city.

Maybe someday, if the writing goes well enough, I could afford....

The memory of frightened, angry voices echoing in the empty house on Trask, his hand pushing the keys through the mail slot, and the taxi waiting in the cold grey day invaded for an instant. He had regained control of himself by the time he reached Lacey's door.

Upon her answering the doorbell, Lacey suggested using her car and tossed him the keys. As they tramped down the stairs into the garage, Black took a guess as to her choice of car. *Something expensive, fast and most likely red.*

Silently he congratulated himself on his accuracy as he got a good look at the red Maserati and ran his hand over the luxurious interior. Black recalled that he hadn't been near a decent car since he had wiped his prints off a BMW in front of a Burger King in San Diego.

"I loved your manuscript!" she said, slipping into the leather passenger seat.

"That's a relief. I'd really have my work cut out for me if you had hated it."

"No, the actress here would be the one doing the work in that case."

"I stand corrected. Buckle up," he said and snapped his own seatbelt into place.

"Yes, Mother."

It took ten minutes to escape the small city's bustle. Then, in the low-slung car that had the quiet hum of a contented panther, Black felt as if he were driving in a road rally through the countryside highway that wound its way toward the coast, twenty minutes farther to the west.

"I was expecting Indians attacking wagons and desperate pioneers crawling on hands and knees through the waterless plains," she said. "The suspense was there, all right, from Page One, but you made me see this area the way it must have been a hundred years ago. Not just the land, but the way the people were. Their values were different. How'd you do that?"

"You mean, how did *Lacey Bonner* do that?"

She hit her forehead with her palm then smiled as he continued, "I've outlined a plan for making you think like a novel writer."

"I'm not going to have to actually *do* any am I?"

"Heaven's no. No insult," he added quickly.

"Suuure!" She pretended a pout.

"I think that if you treat everything I tell you and everything I show you as part of a huge script, you'll do best. The book, for instance—you'll have to virtually memorize it."

"Okay."

"And after you've done that, you'll have to know which details have significance and which don't."

"I don't get that."

"Well, people can notice the darndest things in a story, and they can attach significance where the author didn't intend any. For instance, they might ask if there was some symbolic meaning to having a *white* cat or to having a fly on the wall in Belle's bedroom."

"Hah! I remember the fly! It was there as a symbol of decay, imperfection, in the room of a person obsessed with perfection."

"Very good! Now, Miss Bonner, tell our audience about what the red dog had to do with the story."

She thought for a moment before she answered, "Well, Mr. Talk Show Host, I've been asked about that, but it was just another detail to add authenticity. All farms those days had dogs...."

Black was shaking his head. "There *wasn't* a red dog in the story, Lacey."

She sagged. "I thought I had just overlooked it."

He shook his head again. "You can't just wing it. Any reader hearing such an inaccurate response from you would know there was something rotten somewhere."

"Okay, so I memorize the book and the meaning behind every detail. No problem. What else?"

"The research. You'll have to be at least familiar with the documents I used. I'll develop a list of some of the facts that were woven into the book, and their sources. Saying something like, 'Belle Harmon was loosely based on real-life matriarch, Anna Beaumont, whom I read about in *Claiming the Land*,' lends you credibility."

"Ah, yes, credibility. The bottom line for every actress."

"As for your understanding the writing process itself, you'll be looking over my shoulder as I do the research and start a draft of the next book to come from Lacey Bonner."

Her eyebrows raised expectantly, "Am I gonna get a Pulitzer for it?"

"No, but maybe your 'business manager' will get a decent advance."

He smiled and returned his eyes to the road ahead. In a second there was the feel of her fingers on the back of his neck, gently massaging. He gripped the wheel in a fleeting second of panic. There was Sara beside him in the BMW. The freeway toward San Diego lay before him. The children were in the back.

It took a great deal of self-control for Jim Black to smile as he took Lacey's hand then placed it decisively in her lap.

*   *   *   *

Morro Rock's volcanic mass stands nearly six hundred feet high in the misty skies above Estero Bay. Its rounded form is fittingly reminiscent of the helmets of the Spanish explorers who camped there in the late 1700s. Black parked the Maserati at the base of the looming mass. The mist was kept thin today by the light sea breeze and winter sun.

Jim Black had not missed a day of school due to sickness since a twenty-four-hour flu bug two years earlier. But after a few moments of strolling with Lacey along the road above the bay's rocky shore, he noticed that he felt as if he had been suffering some long-term illness. It had sapped not only his strength, but his interest in life itself.

He noticed that today his very breathing was changed. It was deeper, like that of a man arising from his sickbed after the fever had passed. And he *smelled* the air. He actually *noticed* that the cool breeze had the unmistakable smell of seawater and kelp.

The kelp bed ahead of them had his and Lacey's attention because a brown sea otter had wrapped itself in it. The air-filled pods kept the animal afloat as it lay on its back, holding a piece of rock in one paw and cracking it against a closed mussel shell in the other. Black was fascinated, wondering if any other animal actually used a tool. He made a mental note to look it up in the library when he began the research for the next book.

Correction! When I accompany my student, Miss Bonner, as she does research for her next book.

He watched her, beside him, smiling in the sharp sunlight of a cool January Sunday. Her hair was clean today, no goo, and the light breeze off the water moved the sections in ever-changing patterns, lifting, dropping, sculpting continuously. She was a stunning woman. Half of it at least was her personality—she very nearly *glowed* with intensity. But there was no denying the purely physical half.

Professor Jim Black had noticed her physicality the evening she had arrived in his classroom and slithered into a chair in the front row. Her presence had set off a quake that tore through his body and soul, nearly flattening every wall he had built to protect the tiny piece of the original man left to him. A quake shook him every time he saw her. He suspected she knew it and thus her occasional references to rattling his cage.

He had been able to keep her at arm's length by pleading that any truly intimate relationship would jeopardize his job. Though she had—barely—remained at arm's length for the four months he had known her, he knew she wasn't convinced of his argument. Grayson's frequent flings with students were well known and hadn't endangered his job.

Black sometimes wondered if Lacey knew that he lived like a monk because he was terrified of really caring for another human being again. Today he asked himself how much of his feeling of being truly alive and well was due to finally being able to talk about his writing with someone and how much was due to a growing attraction toward Lacey Bonner.

Just focus on the work. They can't take that from you!

*   *   *   *

Monday evening Black was home after school. The smell of the chicken roasting in the oven was starting to fill the kitchen as he printed out a label that had L. Bonner underneath his name. He carried the label outside and was sticking it on his mailbox when Lacey strode up and read the label.

Just what I expected—she's already stripping both of us.

"Hey, hey, hey! Looks like I should go back for champagne!"

"Afraid not. That's only in case your agent or publisher addresses something in your name instead of your business manager's. What's in the bag?"

"You wanted stuff for salad. There's also Coke, doughnuts, some Chablis. I didn't know I'd need hemlock. You sure know how to cut a girl off at the knees, J.P."

He smiled as he took the bag from her, and they walked inside to the kitchen. "Are you rereading the manuscript?"

"Already did, and I've started on it again."

"That's fast!"

She shrugged. "Just 'cause I can't write doesn't mean I can't read. What smells so good?"

"Just plain old chicken with lemon and garlic. I'll pull tonight's 'homework' together while you do the salad. Just poke around till you find what you need."

"What I need is a map and team of native guides." She looked around the tiny kitchen with bewilderment.

He had started toward the desk but stopped. "You're telling me you can't make a simple salad?"

"Lordy, Miz Scarlett, I don't know nuthin' 'bout birthin' no babies!" she drawled helplessly and wrung her hands.

"What do you eat at home?"

She shrugged. "Food. Frozen stuff or deli stuff when I don't eat out."

He shook his head and returned to the kitchen to get out everything necessary. "Just pretend you're studying for a role as a housewife and pay attention. I'm not going to do all the cooking during our work sessions."

Later, over dinner, he quizzed her on the content of the manuscript. She was definitely a quick study. She already knew every character, no matter how minor, could describe them physically and personality-wise. The reasoning behind some of the events in the plot, however, escaped her. Black considered it a credit to wealthy Lacey Bonner that she simply couldn't comprehend greed as a motivator.

At ten, Black said that class had concluded and gathered up the note sheets Lacey had written, to hand them to her. She rose from the sofa slowly. "Well, since my name's already on the mailbox…,"

"Good night, Lacey," he said with a smile and a shake of his head.

*   *   *   *

Lacey had never taken a note in one of Prof. Black's classes, but Tuesday she sat in the front row, listening attentively. And whenever the professor removed his glasses and cleaned them with a pocket hanky, she scribbled furiously. That little signal meant he was telling the class some writing principal or trick that Lacey could work into her interviews.

They both had Wednesday evenings free, and so he met her after she got off work, outside the library just a few blocks from his apartment on Palm. She was lucky to find a parking space beside the library, on Osos, and he walked over to her car while she put money in the meter.

As they walked toward the entrance of the three-story brick building, he commented, "I don't suppose you know your way around a library any better than you do the kitchen?"

"Untrue, you chauvinist. I've spent hundreds of hours here doing research for different parts. We serious actresses do our homework, too." She stuck her nose in the air for a second before she relaxed and smiled.

"Did any of the parts prompt you to do any research into county history?"

"No, the closest any of them came to that subject was one play about two rival families in early California. But somebody in the cast knew a lot about the history and gave it to us verbally."

"Well, maybe nobody knew it at the time, but dedicated Lacey Bonner also did some library research on the history."

"She did?"

"Uh, huh," he said with a nod and a slight smile. "That's when you developed an interest in writing something of your own from that period."

"Ah, yes! I recall it quite clearly now."

She entered through the glass door he held open, and together they went up the carpeted stairs to the reference desk on the left. There he asked the pleasant, grey-haired librarian to open the glassed-in room nearby.

"Certainly," she answered and reached for the key. "Are you helping Miss Bonner get ready for a new play, Professor?"

Lacey cast him a quick glance. He thought she was suppressing a smile as she wondered how he would respond. He returned the librarian's smile and answered smoothly, "Miss Bonner's a student of mine who's asked me to help her with a manuscript for a novel she's been working on."

"Really!" The librarian's look was not unpleasant, just one of genuine surprise.

"Yes, I developed a bit of an interest when I was studying for 'Golden Heritage.'"

"Ah, how very nice."

The woman unlocked the door and left the two of them in the spacious room, well insulated from the small noises of the other patrons. The long table and its chairs were surrounded on three sides by all manner of books concerning local, county and state history. There were books of law, biographies, newspapers, magazines and historical accounts galore.

"Don't tell me I'm going to have to memorize this room!"

"No, but you'll be here enough with or without me so that none of the staff will be surprised when your book comes out. You'll make it a point that they see you searching through some of the old almanacs and journals. You can study the manuscript here and your own notes. They won't look over your shoulder unless you ask them to. Let's get a look at how the computer reference system works."

"Hah! I could show *you* a thing or two. How do you think I did my own research?"

"Touché!"

Black thanked the librarian and told her they had decided they needed books from the stacks of those that could be checked out, then he and Lacey headed for the far end of the large room.

"Only a few in this section are limited to this county," he said with a short sweep of his hand, "but you'll need info on the state and U.S. life in general, so let's grab a few to give you the idea." He whipped off a half dozen books. Two were thin volumes; the others were quite thick.

She staggered slightly. "Whoa! These are heavy!"

"A chauvinist would offer to carry them for you." He grinned and walked away. "I'll meet you at my place."

*　　*　　*　　*

That Wednesday night's routine consisted of her guzzling Coke, his drinking either herb tea or mineral water, as they ate and worked. Sometimes she literally did as he had said and looked over his shoulder as he sat at the kitchen table. He ran his finger down a book's table of contents or its index as he verbalized his thinking process of selecting chapters that held possibilities and rejecting others.

"These are published by the local historical society. There are lots of possibilities to be explored, judging from the tables of contents. 'Fast horses and *les* girls.'" He bounced his eyebrows in a tease as she smirked. "Bear and bull fights. That could be very colorful. And here's something about a stage robbery on the Cuesta Grade."

He listed page numbers and later carried the books to the computer. There she watched as he typed in notes from information in the books. When he had finished typing in a paragraph from one of the books, she asked, "Are you going to use that quotation in the book?"

"Lacey Bonner doesn't quote history books in her suspense novels. Neither does she plagiarize." He tapped the monitor's screen. "This paragraph contains some really helpful details, like how the dust affected the businesses and then turned around and affected them differently when rain turned it to mud. I've put it down exactly, with quotation marks to remind me it's somebody else's wording."

"Ah!"

"Later, Miss Bonner will change it to her own words if she decides to use it."

"Got it."

Black typed at a furious pace, quoting other chapters and other books or putting ideas and information into his own words. His notes frequently consisted of questions or instructions to himself.

Who was governor that year? Check almanac for rainfall. Might be good to find drought year followed by floods. Could be good irony. Make the river one of the characters—give it personality.

Lacey laughed. "That's a wonderful idea, but how'm I gonna do that?"

"Stay tuned!" he answered and continued hammering happily away at the keyboard.

*　　*　　*　　*

Thursday night she was in class again, intently taking notes. Friday found the two of them returning the library books and picking others before they went to Black's apartment to fix dinner and work.

She had actually made a very good green salad and was studying his efforts with the fish seriously, like a little girl who admired her mommy's cooking. He held her plate toward her and nodded toward her jug of Coke sitting on the table. "If I can wean you from all your sugar sources, maybe you'll get some healthy habits out of this arrangement."

"Give me a break, J.P. I already gave up smoking for you."

"What're you talking about? I've never seen you smoke."

"I know. I gave it up the night I walked into your classroom and found out you weren't a smoker." They stood there, both of them holding her plate, only one step from each other. Her lips moved in a smile of amusement and invitation.

What a chameleon she is! One minute the little girl at 'Mommy's' knee, the next the vamp!

In a second she took the plate from him. "As soon as your cage stops rattling, we can eat."

*   *   *   *

CHAPTER FOURTEEN

The 4th of February, three weeks after Black had mailed the revised contract and the letter signed by Lacey Bonner, he received a check for eight hundred fifty dollars from Rita Armstrong in his Saturday mail. He knew that Lacey would demand a celebration, so he bought a bottle of Korbel champagne to open when he showed her the check.

"We wuz robbed!" she said with an indignant pout. "Where's the other hundred fifty?"

"Your agent, Miss Bonner, kept her commission."

"Less than nine hundred lousy dollars," she said with a shake of her head. "I'm sure getting the better end of this deal, J.P."

"I hope you think so when I start teaching you to use the computer."

"You said I wouldn't have to write anything!"

"I'll write it. You'll input it." He continued as she stood shaking her head, "One of the questions most frequently asked of authors on radio and television is whether they use a typewriter or computer or still write longhand. Do you have a computer?"

"Sure, my friends and I use it for games, and I check financial stuff on the Internet sometimes."

"Well, all the correspondence from Lacey Bonner and all her manuscripts are going to be computer printouts. We don't want anyone raising the question of who does your word processing for you. Let's just keep it simple and straight and teach you enough of the lingo to be convincing."

"Simple and straight? That's a laugh! This role we're playing is the most complicated thing I've ever seen."

You know nothing about complicated scenarios!

"Anyway," Black continued, "your agent and publisher are delighted with the arrangement, even more so than when they thought they were dealing with a male author."

"Seriously?"

"Seriously. There's the letter from your agent," he said, nodding toward the paper on the coffee table.

Lacey read silently until she said with a swagger, "She says I just might be one of a kind."

"I could have told her that."

Lacey opened her mouth to reply, thought better of it, and muttered as she read the rest of the letter.

"While there are lots of women writing Western material, most are categorized as romance writers. And while the number of women writing contemporary suspense novels is growing, neither Wyman Press nor I know of another female suspense writer using the time period covered by you, Ms. Bonner. It will certainly help the promotional efforts to play that up."

Surprisingly to both Lacey and Black, Lacey loved word processing. "I think it's the feeling of power," she said, rubbing her hands and playing the mad scientist. It was late February, and she had been using Black's computer for three weeks.

"Just 'click,' and 'blip,' and out the whole paragraph goes. And doing a global search and replace routine just blows my mind. I love it!"

Her capacity for quickly learning and then retaining were phenomenal, Black had found. Three weeks after sitting down to his computer for the first time, she could use it to perform every function he ever performed, and she could answer every question he could throw at her.

"Do you back up what you've created on the hard disk?"

"Sure, plus on floppies daily, a Zip disk every Friday."

"What kind of printer do you use?"

"An Epson that does near letter quality."

"Not a laser printer?"

"No, but I'm thinking about it."

"Do you use modem?"

"Who doesn't surf the Web? Saves scads of time in research."

*   *   *   *

By late May, the daytime temperature in San Luis was usually hinting of the hot summer to come. This year, however, the weather was mild. It had been some sixteen months since Lacey and Black had begun the work of preparing her for her performance as a writer. Virtually all her free time had been devoted to that task.

Black had observed his fortieth birthday without remark to anyone, working at a feverish pace to keep the painful memories from invading. Still, the questions came.

How would we have celebrated it? At home? A surprise?

No, silly, Sara's no good at keeping....

Sara Thurston's dead, Mr. Black. They're all quite, quite, dead.

And by late May he had completed the bulk of the necessary research for a second book, had actually done a rough draft of the story and was well into the rewriting when the release date for *Trespass Against Us* had arrived.

Several weeks ago, the news had been revealed to Lacey's friends that she had written a book that was soon to be released. Lacey had requested and been granted a leave of absence from her job at the phone company for the three weeks of the promotional campaign.

When Professor Black had let his students and faculty know the news, he had had a hard time getting the spotlight off himself and onto Lacey. He had to remind everyone that it wasn't appropriate for a teacher to get too much credit when one of his students did something noteworthy.

"You forget that the student has had dozens of other teachers in his or her lifetime. The credit is all due to Ms. Bonner."

The exception to that reaction came, not surprisingly, from Grayson Anders, who seemed genuinely astounded by the news from Black over lunch at Michael's. "A book?"

Black had nodded, and Anders had persisted, uncomprehendingly, "I mean not a cyber book or vanity press?"

"Nope."

"An actual printed, published book by a real publisher who paid money?"

"Yes," Black answered with a smile.

"No wonder she turned down the roles I offered," Anders mumbled. Then his mouth flapped open and closed several times before he asked, "Western suspense? Not some Gothic romance?"

"Nope. There's a lot more going on upstairs in Lacey's head than most of us have given her credit for."

"Well, I knew she was bright, of course, but, well, I just find her interest in writing...."

Black resisted the temptation to fill in the blank with,...*a blow to your ego because it meant she was working with me?* Anders never did complete the sentence, and Black made it a point to turn the conversation to other topics over the remaining lunch hour.

The bookstores throughout the county had had copies of the book for two weeks and were anxiously awaiting the dates when the author would be appearing in person to autograph the hardbacks. The first such signing would be this coming Saturday, May 26th. But the curtain on the first act of the Lacey Bonner performance would go up tomorrow morning, when she would appear on KSBY, local television's Channel 6.

Jim Black's stomach went into a knot every time he thought of it, even though Lacey was good. She was, in fact, so good that he couldn't imagine why she hadn't gone to New York or Los Angeles to get some really important roles.

He quizzed her mercilessly all Monday evening, firing questions at her from every direction. She couldn't anticipate whether the question would be about *Trespass*, about the new book she was working on, her growing-up years, the memory capacity of her computer, how she chose the names of her characters, or whether there was any significance to the white cat that followed the postman everywhere.

Her answers were flawless. His mind was trying to gather up more ammunition for another assault, when she groaned and sprawled forward onto her arms on the kitchen table. "I surrender!"

He thought through the questions he was going to ask her, but he realized it was pointless. She knew the answers. Undoubtedly there would be questions that interviewers would ask her that neither of them had anticipated, but he had confidence in Lacey's ability to provide a credible answer. Besides, she had an uncanny knack for controlling a conversation.

Finally, with a great sigh, she pulled herself up off the table and ran her hands through her clean hair as she smiled at him. "Why don't you go boil water or something?"

"You want some tea?" he asked, pushing back his chair, to rise.

"No, silly! You act like a nervous husband outside the delivery room."

*   *   *   *

Tuesday's local TV broadcast was scheduled during Black's morning short story class, and one of the students had brought in a small television, as he had promised. The students crowded their chairs together to see it. Black stood to one side and hoped he didn't have to run out to be sick. He felt as tense as if he were the one to be sitting in the glaring, hot studio lights wishing he were anywhere else in the world.

Suddenly Lacey was on the screen.

Mommy put you on the TV today. Where you been? You missed it.

Black swallowed and forced his thoughts to the present. He had noticed that Lacey photographed even better than she looked in person, and television had the same effect. The classroom was quiet as the announcer introduced his guest to the studio audience. As the television audience applauded, so did the proud students in the classroom. The host gave his television and studio audience a thirty-second summary of the book's story line before he turned to his guest and began asking her questions. Black had his hands inside his trouser pockets, slowly wiping them dry.

"Your background has included a lot of acting. Just when did the idea of writing occur to you? And I'm interested in why you chose this particular genre and time period."

The knot in Black's stomach loosened a fraction. Lacey had the answers. As the questioning went on, he relaxed more and more, as he could see it was going to be a pretty standard interview. He was relaxed enough to chuckle to himself when he heard his words coming out of Lacey's mouth.

"Yes, I do weave in a lot of details in an effort to lend authenticity to the story and sometimes to supply some subtle shading, a second layer, if you will."

"Right down to the fly on the wall," the host said with a chuckle. "That was a nice touch that spoke volumes about the character."

"Thank you. I'm pleased that someone noticed the significance."

Black watched the faint smile of amusement around Lacey's mouth. *She's in complete command and loving it!*

*   *   *   *

It was just before noon when Professor Black heard the wave of excited conversation and applause moving down the hall toward his office. Then he heard Lacey saying, "Thank you, thank you! I'm expecting you at one of my book-signings Saturday," before she knocked and opened the door. He hadn't bothered to gather up the breath to tell her to come in. You don't invite invaders. She closed the door behind herself.

"Was I wonderful, or what?"

"Indeed most wonderful, Miss Bonner."

She did a pirouette, bowed deeply, and slid into the chair facing his desk. "It was a blast! Did you hear the whole thing?"

"Yes, my morning class watched also. You have a whole county proud of you, Lacey. Honestly, you could have a great career on the stage."

"I have the role I want—mostly."

His eyes dived for cover in the student papers on his desk as she continued, "But tonight, I'm going to put *your* acting skills to the test?"

He looked up suddenly. "What do you mean?"

"Five or six of my drama friends are taking me to dinner at Sebastian's to celebrate the book's release. I told them I was bringing the professor who encouraged me and worked with me."

"I don't know, Lacey. I might blow it."

"You didn't blow it to your class. You're coming." She rose. "They've all read the book, and I want you to hear what they have to say about it, first hand. Seven sharp," she said and abandoned his territory as quickly as she had invaded it.

Meals out with Lacey had been lunches only. Working dinners at his place had all been in the bright light of the kitchen or living room. The thought of candlelight dinners with her had always set off too many tremors. Sebastian's seemed particularly threatening to him, since they were famous for their terrace and creekside dining—altogether too romantic to be safe.

But Black quickly found that, in the company of the rowdy assortment of her friends, the usual warnings were silent. While the half dozen actresses and actors at the table overlooking the shallow creek vied for center stage, Black enjoyed being a bit player, sitting on the sidelines to observe, between his few speaking lines. Besides being a rare pleasant time among bright new faces, the evening satisfied him that both he and Lacey could respond to comments and questions as if she had, indeed, written *Trespass Against Us.*

Toward the end of the dinner, talk had turned toward the Saturday book-signings in town. Others would follow, spread out over the county before moving to Southern California, to coincide with other promotional efforts there. Lacey could hardly wait until the book-signings. She was already imagining writer's cramp.

Black had been tempted to tell her that book-signings could sometimes bomb, especially for an unknown writer. Early in the late Bailey Thurston's career, he had several times agonized through two hours in a bookstore, as customers who hadn't noticed the advertising or the poster in the entrance came in for other books and walked on past him.

*   *   *   *

Saturday, just after noon, Black parked his VW two blocks to the east of the Earthling bookstore. Nervously hoping for success for Lacey, he walked back along Higuera. As he reached the store's entrance under the green awning on the corner of Broad Street, he looked up Broad to the side entrance and was pleasantly surprised to see a handful of people clustered around the entrance, trying to get in. He entered through the uncrowded front door, thinking that the small crowd was most likely a group of drama friends or else her fellow students from Cuesta College.

Black had told Lacey he would be coming but that she was not to point him out. He wanted to hang around on the fringe for a short while, listening to see how she handled the interaction with the store patrons. Their comments and questions, he had pointed out, could be quite different from the media's.

"You can expect, for instance, comments like, 'I love Louis L'Amour. Is your book as good as his are?'"

"Who's he?" Lacey had asked.

"Only about the most successful writer of Western and pioneer novels who ever lived."

"Oh! How do I handle it if they want a comparison with a particular work of his or of some other guy I've never heard of?"

"Just admit you've never heard of them. You can claim quite honestly that you've only recently acquired any interest in something besides drama."

"Okay, what else?"

"Well, since most women writing Westerns write romance, you can expect some women readers to assume that about *Trespass*. You have to decide whether or not you want to point out that it's not romance."

"Hey!" she said with a smile and a shrug. "If they want to buy the book, why should I talk them out of it? I intend to sell out the printing before the three weeks of promotion are up."

"I like the attitude, but just don't feel you've failed if that doesn't happen. It almost never does with an unknown."

"Just how do you know what to expect at a book-signing?"

"As an avid reader, I've been in bookstores during lots of them."

Black dawdled near the front of the store for a moment before moving toward the rear and up the ramp to the elevated half of the space. The captain's chairs that were usually clustered around the circular rock fireplace where patrons were encouraged to gather had been removed. Their space was taken up with patrons clustered around the fireplace waiting to get their copies of *Trespass* autographed or discussing their already-signed books.

Black worked his way to the table and took a copy of the book from one of the stacks on the table where Lacey sat. She finished signing her name with a flourish in another copy and looked up. She gave him a smile and a generic, "Hi!" before she handed the book to the woman in front of her.

The woman was thumbing through the book as she asked Lacey, "How many of the characters are from real-life county history?"

Black was pleased to hear her answer smoothly, "None. Only Belle Harmon is based very loosely on Anna Beaumont, matriarch of a pioneer family. The geographic details, though, are drawn from actual history—the street names, real stores and schools. You'll recognize the mission, the Dallidet Adobe."

Black took the book with him to stand a few yards away, where he could still hear as he appeared to scan the book. Over the course of the half-hour he hung about, the crowds coming in to buy an autographed copy of Lacey Bonner's first novel remained steady. It pleased Black. Lacey would have hated playing to an empty house.

And the crowds were not personal acquaintances of Lacey's, as it turned out, just fascinated locals, for the most part. Black discovered from their comments that these small frogs suddenly saw themselves as bigger, in the reflection of their small pond contained in the book. Lacey Bonner was, of course, quite the giant, queen frog and the moment.

Black was about to leave. The bookstore manager had bumped into him for the seventh time. Pretty soon he was going to notice how long the blond customer had been sullying the pages of the hardback book. Black had told Lacey he wouldn't follow her from place to place for the rest of the local signings. It might raise questions if he were noticed by any of the people he had told so emphatically that he didn't want any of the credit. Two of them had just made their way up the ramp: Grayson Anders and hefty, bald Ray Yost of the music department.

Yost's navel—an inny—was peeking out through the gap between two straining buttons, like a curious eye from behind the curtains. Anders nodded to Black and turned his attention toward Lacey. She did a convincing act of a woman responding to an invisible man.

"Yo, Black!" Yost called as he waddled toward the table where Black had been trying to put the book back on the dwindling stack. "The proud professor is getting his autographed copy, I see. Congratulations on your part in it."

"All the credit goes to the woman behind the table."

"Why thank you, Professor," she said, reaching for the book in his hand. She began scribbling with the expensive fountain pen she had bought for the occasion, before he could object. With nervous concern for the content of her inscription, Black watched helplessly as Yost and Anders leaned in to read her note: *With extreme gratitude for your invaluable part in the writing of this book, Lacey Bonner.*

"Very nice, very nice!" Yost said with a slap of Black's shoulder.

"Indeed," Anders added. Black noted the flatness of the comment, bordering on sarcasm.

Black wished Lacey well on the rest of her appearances and excused himself to pay for the book—an odd feeling in itself, especially since he had five of the ten free copies from the publisher at home. He wondered what Anders in particular would think of the message Lacey Bonner had written in one of those: *For the man in the cage, from the woman who keeps looking for the key.* It would be the copy from the bookstore that would lie out to be seen by any visitors.

*   *   *   *

CHAPTER FIFTEEN

Not only was Lacey Bonner's seductive face on the back of book dust jackets across the county, but over the days and weeks that followed the book's release, differing versions of that face greeted Jim Black and the other citizens of the county and state from newspapers and magazines. Articles were taped up in bookstore windows and tacked up on the bulletin boards at the college and at places mentioned in the book that still existed.

The library proudly posted articles, as did the historical society's museum where she (and unobtrusive Professor Black) had done considerable research. Besides the feature articles, every county publication carried ads emphasizing Lacey's uniqueness and the book's local setting.

Jim Black read the feature articles carefully, looking for and grateful not to find a slip-up on Lacey's part. She played the role perfectly. This continued to be true in her local radio and television interviews.

Witnessing her appearances in Southern California was an impossibility except for the two carried nationwide: 'Connie Martinson Talks Books' and Phil Hunter's talk show. The latter one would air during Black's morning short story class period. He toyed with the idea of programming his VCR to tape it while he was in class, then decided he was too nervous and impatient to wait until the end of the day to view it. It would conclude the promotional campaign. And, assuming that Lacey was as flawless as she had been, they would both consider it a very big Mission Accomplished.

He confessed his desire to see the broadcast live to Carol Quinn, a literature teacher. She recognized the broad hint and volunteered to take his class.

He was home, sitting on the sofa, squirming and rolling the sweating Calistoga bottle between his hands as the show began. When Hunter was introducing Lacey, Black had to remind himself that she was feeling none of the chest-paralyzing anxiety he was feeling.

Looking into the screen, into the very broadcast studio where Bailey Thurston had been, at a man who had looked him in the eye for fifteen long minutes, Black had the sudden, paranoid feeling that Hunter could see into his living room.

I know he can see right through my changed appearance. I know that look on Hunter's face—he's about to ask what in the world a dead man is doing staring at him from an apartment in San Luis.

Five minutes into the interview, Black was sitting back smiling over how Lacey had Hunter in her spell. As if he had forgotten he was the host and therefore responsible for directing the events, his elbow was on his desk and his chin was resting on his open palm as he stared raptly at his beautiful guest.

"You see," Lacey said to him, her fingers measuring the air in pinches, "characters are most finely drawn in the strokes of their tiniest, most ordinary actions."

Black heard himself chuckle as he recognized the statement as his own. He must have made it during one of his lectures. No problem. Any of his students hearing the broadcast and also recognizing it would only be impressed with how well Lacey had paid attention.

*   *   *   *

Professor Black was in his office, organizing the work he would take home in a few minutes, when the phone rang. "Hey, J.P.!" came Lacey's elated voice through the receiver. "I just got back, and I'm holding you to your promise."

He sighed, wishing she had forgotten, but she rattled on without giving him a chance to object.

"A couple of weeks ago, I tried the menu out on my drama cronies to be sure I wouldn't poison you. They lived. Drinks at seven. I have tons of clippings to show you. Bye!" There was a dial tone.

Black put the phone down shaking his head and saying sarcastically to the air, "Sorry, ma'am, but you have a wrong number."

A few moments later, as he was standing at his desk, putting papers into his briefcase, he looked up at the sound of tapping on the door. Grayson Anders was standing in the now-open doorway, holding a copy of *Trespass* in one hand and a cigarette dropping ash in the other. He looked as serious as if he were about to deliver Hamlet's soliloquy.

"Hello, Grayson, I see you got yourself a copy sometime after I left the book-signing."

Anders came into the room with a distracted look and sat down. "This is very puzzling." He took a drag, shook his head and held the book in the air for a moment.

"The plot? I thought it rather straightforward."

"No, this coming from Lacey."

Black smiled. "As I said before, Lacey's capable of much more than we've credited her..."

Anders was usually fastidious in his manners. Just now he interrupted Black and didn't seem to notice the ashes that were filtering down onto his trousers. "No, I mean, all those times you and I talked about character development and how the characters are revealed by the details of their behavior. I mean the meter...." He waved his hand as a question. "It's not hers. It's more like...." He didn't finish, and he was squinting at Black in concentration, like a man trying to see through a one-way mirror.

Meter! It was something that few readers noticed, yet it was frequently a characteristic mark of an author. Faulkner's slow, leisurely meter, for instance, would never be mistaken for the more abrupt pacing of Hemingway's narratives. Playwrights were particularly careful to give each character a slightly different meter. Black realized with horror that he had totally overlooked Anders' well-developed actor's and director's ear.

He swallowed and shuffled the papers in his briefcase as he said, "Well, Grayson, I'll admit the book doesn't reflect Lacey's typical thinking or conversation patterns, but somewhere along the line somebody got her excited about that time period. Like any good actress immersing herself in a role, I guess she just submerged her own personality." He looked at Anders and shrugged casually.

"You think so?"

"Oh, sure. I don't think you've given yourself the credit you deserve as her drama instructor." He smiled and hoped the flattery would get the man's mind off examining the issue, then he further diverted Anders with questions about rehearsals for the amateur production to open in a month.

*   *   *   *

Black had been as far as Lacey's front door and garage several times when he had come to accompany her on some location research errand or other. This evening, in the unseasonably cool June weather, he felt like a man walking straight into a trap. Ordinarily it was the men doing the setting of traps for big, dangerous cats.

Lacey Bonner was sensual enough when she arrived in class wearing the conservative clothes required by the telephone company. As he walked up the few steps toward her door, his breathing was already ragged from the anticipation of seeing her in some dramatically sexy outfit.

It will fit her like a second skin, plunge to the waist, and be reeking of musk.

He could barely hear her two-note doorbell above the clanging of alarms throughout every quarter of his body.

She answered the door wearing sneakers, blue jeans, and a sweater so big on her that he wondered which of the Chicago Bears had owned it first. Still, it didn't entirely quell the alarms.

"Some champagne to toast the successful conclusion of your incomparable performance!" he said a bit too loudly and held out the bag with the cold Korbel.

She bowed and took it, telling him to come in and follow her to the kitchen. He was relieved that there was still plenty of daylight in the living room, the candles in the dining room they passed through hadn't been lit and the kitchen was ablaze with nice, safe, bright light.

He almost couldn't get a word in for the next hour as she related the details of her various interviews and personal appearances. She had such a good memory for dialogue that he was certain he was getting close to a perfect replay.

All the while, she ordered him around the small, expensively equipped kitchen, thrusting the bottle of champagne and a cork puller at him, pointing toward the glasses, telling him to follow her to the living room and to sit for awhile as she showed him the stack of clippings.

The ads, articles and the reviews she had clipped were a pale shadow of those that had greeted the release of any of the late Bailey Thurston's later books. Instead of a full-page feature in the Calendar or Book sections of the *Los Angeles Times*, plus a lengthy, favorable review, there was a one-paragraph mention under new-releases.

Lacey's photograph and a two-column article in the *Daily Breeze*, which covered the coast from Santa Monica to Palos Verdes, represented the splashiest coverage. Yet there was lots of it, lots of little favorable mentions in local newspapers and magazines.

A very respectable showing for an unknown. Very respectable.

The dinner she had prepared was virtually a tribute to his efforts to teach her some simple cooking: a green salad, broiled monkfish, broccoli with lemon butter, dark brown rolls, and sliced honeydew on the side. He tensed when she lit the candles, but she made no cat-like creeping attack.

Later, she insisted that he sit while she cleared the table then brought more champagne and dessert, a cop-out, store-bought cheesecake. As he was nearly finished with his, she was talking about Hunter's comments on this morning's program.

"He raved, J.P.! *I've* never had such rave notices."

"You deserve them. Just imagine if he had known what a performance you were *really* giving." He smiled and took the last bite of his cheesecake.

She blinked several times, shook her head and laid the silver fork down on the plate with her unfinished dessert. "You don't get it at all, do you?"

"Get what?"

"I wasn't talking about raves for my performance. All evening, all you've talked about is my performance as an actress."

"Lacey, you've done such an outstanding job," he mumbled with confusion.

She shook her head again. "All evening—in fact, since the book came out!—I've told you all the wonderful things people have said about *Trespass*."

"I know, Lacey. You've done a wonderful job."

"Damn it, J.P.! You seem blind to the fact that *you're* the one they're raving about!" She was quiet for a few seconds, studying him before she said, "I guess you really don't realize what a fabulously talented writer you are."

Confused because the evening hadn't gone as he had anticipated at all, and uncomfortable with such lavish praise, he said a quick, "Thanks," and forced his way on with, "I'm really far along on 'Horn of Joshua.' Did you get enough applause for yourself from this crazy arrangement to be willing to do it again?"

A look of pain flashed across her expressive face as she said, "I didn't do one thing for applause for myself, J.P."

Her low tone contained so much sadness that he wondered what he had said to insult her. Even the look on her face was one of despondency as she picked up the remains of her dessert and his empty plate to carry them from the room.

He was so shocked and confused by her reaction that he couldn't follow her into the bright light of the kitchen and ask the simple question of what was wrong with assuming that she had conducted her elaborate charade for the kind of praise any actress would love.

What did she do it for, then?

Sitting alone at the candlelit table, he reminded himself to back up a step and ask the *what* of all she had done before he could answer the why. In listing events of the last year and a half, he realized that he had gotten so caught up in his drive toward full-time writing that he had overlooked the astoundingly obvious: *Good Lord, she laid herself at my feet as an offering!*

Completely, unreservedly, she had dropped her goals, to help him pursue his. She had quit her drama class, rejected all the parts that had been offered her, to his knowledge had dated no one. She had given up smoking.

A woman with the mere hots for a professor might have quit smoking for a week or two. She might have gone along with the little game of 'becoming a writer' for a few weeks until she could worm her way into the professor's bed. But someone with the hots who hadn't been able to get him into bed would have turned cold long before now.

No, a case of the mere hots was to serious love what the twenty-four-hour flu was to a permanent, incurable disability. Knowing this, Black realized that there was only one possible explanation for Lacey Bonner's behavior. She was actually in love with J.P. Black.

That was disaster enough. The cataclysm was in his sudden realization that, throughout her whole miraculous performance, he had translated all the public praise for the book into an anthem to *her*, simply because he had fallen in love with Lacey Bonner.

Jim Black sat alone, paralyzed in the dining room chair for more than five minutes. Barely able to breathe, he analyzed the unexpected terror over something other people *prayed* for. He decided that only someone who has stood at the edge of an abyss that goes to the center of the earth could understand the basis of such terror.

He felt almost too heavy with fear, and with the guilt of being so blindly obsessed, to lift himself from the chair and walk into the kitchen. She was at the sink, her back to him. Her hands were wide apart, resting on the white tile counter, and her head was down. With the too-large sweater, she looked like a hurt little girl. He spoke her name in a husky whisper. Her dark hair whipped in the light from above the sink as she shook her head harshly.

In the months he had known her, he had made and kept very strict, unspoken rules for himself about not allowing physical contact. All her attempts to violate those rules had stopped shortly after they had begun working together to prepare her. Now he was the one reaching for her. He expected resistance when he tried to turn her, but there was none. Neither did she try to hide the tear-washed face she turned stonily toward him.

He swallowed and began, his hands still on her shoulders. "You're look-ing at one of the stupidest men ever to draw breath." The quick cocking motion of her head and the shift in her eyes bordered on agreement.

"I feel so stupid right now, in fact, that I'm almost afraid to say any-thing at all. I misunderstood your motives for investing all these many months. I'm sorry. I'm…." He swallowed, threw his hands up in the air and let them fall. "I'm sorry."

She stood still a moment before her body began the small, rapid rocking of someone who was fighting hard to contain the volatile result of mixing pain and fury. He nearly raised a hand to defend himself when she lunged forward unexpectedly, but she was merely ripping a paper towel from the dispenser behind him.

She spoke in an angry, broken voice after wiping her face and noisily blowing her nose. "Listen, J.P., I was in love with you from very early on—maybe from the first time I wondered what kissing that mouth that hadn't been fouled by tobacco smoke would taste like."

He tried to escape the emotional threat represented by her admission by looking away, but her vehement voice brought his gaze back to her intense face as she continued, "I figured that if there was someone else in the picture, she—or he—would have crossed paths with me by now. If they hadn't crossed swords."

"No, Lacey, there's no one." He found that 'else' wouldn't come out.

"And I figured that, if you had some kind of physical…deficiency… you would simply have told me about it to cool my heated interest in things intimate. I had certainly demonstrated my ability to keep a secret. But I know it's nothing as simple as any of those. There's something about your past that has you living someone else's life."

He felt as if he had been hit in the chest by a wrecking ball. "What?!"

"Your apartment alone says you can't decide who you are. You're such a decisive man, yet it's a hodgepodge of styles."

"So I'm a bit tasteless," he offered lamely.

She shook her head. "There's also no personal history there, J.P., no stupid college trophies or scrapbooks or souvenirs from your supposed trip around the world. And for a self-proclaimed avid reader, your personal library is pitifully small."

"I lost everything…."

She held up her hand and shook her head. "I don't want a story. It's obviously something really extreme, probably something life-threatening that has a man with perfect vision wearing fake glasses, a dark-haired man faithfully maintaining the strawberry blond impression from the neck up."

He flinched, and his hand went to his hair automatically as she continued, more quietly, "I saw your bare chest the first night I came to your place." She looked at him for a moment before she turned and did a slam-dunk with the paper towel in the open trash can near the sink.

Stupid! Careless! His throat felt nearly closed as he tried to sound casual about everything. "So you found out I'm a little vain in that department. Besides, I had always heard that blondes have more fun."

She whirled. "Then why aren't you having any?!"

They stood in the glaring light of the kitchen, staring desperately at each other for a good, long while. He couldn't run the risk of answering her implied question of whether he was in hiding for his life. Yet, after all she had done, he couldn't let her think she was in love with a murderer in hiding from the gas chamber.

"Lacey, you have nothing to fear from me, if that thought has been on your mind." She gave no reaction, and he went on, "All I can tell you is that something happened to me so devastatingly painful that the only way I could go on living was to consider my past dead, right down to my stupid hair color."

"A woman?" she asked quietly.

"Dead now." *She and all the others, dead.*

Lacey's slow exhaling and the relaxing of her face showed her relief. After a long, awkward silence in the bright light of the kitchen, Lacey walked to the living room and sat in one corner of the deep green velour sofa. Lights of the city below were sparkling outside the dimly lit room. Black came and slumped morosely in the other corner, studying the texture of the carpet. After he had sat in silence for more than a minute, he looked at Lacey.

All pretense had been drained from her. Her arms were stretched along the back of the sofa. Her chin rested on one arm, and her eyes were focused on him, searching intently for the real man beneath the fake glasses and hair color.

Even in the baggy sweater, she couldn't hide her cat body. Black was aching with the desire to pull her to himself and spend the next week on this sofa exploring her. She was more than willing. He was more than starving for such intimacy! But Lacey's admission of her love had brought him to the great abyss again. It yawned before him in the dark, empty space between them on the sofa.

A line from a Bailey Thurston mystery was echoing in his mind. It was a line from a cop character closely resembling Det. Hugh Larson: *Risk only ends when life ends. Risk reminds me every day that I'm alive.*

The breath that Black took as he sat up slowly was deep, as if he were going to dive to a very, very great depth.

"Lacey, you know enough about writing and about the new book that we don't need to continue working on your performance before it's released—if you're still willing to pose as the writer."

She swallowed, and he saw the pain of her assumption that he wanted only to continue using her that way. He went on, "And because we don't need to work on your performance anymore, it would leave us time to be two ordinary people trying to decide whether they really are in love."

Her eyes were blinking rapidly as the tears suddenly flowed, yet her face looked as if a stagehand had turned a light toward it.

"I can never, ever tell you about my painful past. It might...." He looked away quickly.

"Nothing could make me stop loving you."

He smiled sadly and explained, "I won't tell you about my past, because it would put you and maybe others in danger. Lacey, I'm scared out of my mind to risk loving someone again."

"I'll never leave you," she said, reaching for his hand.

"You might never mean to, but loss can happen other ways. For right now, though," he told her with a nervous laugh, "I need at least a couple of days to get my very soul to stop shaking! I feel like a nine-point quake just hit the fault that runs right through me."

She responded with a speechless nod of her face that beamed through the tears.

"Maybe we could make the first step our going away somewhere together for the weekend. Monterey would be a nice drive. What do you think?"

She nodded and whispered, "Yes! Oh, yes!"

The lingering kiss he delivered to her wet and salty mouth revealed the intensity they both felt before he left her crying contentedly on the sofa.

*   *   *   *

Bailey Thurston had numerous times received flowers from Mary Zada or his agent or publisher. Jim Black was stunned on Wednesday to have the florist deliver an enormous display of brilliantly colored flowers to his office at school. The scrawled note said, *Put these in the empty cage!*

The looks that Black received from Yost, Anders and other faculty told him that Lacey might as well have carried them in herself with bass drums and cymbals announcing their arrival.

While waiting for Friday evening to arrive, time would sometimes seem to drag as Black thought of being with Lacey. Then, unexpectedly, while walking or driving he would be in a state of panic at the arguments warring in his mind.

You have a wife. Her name is Sara Thurston, mother of your children.

Her name's Turnbow, and she's dead.

No she's not. It's you that have been playing dead. She's alive and well, and you're plotting to run off with some woman.

She's dead! They're all dead!

He forced his mind back to the present as he did the mundane preparations for a romantic weekend away: laundry, ironing, doing the routine hair coloring before he went to the barber for a trim. He shaved more carefully than he usually did. This was no time to have something as unattractive as several razor nicks.

Lacey phoned him at home Wednesday and Thursday evenings, and their conversations were low, long, and had him wondering whether he could wait until the weekend to be with her again. Fearful—and ecstatic with joy!—he lived until class let out at four on Friday. As he drove toward his apartment, the rain from an unexpected summer shower was pouring down, and a chilly wind was buffeting the car.

Simply a glorious evening! he thought as he hummed along with the radio.

They were to take Lacey's car. And, since the garages and visitor spaces in Lacey's development were being spray painted over the weekend, she would come his direction right after class dismissal. He had been packed since that morning. His small suitcase was sitting in the living room, by the front door.

He brushed his teeth, brushed his hair, put on more deodorant, opened and closed the refrigerator four times before walking to the front window. He checked his watch: five-fifteen. Lacey wasn't exactly a fanatic about punctuality, so he phoned to see if she was doing some silly woman thing like washing her hair at the last minute or doing her polish over.

No answer. She's on her way, then, and should be here within ten minutes.

It took the hands on his watch an imagined three hours to creep around to five-forty-five. He phoned again. Again no answer.

With the rain and the wind and with her excitement.... Oh, God, not an accident! No, no, not now!

He phoned again. Again no answer. He scribbled a note saying he would be right back and taped it to his front door. Pulling up the collar of his raincoat and opening his umbrella, he hurried to his car behind the apartment.

Friday nights were always more congested. Adding a storm to the routine only ground traffic to a slower pace approaching a standstill.

Watching fearfully for signs of an accident, even one whose wreckage had been removed, he clutched the wheel and tried to control the sickening knot in his stomach. The normal six- or seven-minute drive took him thirty minutes. Her garage was open, the car there and the trunk open. He collapsed onto the steering wheel shaking with relief.

Feeling childish over his concern, he parked in the visitor space and bounded through the rain and up the steps to her front door to see if she was running late because she needed help with something. His hand went for the doorbell, but he froze at the sound of some man's deep laughter from inside.

Oops! What to do? Don't want her to think I was checking up on her, that I don't trust her. Who is that with her? Vaguely familiar....

The man laughed again, and Black wondered if it was one of the actors he had met. Or Grayson Anders.

I know I know the voice. There were several cars and a white van along the street, but Anders' black Porsche wasn't among them. Black didn't know what kinds of cars the other actors drove.

Who else? Maybe that's the maintenance engineer's van. He came about a leak once before when I was here. Didn't see his car, though.

The best was to go somewhere nearby and phone, he decided, and so he hurried back to his car and sped down the hill the few blocks to French Hospital. He felt bad about dripping rainwater on the lobby floor as he dialed Lacey's number. Ten rings and no answer.

Okay, so they finished their little get-together or fixed the problem and she's on her way.

Breathlessly, he hurried outside and through the parking lot puddles to his car. He hoped he could make it home before she did. Then he chuckled. *Suuure! A VW beat a Maserati in the rain?*

Her car was nowhere in sight when he pulled into the driveway beside the apartment, parked in the rear and went to his door. His note was there, fluttering wildly in the wind. He pulled it down, asking himself, *Why isn't she here?*

He hurried inside and phoned, letting her number ring twenty times. *Surely if they're in the middle of some leak or plumbing problem one of them can stop long enough to answer a demanding phone.*

He phoned every five minutes until after seven, with no response. He was trying desperately to remember the name of the maintenance engineer so he could look up his number. His chest was heaving with confused worry when he laid the phone down.

Repeated calling did no good. It made no sense that Lacey hadn't called to explain the delay, and so self-doubt slashed in like lightning, joining the fear.

What if gifted Lacey Bonner was only acting when she confessed she loved me? Her car was ready to go somewhere—but not necessarily with me. It's never made sense that she would chose me over Grayson. They're probably both laughing at me.

He was sitting in the kitchen chair by the phone, rocking like a confused little boy, when he heard a thumping at his front door. Nearly in tears from relief, he charged through the kitchen and across the living room to the door as the thumping continued. He tore the door open expecting to find her soaked and with her hands full as an excuse for not ringing the bell.

The huddled mass that fell in on his feet was wet and bleeding. The hands were tied with tape, the wrists bleeding. Strips of tape were over the eyes and mouth, and so only the flaring nostrils on Lacey Bonner's twisted face could reveal her terror. The

cigarette burns to her naked upper body and the thin, bleeding slice to her neck revealed to Black just who had done this.

*   *   *   *

CHAPTER SIXTEEN

Black was in such a state of panic that he later wouldn't know in what order things had been accomplished or even by whom: the calling of the paramedics and the police, the removal of the tape, the wrapping of the tormented woman in a clean sheet. The screams of pain and terror seemed to him about to turn Lacey inside out as she clung to him, in spite of her painful wounds, and screamed and screamed and screamed.

The screams of the police sirens were added to those of the ambulance as Black rode to Sierra Vista Hospital holding Lacey Bonner's wild-eyed, screaming face in his hands. He wasn't sure she even saw him. She had the same look of blind terror he had seen on another woman's face—the woman on the far side of the abyss.

But how had Levi found a way across?! How did he connect Lacey with the dead Bailey Thurston? How had Levi even known to look for Thurston?

The red-haired paramedic was tapping at the side of a syringe. "Morphine. This'll knock her out."

"No!" Black gripped his arm. "Ease the pain, please, but you can't knock her out! We have to question her about others in danger."

"You a cop?" The paramedic squinted in question.

Black evaded the question with, "Remember the Levi killings six or so years ago?"

The paramedic's glance shot toward the slice to her neck and the burns on the patient's bare shoulders above the sheet before it returned to Black, who said, "If this was really him, we'll have to warn a family in Los Angeles." He turned his back to the paramedic and stroked Lacey's sweat- and rain-soaked hair, waiting for her screams to ease a bit under the morphine.

The arrival at the hospital was a blur of movement as they raced with the gurney from the ambulance and through the big doorways that sucked their way open with a hiss and a thump. Bright light and the sound of feet racing on rubber soles across vinyl registered only vaguely with Black, as did the terse command, "You can't go in there!" Someone grabbed his arm. He shrugged it off.

Various voices clamored over one other in Black's ears as he raced beside the gurney and into the examining room. Inside the curtain that was whisked around the area, the paramedics were exchanging medical information with the small female who had joined them sometime in the race through the E.R., Dr. Somebody.

The fiftyish woman nodded curtly and said, "Get a female police officer in here and get this guy out."

"I'm staying!" Black said harshly. Lacey was looking his direction in desperation. He still wasn't sure she saw him.

"Till we know for sure who did this," the physician said in a harsh whisper while pinning him with a glare, "you will get out and stay out!"

"All right, all right, but please listen to me and don't knock her out till the police have found out what the guy said to her."

"Who the hell gives a...?!"

"A whole family might be in danger, only they won't make it to the E.R. before the morgue." He nailed her with a glare of his own before he ran a shaking hand over Lacey's whimpering face and walked out.

Jim Black hurt everywhere, from the tension, the awkward position sitting in the ambulance, from Lacey's strong fingers digging into his arms and his back. He was also bloodstained and received stares as he walked back toward the entrance. A blond female police officer was jogging past him in the opposite direction. He couldn't find the breath to tell her to get the crucial information fast so Lacey could escape into painless, dreamless sleep.

"I need a private phone," he said to the clerk at the E.R.'s front desk.

"There's a pay phone. We don't let…."

He demanded quietly through clenched teeth, "I have to stop a murder! I need a private phone."

Her eyes widened, and she let him into a tiny office no bigger than a large closet, used for completing insurance information and providing the E.R. personnel with confidential information. His dialing of the Pacific Division station of LAPD was automatic, in spite of the intervening years. The desk clerk said Det. Larson was at home.

Afraid that Cynthia might answer and recognize his voice, Black told the clerk, "This is an extreme emergency. Please call Larson and tell him Jim Black has fresh details in the Levi case." He gave the number and sat shaking like a tree in a strong wind until the phone rang less than three minutes later.

"That you, Human?"

"Yeah! What's happened?"

Black hadn't realized that it would take him nearly ten minutes to relate the complex story of his and Lacey Bonner's charade. "I don't know how he connected her to me. The book isn't contemporary. There isn't even a murder in it. None of the interviews brought up the name of Bailey Thurston. She avoided even mentioning J.P. Black in interviews."

"It could be random."

"No! Every detail is the same—except he stopped short of the last step. And why would some random sicko dump her at my door?"

"All right, all right. In case you're right, we'll slap cover around the Turnbow house—same address on Trask." Larson added the last in a low voice that said he knew how hard it was for the man in San Luis to hear his house and family described by some other man's name.

"Hume, you can't let them know why they need protecting. Sara has a new life. They all do. If I'm wrong about Levi and this was just some local maniac jealous over our relationship, it would just be another calamity to let them know I'm alive. You'd be letting Levi know, too."

"All right. I can think of something. What're you going to do right now? Are you going to be all right yourself, Bailey?"

He hadn't been called that name in five years. "I'll stay with Lacey—when they'll let me. The doctor so much as said I was the prime suspect."

"S.O.P., Bailey. Don't take it personally."

Shortly Larson hung up to get things into motion. There was neither time nor mood for chitchat. You don't chitchat across the abyss.

Black went to the desk. The doctor was still examining the patient. No, he couldn't come in. He went to the men's room and saw the look of fear and guilt on his bloodied face. The metallic smell of blood and the stench of Lacey's charred flesh finally made their way from Black's nostrils to his brain. He went and threw up in the toilet.

*   *   *   *

It was after nine, more than an hour after he had been ordered out of the examining room, before Dr. Lois Miles came to the front and motioned for him to come with her and the rather chunky female police officer, Pamela Courtney. Black felt as if he had been three days without sleep. He followed the women to a large, unoccupied supply closet, where they went in and closed the door.

"Sorry I don't have a glamorous office to offer," Miles said and ran her fingers through her short, greying hair.

"Just how is Lacey?" he asked tersely.

"We got over the first hurdle by not letting her slip into shock. The next hurdle is avoiding infection, and we're obviously addressing that. While they're finishing dressing her wounds, I put her under."

"Oh, God!" he groaned and turned his face up to the ceiling.

"Not before I questioned her, though," Courtney said quickly. Black's head spun her direction. She had one hand raised defensively before she flipped open her note pad. "We don't know how much is fact and how much hallucination. When something that painful goes on that long...."

"What did she say?!" he demanded in a whisper. He wanted to cut off reminders of what had been going on while he was counting the rings of her phone, reminders of the fact he had been just outside her door. Listening to the butcher's laugh.

"She said, 'Levi did it.' Does that mean anything to you?"

He slumped and nodded. "A psychopath. LAPD has the file, Det. Larson at the Pacific Station. Did she describe him?"

"No. She said he got in her garage somehow, came up from behind." Courtney looked at her notes again. "She said, 'He wanted Thurston.' Here's a place in her testimony where we're not sure. The victim said, 'Levi knew Thurston wasn't dead because of bus pass'—or maybe it was 'dress pads.' Does that make any sense to you?" she asked of Black.

"The word was *Trespass*. Her book title."

Get the pronoun straight, Black. It was your book that somehow led to this.

Both the physician and the officer blinked in shock and looked at one another before the physician said, "I knew I'd heard her name."

The officer was studying her pad, squinting in concentration as she said, "The victim wandered off a bit, and when she was coherent again, she said, 'Levi wanted Thurston's name.' That made no sense to me. I mean, if he wanted Thurston's name, then he *had* the name, right? Anyway...." The officer shrugged and looked back at her pad again.

"Wait a minute!" the physician interrupted and looked at Courtney. Black was glad she wasn't looking at him. "Thurston! Wasn't that the name of another writer? The mystery guy who was killed after some psycho named Levi....?" The confused physician trailed off as her gaze turned to Black.

He tried to ignore the question on her face as he asked of the officer in a husky voice, "Did she say why her book made Levi think this Thurston was still alive?"

She thumbed through her notes a moment before she nodded, "It was funny. The victim actually smiled for a second when she said, 'Levi said he couldn't miss Thurston's literary fingerprint.' She mumbled that the perp heard her make a statement on a talk show that he recognized as Thurston's."

Oh, God! She listened too well.

"The victim went on to mention some stuff about meters and synapses and symbiotic meaning to flies on walls. Hallucination, as I said."

Meter and syntax and symbolic meaning to the blasted fly on the wall!

Black's head was spinning as he tried to connect the ideas of Levi and the Southern California murders to meter, syntax and San Luis Obispo. Grayson Anders' face staring intently at him rushed to the front of Black's consciousness.

"Meter!" he mumbled and suddenly understood why he had suggested to Larson that perhaps some jealous local nut had tortured Lacey.

Anders as Levi? Is that possible?

Black searched his memory for Anders' background and realized the man had been an actor in Los Angeles for several years before moving to San Luis. He had been in Los Angeles, in fact, during the period of the Levi killings.

"Listen," Black said to Officer Courtney, "I have absolutely no evidence, but can you check into the whereabouts of a local man, Grayson Anders, tonight?"

"The actor/director?" the officer asked with a gathered brow.

"Yes, it might not mean anything at all, but he mentioned the meter of Lacey's writing just a couple of days ago."

"All right," Courtney said, "but are you suggesting he is the serial killer?"

The doctor looked seriously between Courtney and Black before he answered, "I'm suggesting that if Anders was abnormally jealous over our relationship and wanted to punish us both, mimicking Levi would just throw you off his trail."

Black wondered when it would occur to the others to ask his question: Whether it was Levi or merely a copycat, just why didn't he kill Lacey Bonner?

"Listen," Black said as he exited the stuffy room with the two women, "I understand your concern over not knowing whether *I'm* Levi...."

"We didn't suggest that!" Courtney said, suddenly rigid. "Why would you suggest that?"

"Because I spoke with a cop friend of mine, and he said it's S.O.P." Both women studied him for a moment before they looked away and he continued, "I'm willing for any police officer to hold a gun to the back of my head the whole time, if you'll only let me sit with Lacey."

Dr. Miles squeaked her high-top running shoe around on the vinyl floor a moment, crushing some vermin Black couldn't see, before she looked at him. "I've seen some pretty remorseful, smooth-talking insects come in here claiming some other guy put the woman in critical condition."

"I believe you," Black answered quietly.

"And I've seen the effect it can have on the patient—the victim—to wake up seeing the face that put them here."

"I understand."

Dr. Miles breathed heavily several times before she said, "If Officer Courtney is willing to sit next to you in the room for half an hour while the patient is completely under, I'll permit it as long as you don't so much as speak."

Courtney nodded, and Black said, "I'll take it."

"After that," Miles added, walking away, "the attending physician on the second floor will have to ask the patient whether she wants to see you or not."

"I understand." Black could barely control the urge to collapse in a heap of guilt and to scream, *I caused this! It's all my fault!*

He had to return to the lobby and wait with the crying earaches and the dull-eyed fevers, the moaning Friday night blackened eyes and the split-open knuckles for another half hour, while the E.R. nurses completed their treatment and arranged for the transfer upstairs of trauma patient Lacey Bonner.

Pamela Courtney had reported to the chief investigator by phone before she came to fetch the shattered man in the bloodied clothes from the lobby. He walked beside the gurney, too devastated even to ask to hold the bruised and bandaged hand that was exposed on the top of the blue blanket because of the IV connection.

Once in the room, once the patient had been transferred to the bed and the lights were dimmed, all he could safely manage was to sit in the prayer position of a man he had considered dead years ago across the great abyss.

Then Officer Courtney drove him home.

*   *   *   *

Black didn't sleep but lay on his bed trying to rewrite every move he had made since he had known Lacey Bonner. *If I had picked anyone but her to play the charade...,*

A defensive argument came from some sane voice he didn't recognize as his own: *But Lacey was the one to conceive of the idea, the only one you have ever met who could have pulled it off.*

Ah! his accuser continued, *she pulled off her part. And don't try claiming it's San Andreas' fault again. It's your work, your own words that led him to Lacey.*

He lay in the silent darkness and hated the reminder of a boy looking out from under a family room coffee table, a boy still frightened by an earthquake. He hated the reminder of a life that had once flourished on the other side of the fault that had ripped through Bailey Thurston's world.

*   *   *   *

Officer Courtney called Black's apartment just after eleven that evening. "Sorry to call so late," she began, "but we finally tracked Mr. Anders down and he's off the hook."

"An alibi?"

"Yes, a good one. About a dozen actors and stage hands said he had been running them through the mill nonstop since about five-thirty."

Black slumped and felt a sudden, sickening reminder that he had been equally disappointed when nice Ramon Rodriguez had turned out to be just that.

Courtney continued, "We thought maybe you could suggest someone else who might have a motive."

"No, but if I think of a name, I'll call right away." A name he hadn't thought of in years came to mind: Brad Nollan. Black called LAPD at midnight. Larson was, as anticipated, there.

Black explained, "Lacey confirmed that her attacker was Levi. He told her he knew Thurston was alive because he recognized a quote of his when Lacey was on an L.A. talk show. That and Thurston's literary fingerprint, unique style."

Neither Black nor Larson commented on his talking as if Thurston were a stranger. Black continued, "I had hoped Levi was a local fellow here that knows me and Lacey, but the police checked and he's been eliminated as a possibility."

Larson sighed heavily then said, "It'll all have to come out about your being alive."

"I know."

"We'll leave things alone for now, though. Protection's in place."

Larson had stuck his usually righteous neck out another unrighteous mile for his dead friend by falsifying a report of a burglary in the Playa del Rey neighborhood along Trask. At Larson's instruction, plainclothes officers were thick in the area—thicker than usual for a burglary, because the report included mention of a stabbing victim. Uniformed officers were going door-to-door warning residents to stay inside, to lock every possible entrance and to call 9-1-1 at the slightest provocation.

"Hume, if this all comes down on your neck, you've blown your retirement."

"You asked me once about priorities, as I recall."

"Besides the protection, what else have you done since I called? Questioned anybody? Brad Nollan, maybe?"

"We're trying to locate him, Bailey, but the trail's awfully cold, I'm afraid. How's the patient?"

"In the arms of Morpheus—literally. They won't let me see her again till she gives her permission."

"She will."

I'm not sure of that...at...all!

Black phoned the hospital at one in the morning, three and five. No change. Still sedated. The patient's temperature was elevated. That was to be expected. Her body was fighting infection.

What else is she fighting? The painful humiliation of knowing she suffered all this because she entrusted her entire self to the stupidest man ever to draw breath?

*   *   *   *

Black hadn't been aware that he had somehow dropped off to sleep, so he jerked awake like a man who had been hit with a high-voltage line when the phone rang next to his bed.

"Yeah?!" he croaked and looked around, trying to figure out where he was and how much had been a nightmare.

"Mr. Black?"

"Yes?" He sat up. *Levi?*

"This is Dr. Nichols. I'm the attending physician for a patient, Lacey Bonner."

"Yes, yes! How is she?" Black squinted against the morning sun piercing the clouds and his bedroom curtains. The clock radio said it was eight-eleven.

"The patient is asking for you. In fact, she is so agitated that I would appreciate it if...."

"I'm on my way!"

It only occurred to Black as he stumbled down the second-floor corridor that his disheveled appearance might only further disturb Lacey. He hadn't even bothered to change from the bloodstained clothes before he had fallen onto his bed. He hadn't washed his face beyond splashing it in the hospital men's room last night. He hadn't thought to brush his teeth, and the residual vomitus from that same restroom visit was reminding him of what a piece of garbage he truly was.

His hazy recollection of Dr. Nichols' aborted telephone discussion had Black expecting chaos as he neared Lacey's room. There was only the customary hushed level of a hospital's morning activity. The exception to the customary picture, however, was the uniformed male officer outside Lacey's room. He was a compact, no-nonsense black man, early thirties, sitting alertly with a cup of steaming coffee in his hand.

J.P. Black saw the officer see him and saw the officer recognize the classic profile of ᴧ crazed man coming toward the room he was guarding. Black saw him put down the coffee, rise and put his hand on the leather holster at his hip. Black slowed and put his hands slightly in the air in surrender.

"Dr. Nichols wants me here. I'm Black."

The serious man with the cynical look and his hand on his holster didn't have to voice his response: *Sure, man, like I'm white.* The officer pushed open the door and cast a quick glance inside. His call into the room was in the same tone as an officer calling for senior back-up: "Dr. Nichols! Out here, Sir!"

Dr. Nichols emerged in the rumpled, sweat-stained jogging suit of a man who had been called from home and never allowed to sleep or change. Dark circles ringed the eyes of the otherwise athletic looking man of about fifty-five. J.P. Black gave his name as he ran his hands futilely through his dirty hair before he pulled his wallet from his hip pocket to show his driver's license.

Dr. Nichols nodded his acceptance of the I.D. and spoke rapidly in a low voice, while blocking the room's entrance. "She's been through a lot. And while we're trying to keep the pain level down, we have a policy of not sedating too heavily. Trauma patients have to verbalize their emotions—fear, guilt, anger...."

"She has every right to be angry."

"I'm afraid her immediate problem is with self-blame. I was hoping you could help."

Black was shaking his head. "Self-blame? That makes no sense."

"Not to me either." Nichols swept the door open with his arm and a pleading look toward Black before he led the way.

Thin Lacey Bonner looked as if she had lost twenty pounds overnight. The skin that covered her face was not the familiar coffee-and-cream shade. It was whiter than pure milk—where it wasn't black or purple or scabbed over from the tape's damage. Today she looked more emotionally damaged and terrorized than she had last night when he hadn't been sure she even knew he was there.

She saw his face as he approached the bed, and a sob broke from her throat. Both her bandaged hands, hands that showed blackened bruises where they were exposed, reached feebly for him.

"Oh, please, oh, please!" she cried weakly to him. As he cupped her face with his hands and let her arms grasp his, the sound of, "Oh, please forgive me!" pierced him like a knife.

"Hush!" Black whispered as he gingerly stroked her agonized face. Her forehead was gathered in pain, and her eyes that swam as they searched his face showed the dulling effects of painkillers.

"Just hush, Lacey! This is all my fault!" He heard the female officer behind him, sitting to one side, stand suddenly.

He leaned close to Lacey as he continued, "I should have anticipated this."

The officer eased her stance only slightly, and she and the physician both continued studying Black with tense concern. Afraid of causing Lacey further pain, Black limited his touches to her face and hair.

"I had to tell him, J.P. He kept it up and kept it up." She was clutching the sleeves of Black's shirt.

"It's *my* fault, Lacey! I never imagined he could see through all the changes in style."

"I had to tell him who wrote it."

"Shh! I know, I know."

"And he brought me to you so you wouldn't think it was a copycat."

So that was it—the vanity of the psychopath who wants all the credit for his 'work'!

Ironically, it was what had saved Lacey from the final, fatal step, which everyone *would* have blamed on a copycat. With Bailey Thurston dead, the real Levi had no reason to kill.

Lacey's eyes were wandering a bit more, and she had lost her grip on Black's shirt so that one hand had fallen onto the bed, limp.

"J.P., he said to tell you he's going for them all. Who are they? I thought she....? I thought that everything...."

He hoped that neither of the other two in the room heard. "I had a family, Lacey. I was playing dead to protect them. They didn't know."

He straightened up. Her eyes searched his face. He wasn't sure Lacey had ever heard of Bailey Thurston or of Levi before her attack. Now it was too much for her to grasp who Black really was and the reason for *his* elaborate performance, when she was sedated and still in pain.

He hoped she understood him when he smiled wearily and said, "You did the right thing to tell him. If you had let him kill you, I couldn't live anymore." His voice broke and it took him a moment before he got enough control to add, "Besides that, we never would have known to protect the others. You did the right thing."

Her bruised chin wrinkled up, tears ran out the sides of her eyes as the lids slid closed and Lacey succumbed to the painkillers. Black sighed with relief that she was resting and turned to the physician, who was asking, "What was that all about?"

Black swallowed over and over, trying to find some wording that would avoid the complete truth.

"Mr. Black," the officer said quietly, "we know from the victim and from two witnesses outside your apartment when you opened your door, that you didn't do this." He slumped with relief, and she went on, "Still, it sounded to me like you have some material evidence in this case that you're not sharing with the investigators."

He finally nodded heavily.

*   *   *   *

CHAPTER SEVENTEEN

Within fifteen minutes, the chief investigator in the San Luis torture case had arrived at the hospital. In the privacy of an empty counseling room, Black confessed to him and Dr. Nichols the astounding news that he was the presumed-dead Bailey Thurston.

Both men were understandably confused and skeptical. The detective acted initially as if Prof. James Paul Black were a bit of a psycho himself. But Black talked him into calling the LAPD investigator coordinating the Levi case, Det. Hugh Larson, for confirmation.

After the call, the shocked San Luis investigator agreed to keep the news to himself until Larson notified him that Thurston's former family in Playa del Rey had been informed. He agreed that spreading the word that Bailey Thurston was alive would not advance the investigation into who and where Levi was.

Knowing it, however, did have the desired effect of convincing the investigator to keep protection around Lacey Bonner. Levi just might decide to finish the job to further torment Thurston now that the message had been passed that Levi was on to him. Bailey had not been lying when he said he couldn't go on living if Levi had killed Lacey.

Bailey named Brad Nollan as the only suspect being sought by LAPD for questioning, and he emphasized that, aside from Nollan's size eleven feet, the rest of his appearance might be totally different from when anyone on the case had seen him last.

Dr. Nichols was a compassionate man, and Black trusted him to give Lacey a proper understanding of what had happened and why J.P. had to be away for a few days instead of at her bedside.

"Tell her," Black pleaded with him, "that I *will* be back. No matter what happens in Los Angeles, I'm coming back to see if she still wants me."

Black went to his apartment, showered and changed before calling LAPD again. Larson was there, and Bailey told him, "Since it's going to come out that I'm alive, I want them to hear it from you first, Hume."

"All right, Bailey, I'll tell them."

"But could you wait till I get down there? I want to explain face to face right after they know."

"All right. I'll tell Cynthia, so she can help."

Black....Bailey was to come to the Larson house in Culver City. He could wait there while Hugh and Cynthia went to the house on Trask, ten minutes away, before he joined them. Bailey's suitcase was already packed, ready for the Monterey weekend. Angry and guilty, he snatched it up and threw it into the VW.

He wasn't hungry, but he hadn't eaten since lunch the previous day, and so around 11:30 that morning, he began to get shaky. Reluctantly he pulled off the freeway in Buellton and got an iced tea and two tacos at the Taco Bell's drive-through window before continuing south.

Throughout the several hours of the drive, he tried to replace the self-condemning questions of why he hadn't done everything differently, with more constructive questions. He thought back to the very first calls from Levi and tried to recall the exact wording, the sound of the voice. As many years as it had been, he clearly recalled the sound of wicked laughter coming over the phone.

Laughter that I should have recognized when I heard it through Lacey's door.

He forced his thoughts back to what Levi had revealed about himself. Certainly in his action with Lacey he had revealed that he had a huge ego, and he wanted Bailey Thurston in particular to understand it. The whole idea of torturing people close to Bailey then Bailey himself was to punish him because he had not appreciated Levi.

And Levi had revealed that he was not only a regular reader of Bailey Thurston's work and had heard him talking in detail about his work, but he was a very astute reader of other material as well. Not just everyone recognized the presence of meter and syntax much less recognized the pattern of a particular writer.

But what of Levi's 'fingerprint'? What of his meter and syntax?

Bailey thought back to Grayson Anders' mystified comment that the meter of *Trespass* wasn't Lacey's.

Levi's meter, his syntax! They're not Brad Nollan's at all! That's what wasn't right when I listened to Hume's tape of Nollan. And what was Levi's wording? Something about irreverence and, 'You don't appreciate me! You got everything backwards!' Something like that.

Bailey tried to examine the logic of the killer. Levi was so insane that he actually conceived of himself as a holy man, one deserving of reverence, possibly even worship. Such a man would be offended by being portrayed by a writer as evil. While the book never actually labeled Ralph as evil, the implication was there in the idea that everyone wanted him stopped. Thurston had gotten it backwards that a holy man should be stopped. What else was there to get backwards?

"Oh, God!" he heard himself say aloud. *What if that wasn't what I got backwards at all?! What if what offended Levi, what I got backwards, was the physical description? The physical characteristics were all reversed!*

Bailey looked around frantically to see where he was. He had unknowingly gotten as far as Westlake Village. The off ramp ahead didn't look as if it held promise for a phone. In only a couple of moments, however, he saw a gas station at the top of the ramp exiting at Reyes Adobe Road and pulled off, still some forty minutes from Culver City.

He got change from the attendant and dialed Larson's house. Cynthia answered. She had been given the news and spoke in the breathless, rapid voice of someone who is both shocked and deliriously happy.

"He's sleeping, Bailey. Oh, Lord, Bailey, I was so glad to hear you're…!"

"Cynthia, please go get him up! I think I know what Levi looks like."

"What?! Okay, okay!"

The phone clunked loudly, and he heard her voice fading as she ran away from the phone, calling Hugh's name. In a moment, the exhausted man picked up the bedroom extension.

"Listen, Human, you can forget about Brad Nollan."

"I know, but how did you hear so fast?"

"Hear what?"

There was a pause, then Larson answered, "That he committed suicide in Mexico a couple of years ago. We found out about an hour ago. But if you didn't know that, why were you saying…?"

"Never mind, just listen." Bailey hastily explained his thinking about the reversed physical description.

Now alert, Larson said, "Yeah! Maybe so, maybe so. I forget the details, Bailey."

"Me, too. I've blocked the whole thing out. Do you still have a copy of the book?"

"Of course. Hold on." There was another clunk and a minute's delay before the phone was picked up and Larson said he had the book and was trying to find where Ralph was described.

An agonizing two minutes later he shouted, "Bingo! Dark, oily hair and skin, pockmarked, overweight, B.O., and smokes. Are there more details elsewhere, Bailey?" There was the sound of pages being turned.

"I don't think so. The opposite would be light hair, someone slim, clean and healthy, a non-smoker," Bailey answered.

"Sound like anybody you know?"

"Too generic. Besides, we know that Levi smokes—at least sometimes. I suppose I could go through some mug shots," he offered with disappointment.

"Whoa! We can do better than that, maybe. I've always bet my retirement fund that Levi was at your funeral. All the shrinks said so, too, at the time."

"From what I know of his ego, I agree. He probably considered the entire service one big tribute to himself. Can you call the *Times*, ask if they can dig up their pictures?"

"You're forgetting we had our own guy there." Larson asked where Bailey was before he told him to meet him at the station instead of the house.

It was 2:15 in the afternoon when Bailey's VW screeched into the Pacific Division's parking lot. He jogged to the lobby. In the familiar environment, with Irv Deacon and his luxurious walrus mustache behind the desk looking very much as they had more than five years ago, Bailey very nearly charged on past and into the back room.

Deacon showed no signs of recognizing him when Bailey said breathlessly, "Det. Larson's expecting me."

"Are you Mr. Black?"

I have no idea! "Yes."

"I'll just get him," he said, reaching for the phone.

"I know my way. This is urgent." He charged into the bustling room when an officer exited, and hurried past the blur of semi-familiar faces.

The air in Larson's office looked as if they were trying to clean up the L.A. basin by pumping all the pollution into this small space. Larson was behind his desk in the murk. Two plainclothes men were sitting with their backs to the glass-topped door. All three were using magnifying glasses to study black and white eight-by-tens.

As Bailey put his hand on the doorknob, Larson looked up. There was a long moment of non-recognition before that tortured piece of pavement that Larson called a face smiled and took a very deep breath. Bailey opened the door to the room that stank of smoke and sweat and too-strong coffee. He entered, waving a path in the foul air with his hand.

Larson rose and greeted him, "I haven't had time to explain about you. All I had time for was to give them your idea."

Larson had come from behind his desk to envelop Bailey in a bear hug while the two officers looked on with curiosity. Larson shoved the door shut and said to them, "Gentlemen, I'll make believers out of you yet. Say hello to the resurrected Bailey Thurston."

The two officers in Larson's office had known Bailey. And so, after a moment of stunned staring, they were able to see through the changed appearance. They had changed somewhat themselves, one now quite bald on top, the other carrying fifteen extra pounds. Larson himself showed the years in the deepening of his wrinkles and in the beginnings of white hair at his temples.

They added a chair to the crowded space, and Bailey joined them in poring over the numerous shots. Bailey thought his heart would break—again—when he saw the close-ups of his family huddled together. Sara's face was one of exhausted grief. Mike's shined with his tears. Scott looked betrayed.

Bailey's tired eyes watered and blinked, itched, burned, then ached in their sockets. There were several blond men in the pictures who looked slim, clean and healthy. Their faces were as unfamiliar to Bailey and the detectives as they had been years ago, and there was no way to know who they were or how to contact them.

They had all been over the pictures countless times when Larson rose, arched his back and suggested someone go get some food. It was 8 p.m.

Bailey was alone in the stinking room with Larson, who had pushed his swivel chair back and was praying. Bailey sat opposite, praying that Larson's prayers would be answered, since none of his had been.

Larson sighed, looked up and scratched his stubbly dark face as he growled, "You know, Bailey, I just keep having this feeling in my gut that we're staring the guy right in the face. I'm sure he had to be there." He shook his head and gestured at the pile of pictures scattered on his messy desk.

Bailey nodded. His gut told him the same thing.

Larson mumbled, almost to himself, "Practically all of L.A. was there. More than three thousand. Somebody had a count. Every face that was there is in those pictures. We made such a point of it with Victor."

The electricity down Bailey's spine jolted him forward in the chair. "No, no, Human, there was one there that's not in any of the pictures!"

"Who?"

"The man behind the camera, your Victor fellow. I forget his first name."

"Tony." Larson's eyes were darting around the room, his mind racing through the possibilities.

"What does he look like, Hume? I forget."

Larson mumbled, "Blond, smokes....," then looked at Bailey and slumped. "But he's overweight, and he's very fussy about his appearance." He shook his head. "He doesn't quite fit Ralph whether you describe him backwards or forwards. Besides, when you were so paranoid about somebody in the department, I made everyone in the station—men and women—show me their shoe size. The one he took off was a ten. One size too small."

Bailey's heart had begun to beat wildly when the idea of Tony Victor as Levi had occurred to him; now disappointment had begun slowing it to normal, and he sat slumped in the chair. Bailey thought with pain of Lacey. And, as he mixed thoughts of her with thoughts of Levi, he recalled the funny picture Lacey had painted for his class that time she had described the confused caller looking for 'Martial's' last name.

Asking himself what one could know about a person you've never seen, he turned again to thoughts of what Levi had said. It was obvious that Levi believed Bailey had patterned his engineer character Ralph after him. Bailey snarled with frustration and looked across at equally frustrated Larson, the model for one of Bailey's cops.

With that thought, Bailey started shaking. "Hume! What if we've been wrong all along that Levi identified with *Ralph*? I pattern characters after cops sometimes. What was the cop like...?" He slumped again. "A woman."

Larson's eyes were darting around as he thought. Bailey got the idea the same time Larson did and said, "But there was a police photographer in the story for the first time!"

Bailey snatched the hardback copy of *In the Shadows* from the edge of Larson's desk and rifled through the pages. "Stupid! Can't remember my own character."

He found the spot, and his eyes scanned rapidly as he read aloud, "'Martin Lightner laid the grainy black and white on the captain's desk. "Damn," the captain said. "You've got damn expensive equipment, Lightner. Learn to use it. This is just more of your useless garbage.""'"

"Hume, Levi said he was an artist, and he was angry that everyone thought his work was a result of the equipment. I thought he meant Ralph's engineering equipment. Stupid! Throughout the book, I had the photographer bungling everything...."

"Bailey, Bailey," Larson said, shaking his head, "His shoe size is all wrong. I saw it myself, like I saw all the others."

"But he could have been wearing larger shoes when he made the footprint."

"Why," Larson asked, "when he didn't know he was going to leave a print?"

Larson resumed his prayer position. Bailey threw himself back against the chair and studied the ceiling. He was so fatigued that his thoughts began to wander, and he felt guilty at some of the avenues. There was the angry, selfish thought that he should have been in Monterey with Lacey, driving her car along the spectacular Seventeen

Mile Drive. From there, his thoughts drifted to her car, his battered VW, the gorgeous BMW abandoned in San Diego and to his beloved Jaguar.

Where is it now?

He had put so much personal effort into it. That is, all but the few things he couldn't do himself, like upholstery and the creation of a fender from scratch. His mind jumped to alcoholic Angelo Hayes and how, unexpectedly, the young mechanic, Randy, had installed Hayes' new fender so quickly. That had been a surprise, not so much because of Hayes' drinking as because it followed immediately Randy's observation that no two sides of cars....

And people!

The other two officers were just walking back into the office with packages smelling of fried chicken from Dinah's, when Bailey sat up and barked at a startled Hugh Larson, "I don't suppose you looked at the size of *both* his feet! They don't have to match, Hume. Randy's don't."

"What're you talking about, man?" the balding officer asked and closed the door.

"Tony Victor. Hume's eliminated him just because he showed him a size ten shoe."

After a second of confused silence, the overweight officer stammered, "Victor complained once about having to buy two pairs of shoes because one's a full size bigger than the other."

"Okay," Bailey said, breathlessly, "with that argument eliminated, does he fit the picture, Hume?"

Larson was breathing rapidly as he hunted and pecked furiously through his computer's roster. "Victor was an avid fan of yours, Bailey. I think you saw him here more than once...."

Bailey felt the blood drain from his head at the realization. "I was in his presence at least twice after the threats. The first was when he laid some gruesome pictures on this very desk. My God, right next to the authorization for a tap on my phone!"

Larson groaned and Bailey continued, "And then he has the flippin' gall to ring the bell and march straight into my kitchen." Bailey shook his head at his own stupidity. "No wonder both times our paths crossed after the phone calls started that he had a throat problem. I couldn't recognize his voice through a hanky and all that coughing."

Larson was shaking his head, still scrolling through the names. "He read everything of yours in detail, always making a point of trying to figure out if any of your characters was based on one of us. No wonder he was mad. And no wonder Levi could jerk us around so well." Larson stopped typing and clawed the phone out of its cradle.

"Who're you calling?" Bailey asked.

"His lab. If he's there, I'll ask him to wait there for some reason." Larson had his hand over the phone and spoke rapidly during the sixty seconds of letting the number ring. "I sent him in ahead of the lab techs every blasted time! Me!"

The men waited a full minute before Larson slammed the phone down. "He's not in his lab. Get personnel to give you his home address…"

The balding officer was already in motion toward the door. "I know where he lives. I had to give him a ride one time."

"Okay, go on, but send a black-and-white ahead to be sure he doesn't skip while you're at it. Let me know before you go in." The detective dumped his packages of food on top of the pictures before he hurried from the room.

Larson turned to the other detective. "Get the captain to push a warrant through. Tell him I can supply motive, means and opportunity."

"Gotcha!" the man said before he, too, dropped his packages and ran from the room.

*   *   *   *

CHAPTER EIGHTEEN

Larson had the phone in his hand again and was punching in a number as he commented to Bailey, "I'll have dispatch notify the surveillance on Trask of who they're looking for, just in case."

Bailey nodded and wiped his sweating palms on his trousers several times as he listened to the conversation between Larson and the dispatcher.

It was in the hasty, clipped, professional manner of conversations between two such veterans of police procedure, until Larson said, "You're nuts! There's gotta be a response!" His eyes were looking frantically between Bailey and the photos on the desk.

After Larson had listened to the dispatcher for several seconds, he shouted at her as he rose from his desk, "Get the black-and-whites rolling! I don't know how he did it, but Victor's cut us off from the stakeout, which means he's probably inside!"

It felt like Bailey's heart would explode from his chest as he ran behind Larson to his car. Larson threw the portable light onto the roof as he got in. The siren was screaming by the time they shot out of the parking lot like a missile barely under control.

"You gotta stay in the car, Bailey. I can't let you mess things up or get yourself hurt."

"I couldn't possibly mess things up worse than I have. Besides, you're forgetting I'm already dead."

Larson didn't take his eyes off the road as he swerved wildly through the traffic, one hand on the horn and running every light and stop sign in the two-and-a-half minute trip. It ordinarily took nearly six. The black and whites were screaming up the hill behind them by a few seconds, tires protesting the unsafe turns.

"That's ours," Larson said, pointing to the electrician's van parked in front of the Thurston…Turnbow house. He screeched to a halt and threw the car into Park. Bailey was out of the car before Larson was, running toward the house, his hand in his pocket, fishing for his keys.

He was running along the driveway, toward the rear door to the kitchen, when he heard Larson's voice from behind him shouting toward the street, "Get the paramedics! Looks like Ruger's been poisoned or drugged!"

The running man reached the back door of what used to be his house. Fumbling with the key he heard Larson calling out as he ran toward him from behind, "Don't do it, Bailey! You'll scare the hell outta Sara and the kids. Stay outta there!"

Bailey's hand was shaking almost too badly to get the key inside the lock. Inside, the lighted kitchen was empty, but he could hear the piercing female screams from what sounded like the family room.

Larson nearly knocked Bailey down as he shoved his way past him in the kitchen doorway. His revolver was drawn, and he charged into the house and along the hallway with his voice thundering, "This is Larson, Victor! Sara, it's me!"

"Stop him! Oh, God, stop him!" Her voice exploded from her throat, above the other female screams.

Larson made the family room door first and stopped abruptly. Bailey ran into his back and hit him several times with his fist before the reason for the abrupt halt and restraining of Bailey penetrated.

Sara was across the room and on the left, her terrified eyes focused on the overweight blond man inside the room about a dozen feet from the door. He held a large knife to the throat of the screaming three-year-old he held clutched to his chest. A cigarette was between the fingers of his other hand. It had been used already. Bailey recognized the nature of the two ugly burns on the child's bare arm. Her screams sounded as if they would burst her throat open.

Marissa again? No, time didn't stop. Marissa would be eleven. She was the child clutching Sara and whose red curls were buried in her mother's chest.

"Okay, okay," Larson said. He raised his hands and let the revolver dangle from his finger. "I'll be cool. Just you be cool. We can work something out here, Tony."

"Yeah," the blond man said with a twisted grin, "like the gas chamber's real cool this time of year. Slide the gun over here," he demanded in the gravely voice Bailey recognized.

"Okay," Larson said, squatting to put the gun down and pushing it across the wood floor with his foot. "But we can bargain on this."

While the two girls still screamed, Sara had stopped and had one fist in her mouth. The other hand was clutching Marissa.

Tony Victor shook his head. "I can see I don't have anything to lose anymore, so I'll just do as much damage as I can before your moronic buddies take me out."

In the flash of a second during which Levi was adjusting the knife to get a better grip, Bailey ducked under Larson's raised arm and shouted, "It's me you want, Victor…Levi! You were right about who wrote *Trespass Against Us.*"

Sara looked about to explode from terrified confusion. She probably thought she had gone insane. Bailey's appearance on the scene had startled Levi, and his vision whirled toward him in the doorway. Larson had slowly stepped to the left, a couple of feet farther into the room, undoubtedly hoping to get out of Levi's line of sight so he could make a move.

Bailey's hands were raised, and he kept his eyes on Levi's hands. "You'll only have time for one victim, and you won't have the full satisfaction you wanted if you chose that child. She's not mine." Levi's eyes shifted as he considered the argument and then Bailey's offer. "You always said I'd be 'dead last.' Let's go lock ourselves in one of the bed-rooms so you'll have a little more time."

The vacillation in Levi's attitude registered in his quickened breathing and shifting gaze. After a few seconds, he dropped the screaming child like trash. She scrambled toward her mother.

"Be quick," Levi said, nodding harshly toward the door.

Bailey turned. Rushing down the hallway and into the open doorway was a blur of plaid and denim. Somewhere in the split second afforded him, Bailey recognized the dull sheen of a shotgun barrel and instinctively hit the floor. The blast was deafening. There was no cry from Levi before his body blew back against the bookcase beside the television and he fell in a bloody heap, dead before he hit the floor.

Above the increased screaming of the two girls, Bailey heard Larson say, "Be cool, be cool, Scott!"

"Put the gun down, Son! Don't do it, Son!" came another man's voice, unfamiliar to Bailey.

Too late! was Bailey's thought as he pulled himself up and to his feet. When he looked toward the doorway, he understood the stranger's comment. The eighteen-year-old with the auburn ponytail had the shotgun aimed at Bailey's chest. All the betrayal that Scott Thurston was feeling was registered on his face as raging hatred. His chest was heaving, and his hand gripped and ungripped the trigger.

Bailey swallowed several times before he could get enough breath together to say in a rasp, "Let's go outside, Scott, so they don't have to watch."

The boy's hand opened and closed four more times—Bailey counted them—before his chin crumpled up, a groan broke from him, and his weakened arms lowered the gun into the hands of the blond man beside him.

*   *   *   *

EPILOGUE

Bailey Thurston peeled the typed label from the sheet of blanks and pressed it to the tab of the manila file folder. The drawer to the file cabinet was standing open, and he wondered how many inches the other family files measured. There were copies of his testimony and Lacey's, letters, court records and renderings of opinions on the efforts to legitimize Sara's marriage to Larry Turnbow. There was the extensive correspondence straightening out the ownership of the property on Trask, royalties and the repaying of the significant insurance settlement that had been made to Bailey's 'widow.' There was the copy of his death certificate.

The den window was open to the warm summer breeze, and Bailey stood for a moment looking out at the San Luis landscape below. It pleased him to know that no one for miles around had suffered anything more than cracked plaster in the strong, five-point quake two weeks ago.

Thoughts of quakes always turned Bailey's thoughts to Levi—*that damned old San Andreas!*—and the many, many rifts he had opened up in Bailey's soul. There had been so many that black night in the house on Trask that he hadn't been sure he could go on living. A small one had opened up at the sound of Larry Turnbow's addressing Scott as Son. Another opened when Sara fell into Turnbow's arms and turned her face away from Bailey.

The biggest, however, had ripped through him when he had stood looking down the barrel pointed at him, questioning whether the shot that he had barely escaped had been intended for him and not Levi.

Turnbow insisted over and over that it was not. He insisted that, when Scott had grabbed the shotgun and outraced him to the family room, neither he nor Scott nor Michael knew that Bailey was alive, much less in the house. Scott had expected to find Levi the only man downstairs.

Bailey still had his doubts—all born of Bailey's immeasurable guilt. Scott carried Bailey's doubts like a millstone. The work to restore that relationship—and the others—would take a lifetime.

Though it had been, ironically, Levi who had bridged the abyss he had created, that bridge was strengthened by the efforts of Larry Turnbow and Lacey Bonner, with help from the Larsons. Quietly, on either side of the rift, they worked to see that all the others knew there *was* a bridge across. Quietly they tried to help them see that, though the landscape had been forever altered by the upheaval, it was still supporting life.

Two years after the night of horror on Trask, a year after the quiet wedding, new life had sprung up on the San Luis side. Bailey smiled and placed his son's birth certificate in the file folder. He and Lacey named him Hugh Thurston, after the man on the other side who had taught them to believe in the miracle of life after death.

*   *   *   *

ABOUT THE AUTHOR

Linda Lane McCall is the author of : *On the Run* and *Tapping at the Window.*, published by Pocketbooks. McCall's work takes the suspense to real locales in Southern California's beach communities, Baja Mexico, the Sierras, Oregon and Virginia. McCall resides in Southern California with her husband and daughter.